Sigrun's Secret

MARIE-LOUISE JENSEN

OXFORD
UNIVERSITY PRESS

OXFORD

UNIVERSITY PRESS

Great Clarendon Street, Oxford OX2 6DP

Oxford University Press is a department of the University of Oxford.
It furthers the University's objective of excellence in research, scholarship,
and education by publishing worldwide in

Oxford New York

Auckland Cape Town Dar es Salaam Hong Kong Karachi
Kuala Lumpur Madrid Melbourne Mexico City Nairobi
New Delhi Shanghai Taipei Toronto

With offices in

Argentina Austria Brazil Chile Czech Republic France Greece
Guatemala Hungary Italy Japan Poland Portugal Singapore
South Korea Switzerland Thailand Turkey Ukraine Vietnam

Oxford is a registered trade mark of Oxford University Press
in the UK and in certain other countries

British Library Cataloguing in Publication Data

Data available

ISBN: 978-0-19-272882-1

1 3 5 7 9 10 8 6 4 2

Printed in Great Britain
Paper used in the production of this book is a natural,
recyclable product made from wood grown in sustainable forests.
The manufacturing process conforms to the environmental
regulations of the country of origin.

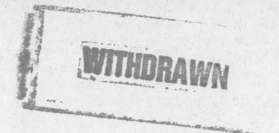
Sigrun's Secret

ALSO BY MARIE-LOUISE JENSEN

✳

Between Two Seas
The Lady in the Tower
Daughter of Fire and Ice

For Karen

CHAPTER ONE

The colt tossed his head nervously as I tried to slip the bridle on.

'Steady, boy!' I said soothingly, stroking his neck. A sudden breeze whipped my hair forward, startling the horse and making him tug at his halter. The wind was bitter today, despite the fact that it was sun month; supposedly the warmest month of the year. It was blowing straight off the sea, whipping up white-topped waves and rippling the grasses and flowers on the open hillside.

I cast a glance out to sea, hoping for a glimpse of a sail. It was my father's sail especially I was looking for. But the broad bay was empty, as ever, and so was the open water beyond it. I returned my attention firmly to the horse.

'I've spent so much time with you,' I sighed, stroking his velvety nose. 'Why are you still so wild? You should have been broken in the spring, but there's only so much I can manage by myself.'

'Surely you won't try to ride him without help, Sigrun?' asked a gruff voice behind me. It was my turn to jump. I turned and saw Erik, my father's most trusted worker, standing there, his back stooped and his face lined with the many winters of his life. He was a freeman like everyone who lived with us. It was my father's house and farm and he didn't hold with slavery.

'He's quite gentle now,' I said defensively, and not completely truthfully.

Erik straightened himself with a grimace of pain and stared at me from under his brows. 'So, in other words, you *were* planning to ride him?'

'Yes. I'd like him to be well-behaved for when my father returns home,' I said.

Erik turned aside slightly, hiding a smile. 'What your father will care about is seeing you in one piece, not how many horses you've broken,' he said, but I knew he understood.

'With Ingvar and Asgrim gone, there's only me,' I said, smiling coaxingly, knowing that Erik was likely to be sympathetic.

Most of the men from our settlement were away. My father had only sailed along the coast to trade at the summer market and would be back soon. Our neighbour Helgi, on the other hand, had been gone for a year, all the way south to Dublin, trading. He'd taken his son and my elder brother with him. None of us knew how long they'd be away. I so wished they'd come back this summer, but I hardly dared hope for it.

Erik sighed, recalling my thoughts from my absent friends and family. 'I'll give you a hand then,' he said, good-naturedly.

'As long as I'm not making you neglect your work?' I asked.

'The others can manage without me for a while.'

'Thank you,' I said with a grateful smile.

Between us we coaxed the bridle and then the saddle onto the colt, which, as yet, had no name. Erik held him steady, speaking soothingly, while I climbed onto his back. The young horse stood there snorting nervously, every muscle in his body rigid with tension. I knew he'd bolt at the slightest opportunity. I'd ridden him twice before and he hadn't relaxed for an instant.

Slowly, carefully, Erik led the horse inland. After jibing a few times the colt allowed himself to be led, pulling nervously at the reins from time to time. I praised him. He pricked his ears up and walked willingly, but he was sweating with the strangeness of it all, his muscles still bunched up tight.

We walked a fair distance before turning for home. The colt was quieter now, beginning to feel tired. He'd had enough for one morning and Erik and I both had other work to be getting on with.

As we rounded the edge of the hill, the view of the bay opened up before us once more. The clouds were clearing and the water sparkled in the strong summer sunshine. Erik and I both gasped.

Gliding towards the head of the bay, their sails filled with the fresh, morning breeze, two ships were sailing towards us. It took only an instant for us to recognize the colours. On one ship, I could clearly see the stripe of green so laboriously woven into my father's sail over two long winters at the loom. And the other was . . . could it really be?

'Brown and yellow. Helgi's returned!' exclaimed Erik, stopping abruptly.

'And father!' I cried excitedly, standing up in my

3

stirrups for a better view. For one critical moment we'd both forgotten I was astride an unbroken horse.

The horse threw his head up, tearing the reins from Erik's grasp. My heart gave a sickening lurch as I realized he was free. I tightened the reins at once, trying to bring him under control, but he was quicker than I was. He snatched the bit, and before I even had time to think, he bucked.

I was no novice at breaking horses. But, unpardonably, my attention had been caught by the sight of those splendid ships, and my mind filled with excitement at this unexpected double homecoming. I hung on desperately, clinging to the saddle with my knees and to the horse's mane with both hands. I was thrown sideways and half slipped from the saddle. And while I was in this precarious position, my mount bolted.

The ground was rough and uneven, the grass growing in huge, unruly tufts. The horse thundered down the steep hillside with no care for danger. I was aware that one wrong step could leave him with a broken leg, no use to anyone. Even worse, he was heading straight down towards the cliff edge.

Slowly, painfully, I dragged myself upright and back into the saddle. My feet sought the flying, twisting stirrups that were probably terrifying the colt, banging into his sides. Once my feet were securely in them again, I dared to let go of his mane and gather up the reins. I fought desperately to get the youngster's head, but he had the bit firmly between his teeth, and could barely feel my tugging. I pushed my feet down, leaned back and pulled with all my strength. But my strength and will

4

were nothing to the power and determination of a horse of three winters, in full flight. He would neither listen nor respond to my commands.

As the cliff-edge loomed closer, I could feel waves of terror washing through me. I pulled hard on the left rein, trying to force the horse to at least turn away from certain death. When he still didn't respond, I considered jumping off his back and letting him go to his end alone.

But I couldn't abandon him. I just couldn't do it. He was a valuable colt. I didn't want to lose him, to let my father down. Surely I could turn him in time?

There was a sudden eruption of brown-speckled feathers almost under the horse's hooves. Ptarmigans, flushed from the undergrowth with their chicks, caused him to rear and scream in fright. He was up on his hind legs, arching his neck, pawing the air, a mad flapping in front of him as the birds took wing, and this was my chance. I threw myself forward, fighting to hold my balance, and gathered the reins tight, regaining that vital contact with the horse's mouth. And then the birds were gone and I'd pulled the horse round. When he bounded forward again, he was racing along the shoreline, still resisting all my efforts to stop him. But his flight was no longer so ungoverned, so frantic and there was no longer any immediate danger. I was slowly gaining control; he was trembling beneath me as we galloped towards the head of the bay.

Ahead of us, the two ships were sailing straight onto the beach. The people from both households were already gathering to welcome them. As I battled to stop the runaway horse, I could see them waving and calling out, though the pounding hoof beats and the wind in my ears drowned the sound.

And, oh, the shame. My father's first sight on returning home would be his daughter on a runaway horse. He'd probably watched the whole, mad flight from his ship. Everyone would see my disgrace: my brother Asgrim, and my best friend Ingvar whom I'd not seen for over a year.

The sight of the crowd ahead slowed the horse. He dropped to a canter and then, in response to my command, he stumbled into an exhausted walk. I saw my father jump ashore. His eyes were fixed on me as I rode up on his valuable colt, the animal lathered in sweat, flanks heaving with exhaustion.

My father walked straight towards me. The colt shied away from him half-heartedly, but was too tired to run any further. The welcoming crowd drew back, turning their eyes on me too, their voices hushing. My father signalled for someone to take charge of the horse. A fair, handsome stranger stepped forward and took the reins, but my eyes didn't leave father's face. It was stern as he took in the state of the horse, and then looked up at me.

'Are you all right, Sigrun?' he asked. To my relief, there was no anger in him, only concern.

I nodded, aware I was shaking from head to foot. 'I was just . . . breaking in the horse for you, father,' I said, unable to keep my voice steady.

And then he laughed and held his arms up to me. I tumbled into them, hugging him, crying with pleasure and relief that he was safely home again.

'I'll teach you to break horses in that way,' he said

mock-fiercely, tousling my windblown hair. 'Look at the state of him. We'll be lucky if you haven't lamed him for life! Is that Erik I see, running after you?'

I looked back, guilty for the fright I must have given Erik. He was running down the hillside towards us, but as he drew closer and saw all was well, he stopped, bending double to catch his breath. 'I'm sorry, Bjorn!' he called to my father.

'Poor Erik,' teased my father. 'He'll be relieved we're all back to keep a closer eye on you, Sigrun.'

He set me on my feet again and turned away. I knew he was looking for my mother. She stepped forward, a woman of some five and thirty winters, retaining much of the beauty of youth in her glowing, happy features. She smiled at my father, warmly welcoming.

'Thora,' he said, the word a caress. He walked to her and swept her up in his arms, holding her close.

Some of the people clapped with delight and cheered. At the same time, I saw our neighbour, Helgi, embracing Bera, who was weeping with joy to see her husband safely back. Other men, our free workers and Helgi's slaves, were also greeting their loved ones.

'Sigrun,' said a deep voice close to me. I turned, looking up questioningly at the tall young man who held my horse. 'If you want to race your horses, you should pit yourself against me,' he said.

There was something familiar about him. As I looked, feeling shy about studying such a fair young man so closely, I caught my breath in surprise. 'Ingvar?' I asked uncertainly.

My childhood playfellow had grown and changed so

much in the year he'd been away that I hadn't recognized him. I realized I was staring, confused and admiring, and felt a little colour creeping into my face.

'If you don't recognize *me*, do you at least know your brother?' Ingvar asked with a smile. He pulled Asgrim forward, taller, and bronzed from his long sea voyage. I hugged him eagerly.

'What's this supposed to be?' I asked, tugging affectionately at a new growth of fluff on his chin.

'Mind your manners, little sister,' he retorted. As we let each other go, Ingvar passed the reins to Asgrim and stepped forward offering an embrace too. I caught my breath, suddenly shy. But before I had time to think about it, I was stopped by a high-pitched keening sound behind me.

I whipped round and saw my mother standing rigid, her eyes glazed over, a faraway look on her face, her eyes glowing blue. She was experiencing the sight, I knew at once.

'Thora, what is it?' my father was asking, still holding her hands tight. 'What do you see?'

My mother began to speak. Not, I knew, in response to my father's question, but because Freya, the goddess of prophecy, had chosen to speak through her. Her voice was deep and musical, as though it was Freya herself who spoke.

'They are coming again. Their garments are black as night. They carry torches in their hands, darkness and anger in their hearts.'

With a convulsive shudder, she stopped speaking and fell forward. My father caught her in his arms and they looked into each other's eyes.

I didn't understand what my mother had seen. Her words meant nothing to me. But I knew she had visions when danger threatened. And that what the goddess showed her always came to pass.

Around us, voices were raised in fear and several women began to cry. I shivered, feeling a dark threat draw over us. The fright I'd just had, my concerns for the colt, and the excitement of the homecoming faded into insignificance, swallowed up in a terrifying sense of dread.

CHAPTER TWO

The preparations for a homecoming feast were usually joyful, but as I helped lay out bowls, shells, and goblets on the tables, I could feel the shadow my mother's vision had cast over us. The older members of the household wore serious faces and talked quietly together. There were no jokes and no laughter. What had my mother seen? The thought made me restless and afraid.

My parents weren't in the longhouse. I found them pacing the dusty ground outside the house together, deep in conversation. As I approached, they stopped talking and looked round, strain etched into both their faces.

'What did you see?' I asked. 'Is there danger?'

My mother looked away.

'We won't be long, Sigrun, my child,' said my father, avoiding my eyes. He gave me a quick hug. 'Please don't worry. There's nothing to be afraid of.'

He was *lying* to me. I couldn't believe it. My parents had always been close, almost as though they knew each other's thoughts and feelings without the need for words. So much so that I sometimes felt shut out. But they'd always been honest with me before. Shocked and unhappy, I walked back into the longhouse, dragging my feet.

'Do you know what's going on?' I asked my brother.

He shook his head and the slight crease in his brow told me he, at least, was telling me the truth.

'No, I don't,' he said. I noticed his voice had deepened in the year of his absence. 'There was some kind of incident at the market. I don't know whether it's connected with what mother saw.'

'What happened?' I asked.

'I don't know. Helgi thought we should stop over on our way home in case father was there. And he was. He'd finished trading and told us he was about to leave, but we all thought there was some kind of scene going on, some hostility. Father wouldn't talk about it.'

More worried than ever, I went to Erik's wife, Asgerd, and sat down beside her at the fire where she was roasting a whole pig for the feast.

'You know my mother better than anyone,' I said quietly. 'What did she mean by her vision? Who's coming?'

Asgerd shot me a sideways glance. She and Erik had come to Iceland with my parents at the time of the settlements some twenty years ago. If anyone knew she did.

'I can't tell you. Your parents will take care of everything, Sigrun,' she said.

I scowled at her, a knot of fear twisting in my belly. 'Why is everyone hiding things from me?' I asked. 'I'm fifteen. Aren't I old enough to be trusted?'

'They'll tell you when they're ready,' Asgerd said. But like my father, she avoided my eyes, concentrating instead on basting the meat over the fire.

I'd looked forward to my father's return so much. Every day that I'd helped with the chores, cared for the horses and accompanied my mother in her gathering of plants for medicines, I'd been counting down the days of sun month until the market would be over and I could expect the ship. And now everything was secrets and fear.

A bustle and voices at the door drew my attention. I looked up to see Helgi, Bera, Ingvar, and his younger sister Gudrun all come into our house together. They'd been invited for the feast, of course. Gudrun was wearing a blue apron dress over her brown kirtle, I noticed immediately. All heads turned, everyone stared and whispered. Gudrun smiled and preened, delighted by the attention.

I felt a small tug of envy, looking at the beautiful blue. It was a colour we couldn't make in Iceland, and showed Gudrun's father had been in foreign lands with money to spend. If my father or brother had brought me any sort of gift, it had been forgotten in the turmoil of the prophecy.

With Helgi were two strangers I'd never seen before. They must have been at the ships, but in all the excitement, I hadn't seen them. What I particularly noticed was that they were smaller than the men here, more my father's height, and dark haired too, like him, and like me.

'Hello again, Sigrun,' said a familiar voice. I got to my feet in a rush, almost tripping into the fire.

'Hello, Ingvar,' I mumbled, glancing up shyly. He'd grown so tall, his features more defined than I remembered. His sun-bronzed skin contrasted with his fair hair, which tumbled to his shoulders in a pale golden mass. And his eyes. Such an intense blue. Why had I never

12

noticed them before he went away? I met them briefly and felt my breath come short in my chest and a fierce heat spread over my face and neck. What was the matter with me?

Ingvar was smiling down at me. It made my stomach flip over.

'Will you sit by me?' he asked. Before I knew what he intended, he'd taken my hand and was drawing me to one of the trestle tables nearby. My feet turned to clumsy lumps of clay with nervousness and my heart was fluttering at the touch of his hand.

'Your mother has set everyone in an uproar,' Ingvar said once we were seated. He leaned close and spoke for my ears only, so that I could feel his breath warm on my cheek, making me shiver deliciously. 'There's something truly other-worldly about her when she sees like that.'

'It's a great gift,' I agreed, fighting to keep my voice steady. I was affected by his nearness, my feelings thrown into confusion. But at the same time, his words touched a sore point. It was my deepest disappointment that I'd failed to inherit the gift from my mother. I'd worked hard to learn the healing skills she taught me, but I always felt like an impostor, lacking the sight.

Other people sat down around us, and to my mixed relief and disappointment, the talk became more general. Several of the women served the food; I was glad it wasn't my turn tonight with so many guests in the house. I was more than happy to sit quietly beside Ingvar, glad to have him home after such a long voyage. Asgerd came around with a large jug of mead, and poured some into my goblet too. I looked up at her, surprised.

I was normally only allowed whey, or as a special treat, watered ale.

'Your father says you may,' she said by way of explanation. I glanced over at my father who nodded to me and gave a tiny smile before turning back to Helgi who was talking earnestly to him. Father was showing me he was thinking of me, despite his worries.

'Bjorn realizes you're growing up,' said Ingvar, with a smile, reclaiming my attention. 'Your very good health,' he said, looking directly at me as he touched his goblet to mine.

'And yours,' I replied shyly. I sipped the mead and closed my eyes as the unaccustomed sweetness spread through my mouth. 'Oh, it's good,' I sighed.

Ingvar laughed, and it seemed to me he radiated happiness, dispelling the gloom that had engulfed me earlier. I found myself laughing too, my worries pushed into the background. I sipped the mead again, noticing that all around us, voices were raised in toasts and chatter. The fear of the prophecy was, if not forgotten, then at least put aside for the time being. The tense, oppressed atmosphere had lightened, as though everyone had decided to revel in being together again after such a long separation. The fear my mother's words had lit in me burned lower, like a fire fading to a gentle glow. Perhaps they had meant nothing so very serious after all.

As well as the pork, juicy and tender, there was roast lamb, cheese, fresh fish and crusty newly-baked flatbread, in honour of the homecoming. We hadn't feasted so lavishly all summer. After the energy I'd expended riding, I ate eagerly, enjoying the flavours of the good food.

'Ah, it's good to be home,' sighed Ingvar, tearing a piece of flatbread and soaking it in the juice that had run from his meat.

I smiled, glad to hear him say so.

Once the food had been cleared, we pushed the tables aside and gathered round the fire. The story telling was about to begin. I felt a shiver of excitement in anticipation of the new tales we'd hear tonight. Ingvar sat beside me once more, his shoulder touching mine, his face lit by the firelight. The knowledge that he was choosing to be near me gave me a glow of pleasure.

Helgi spoke first; he told us of storms at sea, of trading and battles. He described the green land of Ireland, where there was daylight even in the depths of winter. I listened avidly, drinking in the new images, my troubles forgotten in the excitement.

My brother recited a poem he'd written for an Irish chieftain, and showed off the gift of a fine knife it had earned him. When he finished, Ingvar was invited to tell the tale of how the ship had been ambushed by pirates on the way home. He went to stand by the fire to speak, so everyone could hear him. At last I had an excuse to look at him without shyness. I watched his face become animated as he recounted the gruesome battle on the deck, and how they had turned the tables on the pirates. He made light of the fear and the danger they'd all been in. Even so, I shuddered at the thought of it.

When he'd finished speaking, two of the young farm

girls, Halla and Jorrun, beckoned him over to them and to my regret he went to sit beside them. I could see Halla gazing worshipfully up at him as he answered their questions and felt unaccountably annoyed. Halla was nearly my age and far too pretty with her blue eyes and fair hair.

One of Helgi's guests asked him to recount the story of how he'd come to settle in Iceland. He did so, telling of the hauntings that drove them from the east fjords, leading them to settle here, near us.

'And you, Bjorn?' asked the guest when he finished. 'How did you come to settle in such a remote spot?'

My father shifted a little and exchanged glances with my mother. He was a gifted storyteller, but never liked recounting this tale for some reason. Perhaps he had told it too often. His eyes sought out my brother Asgrim, who was in the act of draining a horn of mead. With a slight shake of the head he turned to me.

I clenched my fists tightly in my lap and sent a swift prayer to the goddess. *Not tonight, please don't make me speak tonight*, I whispered inside my head. *Asgrim isn't so very drunk; let him tell the story*.

My father was looking at me now and I looked back at him with a pleading I hoped would melt the stoniest of hearts. It had no effect.

'My daughter Sigrun will recount the tale,' said Bjorn quietly.

A hush fell on the longhouse. There were at least thirty people here, all staring at me. My legs turned to water and my mouth dried up. My whole body shook as I shrivelled up inside with horror. Nothing frightened me more than speaking to so many. I'd rather get back on the runaway horse and face the cliff again.

But I couldn't argue with my father in front of all these people. So I dragged myself to my feet, took a deep breath, clasped my trembling hands together, and recounted the tale I'd learned by heart as a little girl.

'Some twenty winters since,' I began, my voice shaking, 'my father, Bjorn Svanson, was a renowned and prosperous chieftain in Norway. But King Harald Tanglehair had vowed never to comb his hair until he'd brought all of Norway under his control. He found excuses to rid himself of many of the noblemen of the land, forcing them to submit to him or die. Bjorn would not submit.'

I smiled tremulously at my father, pride in my heritage momentarily overcoming my fear. But my father looked away. I'd never understood his modesty over his past. 'So,' I began again, blushing to realize I'd paused, and everyone was waiting for me to continue, 'when he heard the king was marching towards him with his army, Bjorn loaded a ship with all his worldly possessions, and he and his wife, Thora Asgrimsdottir, went aboard.'

I looked over at my mother, but she looked down, a little colour in her pale cheeks. She must still be disturbed by her vision.

'They sailed across the sea, guided by the stars and by Thor, the protector of those at sea, until they reached the new land they'd heard tell of: Iceland.'

There was an appreciative murmur at my words, and I was aware of the strangers smiling at me encouragingly. I spoke on, my voice growing steadier, though my hands still shook.

'The goddess Freya spoke to Thora,' I continued. 'When they reached Iceland, she told her not to go south to the fertile lands, because there was danger in the south. It's never wise to ignore the warnings of the goddess.'

I swallowed hard as I spoke the familiar words, remembering that the goddess had spoken to mother again today. But I had to continue my tale:

'So instead, Bjorn directed his ship northwards, guided always by Thora's vision of a bay of great beauty, ringed with snow-capped mountains and rich in good farming land. And when they sailed into this bay, she knew it at once and everyone on board gave thanks to the goddess for her guidance.

'Then Bjorn threw his high seat pillars overboard, and declared that wherever they washed up, that's where he would make his home. Sure enough, they landed on the beach just below this very spot. Bjorn built the farmhouse here, and named it Thorastead after his wife.'

I stopped, out of breath and drained, relieved to be finished. Everyone applauded, making the blood rush to my face again. I was trembling uncontrollably. I leant forward and picked up my goblet in a hand that shook, only to find it empty.

Asgerd filled my goblet. The liquid eased my parched mouth and throat, but it tasted sickly now. I'd have preferred the sharp, refreshing tang of whey.

I was in a state of restless excitement and confusion. The storytelling had ended, people were chatting together in small groups. I saw Halla giggle and put her hand on Ingvar's arm, and suddenly everything was too much for me. The strain of speaking on top of everything that had happened today had shaken me and I needed to clear my head of the dizzying effects of the mead.

I stumbled across the crowded hall, out of the smoke and fug of the house into the sharp, clear night air outside. It was cold tonight and the sky was heavily overcast, stealing the brightness from the light summer night.

I gulped the chill air and tried to still my shaking as I walked down to the beach. I sank onto a rock, drawing my knees up under me and resting my chin on them. The waves lapped gently at the shingle in the dusk. Every now and then a larger wave came higher up the beach, hushing over the stones. I threw a pebble into the water and then another. They landed with small plops, loud in the stillness of the evening. Distantly, I could hear the merriment drifting down from the house.

Before long, I heard another sound, closer at hand. Feet crunching across the shingle towards me. I thought it might be Asgerd or Erik come to tell me off for running out in the cold, so I didn't look round. But a moment later I felt a hand warm on my shoulder. I looked up, startled to see that the person beside me was Ingvar.

'I didn't mean to make you jump,' he said quietly, sitting down beside me.

I was glad he'd come to find me but nervous too. I risked a swift sideways glance at him. He was staring peacefully out into the bay, his face completely familiar to me and yet strange. We'd spent so many of our childhood hours together, but Ingvar had changed.

We sat in silence a while, and before I could formulate my tangled thoughts, Ingvar's warm hand closed over my cold one, holding it in a comforting clasp. I sat without

19

moving, my heart hammering so hard I felt dizzy. His next words took me by surprise.

'Would you like to see the ship?' he asked me.

'I . . . the ship? Yes, of course,' I replied. I'd seen the ship before. We'd all explored it, Asgrim, Ingvar, and I, before they set sail last spring. Even Gudrun, who so rarely joined in our games, had come with us. We'd played in it, imagining what the journey would be like. But if Ingvar wanted me to look at it again, I was willing to do so. He stood up, pulling me to my feet, and then led the way along the shingle to the tall shape of the boat. It was beached, pulled up high out of danger of unexpected storms.

'Our home for the best part of the last year,' Ingvar said with a grin, slapping the timber side of the ship. He climbed onto a block and vaulted lightly over the side. Then he turned and held his hand down to help me up. I didn't need his assistance, but I put my hand in his anyway. Once I was on the deck, Ingvar stood looking down at me for a moment. I thought he was about to say something, but then he dropped his eyes and turned away. 'Welcome aboard,' he said.

I looked around me. The ship had been well scrubbed since the men's return, but there was nonetheless a whiff of latrines and male sweat about it. I wrinkled my nose a little.

'How unpleasant to be so many people crammed together for so long,' I remarked.

Ingvar shrugged. 'The weather is worse,' he replied. 'When you can't escape the lashing rain, and it's so cold you can't stop shaking no matter how many layers you put on. Or when the ship is being blown before a storm in the darkness, and you have no idea if there are rocks ahead.'

'You must have been afraid.'

'At times. We all were. But it was exciting too.'

I walked along the deck, running my hand lightly along the side rail, worn smooth by use. 'Where did you fight?' I asked Ingvar, remembering the pirates.

With a grin, Ingvar wielded an imaginary sword. 'We fought all over the ship,' he said. 'Here, I was pinned against the side.' He leaned back, acting it out. 'But I managed to kill my opponent with a lucky thrust.' He thrust his arm forward and up and I imagined his opponent falling. 'And here . . . ' he stepped across the deck, 'I was wounded, but I didn't fully realize until later.'

'Wounded?' I asked shocked. 'Where?'

'A gash in the side,' said Ingvar lightly. 'It healed well.'

The realization that he could have been killed in that battle struck me, and I shuddered.

'Are you cold?' Ingvar asked at once. 'I should have brought your cloak.'

'No,' I said. 'I was just thinking battle must be terrifying.'

'It isn't,' said Ingvar unexpectedly. I looked up at him surprised. 'There's no time to be afraid when you're fighting for your life. There were other things I found far worse.'

'Such as?' I couldn't imagine what he was going to say. I saw it was his turn to shiver, and only half aware of what I was doing, I drew a little closer.

'We . . . raided a village,' Ingvar said. 'We sneaked up

21

a river and burst on a peaceful settlement at dawn to kill, steal, and take slaves.'

'You did that?' I asked astonished. My father had strong views on the taking of slaves. I'd understood over the years that he was unusual. Many of the visitors to our farm had told tales like Ingvar's. They considered it brought glory and honour as well as wealth. My father disagreed. He said it destroyed lives. Somehow I'd always thought Ingvar's father agreed with him. He was his best friend, after all.

'Just once,' said Ingvar. 'We were with another Viking ship off the coast of Scotland and they persuaded us to join them. But . . . '

I waited for him to continue.

'Oh, Sigrun,' he said at last. 'The terror and pain we caused them. The men from the other ship fought the men who tried to defend the settlement and killed them. That was bad enough. But then they couldn't stop. They killed the old people too, and captured the children. And what they did to the women . . . '

He turned away from me, in the grip of memories. 'So much screaming, so much blood and death . . . ' he whispered at last.

I was deeply shocked by the tale, and moved by Ingvar's obvious distress. I drew closer, wanting to comfort him, but unsure how.

'It sounds . . . ' I began, but my voice tailed off. I didn't know how to put my horror into words.

Hearing my voice so close, Ingvar turned. I wasn't quite sure how it happened, but we moved together, hugging awkwardly. This was the greeting my mother's vision had prevented earlier in the day. His body was warm against mine in the cold night air; his nearness made my heart beat faster.

'Sigrun . . . ' said Ingvar. He didn't say anything else, just pulled me closer, folding his arms around me, holding me. I hugged him back, my cheek pressed against the rough wool of his tunic, understanding that he needed comfort.

'I understood, that day,' said Ingvar, his voice muffled against my hair, his breath warm, 'that everything your father says about slavery is true. I imagined it was us—you and me and Asgrim, and my sister Gudrun too, snatched away while we were still children and watching while our parents were killed and . . . worse.'

I tightened my arms around him, appalled by the image he described.

'Ingvar!' A voice rang out somewhere near the longhouse. 'Where're you?'

'It's Asgrim,' I whispered. Reluctantly, I let Ingvar go, feeling the cold air rush around me, chilling me where his arms had warmed a moment before. We both shivered, and looked at each other for a moment in the dim light. We weren't ready to be disturbed, but there was no help for it. My brother was heading towards us.

'Is'at you, Ingvar?' he slurred, walking unsteadily across the shingle to the ship. 'What you doin' out here ina cold? Oh, it's . . . ' he broke off, noticing me. There was an awkward silence. I blushed, wondering what my brother was thinking.

'Come on, Ingvar. There'sh drinkin' to be done. Don' wast' the night talkin' to my li'l shishter.'

I'd never seen Asgrim so drunk that he couldn't speak clearly. Perhaps the mead had muddled his eyesight too, and he hadn't seen our closeness of a moment before. I was relieved. I didn't want to be teased and misunderstood for giving a friend a hug.

Ingvar helped me down from the ship and we accompanied my brother back to the house as though nothing had happened. But it had. I was filled with unfamiliar feelings. It was as though I'd discovered something important out there under the summer night sky. I just wasn't quite sure what it was yet.

At home, everyone was unrolling sleeping furs and lying down to sleep. Some picked spots near the fire, others chose the wooden sleeping platforms against the wall. Families curled up together, husbands and wives sought quiet corners. My parents withdrew hand in hand to their sleeping room. No one but Asgrim wanted to stay awake.

I bade Ingvar a shy and distant goodnight, while my brother started telling him a long and incomprehensible story about a fight. I climbed into the loft where my sleeping furs lay. Eventually, peace descended on the house, broken only by an occasional crackle from the banked-up fire and the rhythmic sounds of snoring.

Somehow the peace around me couldn't enclose me in its embrace. Despite the joy I felt at seeing my kin and friends back again, despite the excitement of renewing my friendship with Ingvar, a deep sense of unease disturbed me. My mother's vision hung over us still. Something was deeply wrong.

CHAPTER THREE

I woke with a jolt the next morning. Anxiety gnawed at me immediately, but it took me a few moments to remember why. Then everything came flooding back: the double homecoming, the vision, and the secrets. Happier memories came too, to temper the fears: the walk on the beach with Ingvar and the hug.

It was early. The bright morning light was seeping through a few tiny cracks in the ceiling, but it was still cold. It was difficult to judge whether it was rising time as there was no darkness at this time of the year. But I could hear the cattle lowing restlessly from the pasture so milking time must be near.

I couldn't lie still. Sitting up, I freed myself from my sheepskins and pulled my kirtle over my head. I decided to go and groom the horses, ready to show them off to my father, my brother, and to Ingvar. That would keep me busy and take my mind off the unease coiling itself around my insides. Carrying my shoes, I climbed as quietly as I could past the other sleeping girls. The ladder hadn't been put out for us to climb down yet, so there was probably no one else up.

Removing the ladder from the loft at night was supposed to protect our virtue, all those of us who were young and unmarried. It was a joke really, considering how Hild had crept down to Geirmund every night for months and was only discovered once she was with child. Father was angry at first, but then they were married and everyone forgot about it.

It wasn't too high to drop to the ground. It's what we all did if we needed to relieve ourselves in the night. As I slid down backwards and landed with a soft bump on the dirt floor, a couple of the men sleeping nearby stirred; one stopped snoring and grunted. I placed the ladder so that the other girls could climb down when they woke, and slipped barefoot out of the house.

The ground was freezing cold and the dewy grass bit my toes as I emerged into the bright light of another summer morning. I hurriedly bent and pulled my soft leather shoes onto my feet. Once the sun came up over the mountains it would be a warm day, but there'd been frost in the night to judge from the chill now. It was bad for the grain crop when the night frost persisted through the summer.

I headed for the pickets. Some riding horses were kept nearby, while the rest of the herd were left to roam free through the summer, fattening themselves on the rich grass. The four youngsters were grazing peacefully on their picket lines and all lifted their heads to nicker softly at me. I petted them, frowning at the patches of mud where they'd rolled, and checking their legs to make sure they were sound. In the excitement of the homecoming yesterday, I hadn't seen to the colt myself, which had been a mistake. Whoever had rubbed him down had done it carelessly. There were sweat patches dried into his

26

coat in places, and I detected a slight heat and swelling on one hind leg. That would need to be treated at once.

'You foolish young horse,' I chided him, rubbing his soft nose. 'What a trick that was yesterday. You shamed me in front of everyone, and hurt yourself too.'

Untying him from his picket, I led him to the stables. He went willingly; he was tame enough as long as I didn't try to ride him.

I wanted all the young horses groomed and presentable before father saw them. I'd been looking forward to this but now I worried a little he would take me less than seriously after yesterday's disaster. I sighed. I'd succeeded in breaking and taming three out of the four youngsters, after all. That ought to be impressive enough.

I'd made a poultice for the colt's leg and was rubbing down the first horse when the women walked past to begin milking. They waved to me through the open door of the stable. Once the milking was done, it wouldn't be long until breakfast time and I was hungry already.

Before I'd finished grooming the second horse, a shadow darkened the doorway. I turned and saw Ingvar's tall shape silhouetted there, his fair hair glowing in the sunlight. I smiled warmly up at him, both delighted and surprised that he'd come to find me.

'I'm just . . . ' I indicated the horses, but then dropped my brush. As I bent to collect it, I felt the colour rush into my face at the thought of what a fool I kept making of myself in front of Ingvar. It was ridiculous to be so shy, but he was no longer anything like the little boy I had played warriors with in the pasture years ago. He was a young man.

Ingvar stepped close to me, flustering me. I could smell the smoky scent of the longhouse still clinging to his woollen tunic. But he was merely running his hands over the horse I'd been grooming, apparently unaware of my confusion. I took a deep breath, steadying myself.

'This one's grown very fine,' Ingvar said with a smile that made my heart miss a beat. 'Does he run away too, or can he behave?'

'He's as gentle as the other one's wild. I broke him in the autumn and he's ready to be ridden by anyone.'

As we began to talk horses, I gradually relaxed. It was familiar territory, and it was easier to slip back into our old friendship terms. Soon Ingvar was hard at work grooming and we worked side by side in comfortable companionship until my brother joined us.

'Asgrim,' Ingvar greeted my brother. 'Have you seen how the young horses have grown?'

'Father sent me,' Asgrim said grimly. 'Some men have arrived, interested in buying horses.'

'Well, it's early in the day, but there's nothing in that to give you a long face, surely?' asked Ingvar.

'I've never seen father so agitated,' said Asgrim. He paused, looking at me, and we held one another's gaze for a moment.

'Some kind of trouble?' I asked, puzzled.

'I don't know. They're unpleasant customers . . . they refused our hospitality: they don't want breakfast. We're to bring the four youngsters down for them to look at now.'

While Ingvar and Asgrim put saddles and bridles on the three horses that were groomed, I swiftly brushed the worst of the mud off the fourth youngster. My belly was churning now. What was upsetting my father? Was it the danger my mother had foreseen? As we led the horses out of the stable, I saw the strangers standing with father, waiting for us; one tall, broad, and red-haired, the other fair and slight, with the face of a fox. To my relief, neither wore black. They were simply wearing ordinary homespun clothes in the usual browns and greens.

The sun was up now, and with it had come the warmth of the day, making the ground steam as we made our way down the hill to the three men. My father made no introductions, which surprised me, but instead, spoke to the strangers.

'All four youngsters are broken and for sale,' he said, his voice cold and unfriendly.

The red-haired stranger headed straight for yesterday's runaway.

'This one isn't fully broken yet,' I explained hurriedly. 'He's still rather wild. The others are gentler and fully trained.'

My father frowned slightly. The stranger, after a brief stare at me from ice-cold eyes, remarked: 'This is the only one up to my weight.'

He swung himself heavily onto the horse's back, landing with a bump that had the youngster pulling madly on the reins I still held. His head was up, his eyes rolling back to show the whites and his ears flat against his head. I was afraid for both the horse and the stranger. But the man simply pulled the reins out of my hands, put his heels to the horse's side and pushed him forwards.

With an indignant snort, the horse threw up his head

and started to fight the bit. The stranger pulled at the young horse's mouth and kicked him again, and the horse let out a shrill, indignant squeal. He flung himself into a series of bucks ending by rearing up on his hind legs with a loud neigh. Several people came running out of the longhouse to see what was going on, my mother among them.

She saw the strangers and her expression changed. A look of horror came over her face. Leaving the group of onlookers by the door, she half-ran forward towards us. And then she froze, her eyes glazed. I knew it was the sight, but I also knew she was in danger. The horse was twisting and bucking. He hadn't yet unseated his rider, but he was out of control. A final twist and the rider fell heavily to the ground. The young horse turned to bolt and ran straight towards my mother as she stood help-less and unseeing.

'Mother!' I cried out, trying to warn her. I could see her standing there, motionless, unaware that a mad-dened horse was running straight at her. Her sight was turned inwards; towards whatever it was the goddess was showing her. I ran to her, but I couldn't overtake the horse. Head held high, foam flying from his mouth, he fled across the yard. In his desperation to escape the man who had tormented him, he didn't see my mother.

There was a moment's confusion. Hoof beats and the squeak of leather, then a collision. I saw my mother fall under the legs of the runaway horse, and I heard the sickening snap of bone as the horse trod heavily on her leg. Then he was gone in a thunder of hooves, stirrups flying, and my mother lay crumpled on the ground.

'Thora,' yelled my father, already running towards her, his voice hoarse with fear. He reached her first, dropping to his knees beside her, taking her hand. She clung to him, her eyes clouded with pain. 'Send them away,' she panted through gritted teeth.

'You're hurt,' said my father. As I knelt beside him, I could see all the colour had drained from his face. 'Oh my love,' he whispered. 'No, please, no.'

I was already checking my mother's leg. She cried out as I touched the break.

'This needs to be set at once,' I said, feeling sick at the thought.

'I know,' she gasped, her face white. In a voice faint with pain, she whispered urgently: 'Bjorn, you must send the men away. They aren't here to trade, but to spy.'

Exhausted from the effort of speaking, she fell back. Everything was confusion around me. I heard my father shouting at the strangers, sending them away. Ingvar and Erik carried my mother indoors. Asgerd hurried for splints and Astrid tore strips of cloth. This wasn't the first broken bone I'd set, but I'd always worked under my mother's guidance.

Mother endured the move with gritted teeth. There were beads of sweat on her brow and her hands were clenched at her sides. Ingvar and Erik stood ready to hold her down as I worked. I knew if I made a mess of this, my mother could be a cripple for the rest of her life, her gait marred by an ugly limp. I breathed deeply, trying to stop my hands shaking. My mother reached out and grasped my wrist.

'You can do this,' she said calmly, despite her own pain. 'I trust you.'

'Thank you,' I said gratefully. Her confidence gave me courage, but it didn't last long: even though I worked as quickly and as lightly as I knew how, my mother gave great cries of pain that sent shivers through me, unnerving me. But the task was done at last and the leg tightly bound. I sat limply by my mother's side, trembling and sick from the effort and responsibility. She took my hand.

'Well done, my daughter,' she said, her voice faint. Her skin was cold and clammy and I knew she was in shock. The danger wasn't over. This might be a clean break that healed well. Or there might be complications—internal bleeding, for example, which I could do nothing about. Oh, how I wished I was better at this. I'd worked hard to learn, but I didn't have the favour of Eir, the goddess of healing. And now my mother, who I'd always depended on, was sick herself.

'Put your fears aside, Sigrun,' said my mother. 'What will be, will be.'

I nodded numbly, unsurprised by my mother's uncanny ability to see my thoughts and feelings. She always knew.

'If only *I* had the sight,' I said suddenly, the words escaping me unexpectedly. 'Then I might have been able to prevent you being hurt.'

It was the first time I'd ever expressed such a wish to my mother and her reply astonished me.

'Don't wish for it, Sigrun. It's . . . a great burden to bear.'

'But it keeps us safe . . . '

32

'It didn't keep me safe today. On the contrary. And it comes at a cost. Can you imagine seeing the future, and being unable to change it?' Her voice was a strained whisper. 'So much fear. So much dread. And sometimes it's a glimpse only. Without the context, the whole picture, it's misleading. Things haven't always turned out as I've expected.'

I'd never thought of it like that, but dimly I could see that might be so. 'I thought you were disappointed I hadn't inherited the gift,' I whispered. 'It would be a sign I was a true healer.'

My mother's hands tightened on mine. 'No,' she said. 'I dreaded it coming to you.'

She lay back on her furs, pale and exhausted, her eyes closed. I stroked her damp hair back from her brow, and turned the new thought over in my mind. Mother wasn't disappointed in me. And despite my fears, I felt as though a burden had been lifted from my shoulders.

My father entered the room, his face lined with worry, and dropped to his knees at my mother's side. He drew her hand from mine and kissed it tenderly. 'Thora,' he whispered, his voice breaking with distress. He saw the splint, looked up at me and managed a faint smile. 'Well done, Sigrun,' he said. 'Will it heal?'

'That's in the hands of the goddess,' whispered my mother faintly. 'But, Bjorn, did you send those men away? They weren't here to buy horses.' She was agitated again, and needed to be calm.

'Can I have your keys?' I asked softly, intending to look in the storeroom for some willow bark or elder that I could brew into a pain-killing drink. Mother fumbled at the cord at her waist, untied the household keys and handed them to me.

'Those were the men from the market,' I heard father say softly. 'They . . .'

I paused, hoping to hear more, but my father stopped and glanced at me. Reluctantly, I left the room.

CHAPTER FOUR

As I emerged from my mother's room, everyone looked up. Nobody was working; they were all gathered in groups around the fire.

'How's Thora?' I was asked from all sides. Someone clutched my sleeve, I think it was Hild; I caught a glimpse of her worried face. Someone else was tugging at my other arm. 'Will she be all right, Sigrun?'

I felt crushed by so many expectations. 'I think so,' I said, dazed. 'Her leg is broken and she needs quiet. I think, well . . . I must get her some medicine.' I felt a wave of dizziness come over me, and I swayed a little.

'Let Sigrun alone!' Asgerd ordered the others. 'Can't you see she needs some peace to think about a cure?'

At once there was space and air around me and I could breathe again. I gave Asgerd a tremulous but grateful smile. 'What can I do to help?' she asked, hiding her own concern under a brisk manner.

'I'm going to brew a tea from willow bark,' I told her. 'So I'll need hot water.'

Asgerd nodded and picked up the water pitcher, but it was empty.

'I'll fill it,' said a quiet, calm voice, and Ingvar took the pitcher from Asgerd's hands and left the house.

'Don't mind the others fussing you like that,' said Asgerd in an under-voice. 'They're worried. Your mother's the heart of the household, and we all want her to be well.'

'I understand,' I told her, and bit my lip. All these people, all my family and friends, were depending on me. It was a good thing they couldn't see how I doubted myself and my abilities.

I went to the storeroom, my mother and Asgerd's domain, and unlocked the door with the large iron key. I loved this room, with its rich smell of stored butter, cheese, dried fish and meat, and barrels of *skyr*, the milk curds we preserved the summer berries in. As autumn approached there would be grain and vegetables too, stored against the coming of the long, dark winter.

Today, it wasn't the food that interested me. I went straight to the medicines. The powerful and dangerous medicines, my mother kept in a locked chest. I didn't need those today, thank the goddess. I would scarcely trust myself with them. The willow bark was stored hanging from the rafters with many other dried barks and plants. I broke off a tiny piece, locked the door carefully behind me and took the bark to the fireside.

I stooped to pick up a stone pot and began to grind the willow bark in it. Most people had found tasks to do now, or Asgerd had found some for them, and I was left in peace to work. As I pounded the bark, I found my hands were shaking and had no strength in them. This brought tears to my eyes. Mother needed me to be strong and here I was, as weak as a new-born kitten and now crying into the bargain. Ingvar returned with the water, and gave it to Asgerd to heat. I hurriedly turned my face away so he wouldn't see my tears, but it was too late. He was already crouching beside me, one hand on my shoulder.

'Sigrun, are you all right?' he asked.

I nodded, not trusting my voice.

'Here, let me do this,' said Ingvar, taking the tools gently from me and beginning to pound the bark himself. Like fetching the water, this was women's work, and the surprise at seeing him undertake it stopped my tears.

'Thora will recover, Sigrun,' Ingvar said as he worked. 'My father broke his leg too, when I was just a baby. He doesn't even limp.'

'I know,' I replied, dashing the last tears away with the back of my hand and trying to regain control of myself. 'But he had my mother to set the bone for him. She's told me about it. My mother only had . . . me.'

'You should have faith in yourself,' said Ingvar. 'The rest of us trust you.'

'Do you?' I asked him sceptically. 'Tell me truthfully; if you'd broken your leg, and I and not my mother arrived to set it for you, wouldn't you wish it was her?'

'Absolutely not,' Ingvar assured me. 'I would be pleased you were going to tend me.'

I was certain Ingvar was lying. But his lie sprang from kindness, and I was grateful for it, so I smiled a little and said nothing.

'Here you are,' said Ingvar, handing me back the bark. 'Will that do?'

I shook the finely-ground powder. 'Thank you,' I said.

I put it into a goblet and poured a ladleful of hot water into it, stirring carefully.

'What did the runes say, Sigrun?' asked Asdis from across the fire where she was sitting sewing.

I looked over at her, the flickering orange light dancing on her concerned face, and all my courage drained away again. She was assuming I'd already consulted the runes as my mother always did in cases of sickness and injury.

The runes. Dear Freya, please. Not the runes. The small leather bag of pebbles was lying beside my furs in the sleeping loft. My mother had given them to me for my tenth birthday, each pebble painstakingly painted with a sacred rune. She'd told me their secrets over the years, instructing me in their use, explaining and demonstrating often.

After all these years they still meant nothing to me. They spoke a language I didn't understand. I read them slowly, clumsily, always unsure how to interpret their message. It was a shameful secret I hid even from mother. The goddess knew my failure, but to the rest of the world, I pretended. I became aware I was still staring at Asdis, and that she was waiting for my reply.

'I'll read them later,' I mumbled. 'There's no need to consult the runes over such a simple remedy as this.'

She frowned, but didn't press me. My legs shook a little as I got up to take my mother the medicine. Ingvar's words had soothed me, but Asdis had undone that with her question, and it was with some trepidation that I went in to my mother's room. I hoped she wouldn't think I'd selected the wrong medicine.

38

I found her and my father hand-locked, talking fast in urgent voices. They broke off as I entered.

'I brought you . . . ' I began, and then my voice trailed off as I looked from one to the other of them. 'What were you talking about?' I asked.

'There are plans to be made, Sigrun,' said my father. 'We'll tell you all you need to know soon enough.'

I felt anger rise in me and shut my lips tightly to keep it in. I was frightened and doing my best to help, and *still* they wouldn't trust me with whatever secret they were keeping from me. 'Why won't you tell me now?' I asked, trying, but not succeeding, to ask calmly.

Father seemed not to notice I had spoken. He bent and kissed my mother's hands passionately and then withdrew. I stood frozen. I didn't know whether fear or hurt was uppermost in me as he brushed past me without another glance.

'What have you brought me?' my mother asked. Her voice was so faint and weak that my fear won. She needed nursing, not a confrontation. So I swallowed down the turmoil of thoughts and feelings within me, sat down beside her and offered the goblet. She sniffed at it and pulled a face.

'Willow. I can bear the pain, Sigrun, my dearest, without this.'

'I know. But you need to rest. And there may be fever. It's what you would prescribe to anyone else.'

My mother grimaced and sipped at the liquid obediently.

* * *

The rest of the day was long. My father kept everyone close to the house and set guards to watch the approaches. We ate and worked mainly in silence, a numbing sense of fear and uncertainty stealing over all of us as we realized my father expected serious trouble. A pregnant woman and a mother with tiny children were sent to Helgi's to stay. My father took them himself and stayed a while, probably to consult his friend.

'Can you think why anyone would want to harm us?' I whispered fearfully to Ingvar as we sat down together to eat nightmeal. 'We're on good terms with neighbours near and far. We heal their hurts and deliver their babies.'

'It's as much a mystery to me as it is to you,' he said. 'It must be something to do with those men that came this morning. I'll stay here until Bjorn feels safe again, if you'd like me too?'

'Of course,' I said, and then blushed.

Sleep was a long time coming that evening. The atmosphere in the house was edgy. My father retired into his room to be alone with my mother as soon as nightmeal was over. I lay in the sleeping loft, unable to get comfortable in my furs, endless and frightening possibilities turning over in my mind. Late in the night I fell into a deep sleep, from which a shout abruptly roused me. I sat up, confused and disorientated, my heart hammering.

My mother's voice was speaking below, quiet but agitated. Something was wrong; perhaps she was in pain. I dragged my kirtle over my head and scrambled past the other young women towards the edge of the loft. I could hear other voices down in the main house now and movement. What was going on?

As I climbed down the ladder, there was enough light to make out the men of the household, every one of them up and dressed with weapons in their hands. My heart almost stopped in pure fright. 'Father?' I cried, seeing him standing by the door, peering out through a crack he'd pulled the woollen stuffing out of.

'Hush, Sigrun!' he said, his voice low, but urgent. 'Wake the women and children and take them into the hidden passageway. As fast as you can. Keep as quiet as possible.'

'Why? What's going on?' I asked, feeling my mouth go dry and my hands start to shake.

My father looked at me and hesitated. 'Don't be frightened,' he said. 'We'll keep you safe.'

His words made me more afraid than ever. What was so terrifying that I couldn't even look at it? Giants? Demons? Trolls? I slipped past him, and put my own eye to the gap he'd been looking through.

The glimpse I caught before father pulled me away made my blood freeze in horror: I could see black-clad men on horseback around the house. Some were carrying drawn swords, others had lit torches, the flames flickering and jumping in the wind. My mother's vision had come true.

It wasn't dark out. Instead the world was bathed in that subdued, early morning light before the sun rose. So why did the men need torches? I looked up at my father, frightened, clutching his arm. 'What do they want?' I whispered in a strangled voice. Father laid his free hand over my grasping fingers.

'We'll find out soon enough, but you can see it's nothing good, Sigrun,' he whispered. 'I need you to be brave. Now you've seen, do as I tell you.'

I fought the fear that chilled me and hurried to obey him. Climbing back into the loft on limbs that were clumsy with terror and the need for haste, I woke the young women with hurried shaking and a finger to their lips to hush them before they could speak. 'Don't make a sound,' I whispered each time. 'Dress warmly and come downstairs. We're in danger.'

We were all down the ladder in just a few moments, some girls whimpering in fear. The married women who slept downstairs were already up and dressed, waiting for us, their children clutching their hands. A dreadful thought struck me.

'What about mother? She can't walk with us.'

'I'll take care of Thora,' said my father grimly.

'But . . . can't we carry her?' I asked. I knew as I said it, it was stupid. None of us were strong enough to carry anyone in the confined space of the tunnel; her leg would be horribly jarred.

'Trust me, Sigrun,' ordered my father. He was efficient, decisive, and cool, giving orders and expecting them to be obeyed at once. It was a side of him I rarely saw, but I knew it well enough not to argue.

'Go now. Stay hidden in the passageway.' He turned abruptly. 'Ingvar, go with them, please.'

Ingvar stepped forward from the shadows. 'I want to fight,' he objected, gripping his sword.

42

'It may not come to that.'

'But I . . .'

Father stepped forward and grasped Ingvar's arm. 'I have another task for you, if you have the courage for it.'

Ingvar's eyes flashed in the gloom and he stood straighter.

'When you've taken the women into the tunnel, follow it right along to the far end, take my fastest horse from the stable and ride to your father's for help. Do you dare do that? There's a risk you'll be caught.'

'I dare,' said Ingvar. Swiftly, he led us all to the tunnel. As we reached it, I turned again and ran back to my mother's room. She lay on her bed staring at the ceiling, her hands clenching and unclenching. She jumped as I knelt beside her.

'What are you doing?' she asked fiercely. 'Go with the women, and stay safe!'

I bent and kissed her cheek, and then I ran after the others. Asgerd lifted the false section of wall made of woven sticks and rushes. We all ducked under it and descended the rough steps carefully. The secret passageway had been built for precisely such an emergency as this. It was lined with rocks and clay, and smelt damp and musty with disuse. It led underground, up the hill some distance to a hidden exit just above the stables.

We all halted as the last person entered the tunnel and the wall was closed behind us. It was hard to see who was who in the murky darkness, though I could make out a cloud of indistinct, pale faces. I made my way past them one by one, hoping to find Ingvar.

'Who's attacking us?' asked little Jorunn in a

high-pitched voice, clutching her mother's hand.

'Shhh,' said Astrid, crouching down and hugging her close. 'No one's attacking us.'

There was a buzz of frightened whispers and a few suppressed moans.

'You must be quiet,' Ingvar's voice spoke from right beside me, deep in contrast to the women's voices. 'If you make a noise, you'll give us away.'

The frightened murmur hushed at once apart from a quiet sobbing. I couldn't tell who it was. In the darkness, Ingvar took my hand and pressed it.

'Please be careful,' I whispered. I felt sick at the thought of him riding out alone past all those men.

'I'll be too quick for them,' Ingvar promised. Then he let go of my hand and moved off up the tunnel, his footsteps fading quickly.

'Will we be safe here?' whispered Halla.

'No one will find this tunnel,' said Asdis's voice in the darkness.

'We don't know that,' I whispered. 'It's never been used before.'

'It has,' said Astrid, and even her whisper shook with fear. 'We hid here twice when I was a child.'

I fell silent, realizing there were more secrets being kept than I had any idea of. I felt betrayed. 'Men clothed in black,' I said, remembering my mother's vision. 'What's the significance of black?'

'Vengeance,' said Hild. 'Black signifies revenge.'

'Hush!' whispered Asgerd fiercely.

'Revenge for what?' I asked, ignoring her, a hundred possibilities crowding into my mind.

44

'The greatest danger,' Asgerd whispered, not answering my question, 'is if smoke comes into the tunnel. If anyone smells smoke, we'll move further along. And if it's really bad, we might have to go right outside.'

A spasm of fear shot through me. It clutched my stomach and squeezed it, making me crouch over in terror. So that's what the torches were for. The men, whoever they were, were planning to set fire to the house and burn us all alive. There was a frightened murmur of voices around me as everyone understood what Asgerd had said.

I thought of the men back there in the house. My mother unable to walk. My throat went tight at the thought of them trapped in there, the house blazing. The closeness of the crowded tunnel was closing in on me, suffocating me. I couldn't stay still. Silently, I turned and began to make my way along the dark passageway, following Ingvar. At least from the stable I'd be able to see what was happening.

CHAPTER FIVE

The roof of the tunnel wasn't high enough to stand upright, so I had to stoop as I ran. There was mainly rock above, the ceiling of the tunnel disguised as a stone wall from the outside. I was quickly short of breath and realized it was fear that was affecting me so badly. I'd always suspected I lacked true Viking courage, and chided myself as I walked. I *have* to be strong, I told myself. Fear *won't* help. It'll weaken me. I *won't* be afraid.

As I said this, I stumbled and fell because my legs were shaking so much. I could feel a sharp pain and wetness on my right knee and on the heel of my right hand. Blood. I wiped at it with my tunic and walked on, forcing my trembling legs to carry me.

I knew the exit from the tunnel was hidden behind the stable, so that anyone fleeing would have the best possible chance of getting a good head start before they were spotted. But real cover wasn't possible in such an open, barren landscape. There were no trees that reached above a man's waist. Once Ingvar was outdoors, they would see him and pursue him. Everyone I cared about was in danger and I could do nothing to help.

I emerged behind the stable, blinking and stumbling into the brightness of the early morning. I saw Ingvar crouching down, peeping over the low stone wall next to the building.

'That's more men than Bjorn reckoned on,' I heard him mutter. 'We don't stand a chance.'

His words made my stomach lurch. I crouched down beside him, gazing at my home. Some twenty strangers had surrounded the house, most on horseback.

'Why are you still here?' I whispered.

'They've taken the horses,' Ingvar replied angrily. 'There's only the old mare left, and my feet practically touch the ground either side of her. I'm so sorry, Sigrun. I wondered if I should try to get through on foot, but they'd catch me almost at once.'

Ingvar looked back down towards the house. There were voices drifting up from the longhouse. 'What are they saying?' I asked.

Ingvar hushed me, listening intently.

'I think they're offering to let the women and children out of the house,' said Ingvar, his voice very grave. 'They must truly be intending to burn it.'

My ears were singing. I couldn't hear. I couldn't think straight. My home. My family. They mustn't burn it. 'Why?' I asked in a voice that was half moan, half wail. 'Why would they do that to us?'

Ingvar shook his head helplessly.

'Why doesn't father let them out?' I asked, desperately. 'Mother especially. She can't get out through the tunnel. What's he waiting for?'

Ingvar looked at me briefly and then averted his eyes. He spoke low: 'Letting them out is no guarantee of safety, Sigrun. Death is not the only thing to be afraid of.'

47

I couldn't imagine what he meant. 'What could be worse than burning alive?'

'If you'd seen the way women are sometimes treated . . .' Ingvar's voice trailed off, and I remembered what he'd said to me on the boat, though I still didn't understand what he meant.

I took a deep breath, trying to still my shaking before I spoke.

'I'll ride to fetch your father,' I said. 'The mare will carry me well enough. I ride light.'

'No,' Ingvar said immediately. 'She can't outrun those horses.'

But I'd already pulled away from him and slipped inside the stables. I grabbed a bridle off the hook to put onto the mare. There was no need for a saddle. Ingvar appeared behind me and grasped my arm.

'I can't let you go,' he said. 'Your father will kill me.'

'If I don't go, we'll all die!' I cried, my voice too loud. I saw Ingvar move to silence me and lowered my voice. 'You *have* to let me try, Ingvar,' I said desperately. 'Even if I get caught, perhaps I can alert your father. It's our *only* chance. I'll be halfway there before they even spot me.'

I vaulted onto the mare and pulled her round. Ingvar caught my hand and held it tight. I could see the indecision in his face. He hadn't been afraid to go himself, but he was afraid to let me go. I didn't give him a choice; I pulled my hand out of his and kicked the mare hard. I ducked low over her neck as she shot out through the stable door, leaving Ingvar behind.

I tried not to think about the consequences. About

what might happen to me if I was captured, which I almost certainly would be. My mouth and throat were dry with the fear I'd been hiding from Ingvar. To keep it at bay, I focused all my thoughts on riding to escape the men's notice. As we cantered straight up the side of the hill behind the stable, the hoof beats were muffled in the long grass. No one looked round.

The hillside was steep and the horse was old. She struggled as the slope grew ever steeper, the vegetation fading into a rugged barrenness. Her unshod hooves which had been silent on the grass were now clattering softly on the stones; any minute now we'd be heard.

I steadied the horse a little, letting her catch her breath and place her hooves more carefully. The men below were clearly absorbed in whatever was going on down there. I prayed that might last. I didn't look down to the house, afraid the sight of all those men might take the last of my courage from me. Already my hands were slippery with sweat.

A shout broke into my thoughts, and I realized I'd been spotted. I'd expected it, but had hoped my luck might hold a little longer. Helgi's house was still distant. I was acutely dismayed that I'd covered so little ground before they came after me.

I dropped my hands and kicked the mare.

'Go! GO!' I shouted at her, heedless now of noise. We lurched forward, the mare finding new strength after her short respite. I leaned forward, urging her, yelling, desperate to increase her speed. I pulled her round so that we were no longer going straight up the hillside. We were heading directly for Helgi's now. As we raced along the side of the hill, the mare's pace quickened, and her stride lengthened.

'Good girl,' I urged. 'Faster!'

For a moment, as I drew closer to Helgi's house, I really thought we might make it. But then the mare stumbled. She was flagging. I steadied her, and risked a swift glance behind. Two horsemen, their torches abandoned, were heading up towards us. They were riding diagonally at the hill, intending to cut me off. I felt a wave of pure terror at the sight of them. These were the men who were attacking my home; what might they do when they caught me?

The horse sensed my fear and faltered. 'No! Don't stop!' I said, pushing her on. Her pace seemed appallingly slow as the hooves behind me thundered closer and closer. It was like being caught in a nightmare when you need to run, but your legs will barely move.

The horses were so close now I could not only see and hear them, I could smell them too, sweating and straining to get ahead. And then they'd done it, got between me and Helgi's house. They both slowed, wheeling round, the riders' hands ready to snatch at my reins. As one reached out to grab them, I pulled my horse round so hard she half reared and stumbled again, and then we were through and past them, galloping flat out.

They were after me at once. Hooves thundered below and behind, a blur of noise and confusion. I could hear the men shouting, blaming one another for letting me escape. Helgi's house was ahead and I made straight for it. My horse was fighting for breath now, her sweating flanks heaving, her legs trembling. The two horses behind me were much younger and stronger.

A horse crept into my peripheral vision on either side, sweat drenched, galloping all out to catch us. I leaned lower over my horse's neck and shouted at her to go faster, but she was slowing, completely spent.

One horse was level with us. I could see the foam flying from its mouth. Now the rider was beside me, his knee almost touching mine, focused on snatching the reins and getting control of my horse.

'Helgi!' I shouted with all the breath I could muster. 'Helgi, help us!'

The sound echoed against the mountains, coming back to me and blurring with the noise and confusion of the horses.

The man almost had me. Once more, I pulled my horse aside, and she swerved wildly, almost losing her footing. She recovered, but stumbled and staggered with tiredness, coughing.

'Helgi!' I screamed again, terrified and desperate. The man reached forward and grasped my reins, pulling us to a halt. The old mare stood, head hanging, trembling and snorting with exhaustion.

I slipped off the mare's sweat-drenched back on the side away from my captor and ran towards Helgi's farm. I'd never been much of a runner, but this was life or death. I remembered my parents trapped in the longhouse, and the thought gave me a swiftness I'd never known before. But it was only moments before there were hoof beats behind me. Even a tired horse could outrun a girl on foot. I kicked off my fish-skin shoes and pulled up the hem of my long kirtle to go faster still, but before I'd covered even half the distance to Helgi's farm, the horse pulled up beside me, and the man grabbed me by the hair and twisted it.

'Helgi!' I shouted yet again, the pain making my voice hysterical. Then louder, every last vestige of breath in my body going into the cry: 'Help us! Enemies!'

My captor clapped a hand over my mouth. My hands were still free, so I tore at it with my nails and bit down hard on his fingers. There was a grunt of pain and I tasted blood. 'Vixen!' he snarled.

'Hel—!' I began one more time, my voice ringing in the still air, but the man clamped his hand back over my mouth, cutting off the sound. This time, no matter how much I squirmed and struggled in his arms, I couldn't escape. I could see Helgi's house still some distance ahead, silent and shut up for the night, its solid timber-and-stone walls and turf roof, built to keep out the winter winds, locking out sound too.

The second man reached us and between them they half carried, half dragged me away from the farm, back towards their companions. I thrashed and kicked and fought, desperate to get to our friends, to get help. I couldn't bear that I had got so close and still failed. I'd let my family down.

One man held my mouth closed, almost suffocating me, while the other tied me. I was slung across a horse and taken swiftly back to the longhouse, the breath knocked out of me by the jolting. I fought and struggled against my bonds, but I was a captive.

CHAPTER SIX

When I was dragged down from the horse again, I found myself face to face with a tall young man. I recognized him at once as the man who'd lost control of the colt and hurt mother. He stood quite still, looking me over, while I was held bound and helpless by his companions.

I glared back at him. He had a fleshy face, puckered by a small scar on one cheek, and eyes that were so pale blue and cold, they'd look more at home in the face of a dead fish. I could detect no compassion in his expression. Nothing that led me to believe he'd have mercy on my family.

'Who are you?' he asked.

'Who are you?' I asked back.

The man slapped me, making me gasp. My cheek stung and burned and my head spun for a moment. He was already raising his arm to strike me again, so I had to think quickly. I didn't know who this man was, or what he wanted, but surely the less he knew the better. 'I'm Gudrun Helgisdottir,' I blurted out. If I pretended to be Ingvar's sister, he might let me go.

'And you were riding for help?'

'I was frightened,' I babbled. 'I live over there. I was running home.'

I prayed he wouldn't ask me how I'd got out of the house.

'You're lying,' said the man. Looking back at him, I saw a slow smile spreading over his face, revealing a broken front tooth. 'You were calling for help. I saw you yesterday with the horses. You must be the impostor's daughter. Well, well. A gift from the gods.'

'My father's no impostor,' I said hotly, forgetting caution. 'He's a free man and was a chieftain.'

'He's a runaway slave, a thief, and a murderer,' said the young man, in his strange, flat voice. But his eyes had changed now. They were burning with a fanatical, greedy light. 'And it's time for him to pay his blood debt.'

'I don't know what you're talking about,' I cried, struggling against the man who held me and against the ropes around my wrists. 'You're mistaken. My father's never done anything bad to anyone. He's a good man.'

The leader leaned forward and glared. 'Let me tell you who I am,' he said. 'My name is Halfgrim Bjornsson. I've come from Norway in search of land and in search of my father. My father's name was Bjorn Svanson.'

I stared, confused, no longer sure what to think. Had my father had a child before he came to Iceland? Could this man be my half brother? The man watched my evident confusion without emotion. 'You wouldn't fool a child,' he said coldly. 'You must know that your father murdered mine and fled, stealing his ships and all his possessions. He even stole his name. He's not Bjorn Svanson, and he was certainly never a chieftain.'

A numb feeling crept over me. There must be some

mistake. My father, a slave and a murderer? It wasn't possible.

The man called Halfgrim mounted his horse and I was thrown up in front of him, my hands still bound. Halfgrim caught me round the waist and cantered towards the farm. I was limp and unresisting, my mind in turmoil.

'Hey, impostor!' shouted Halfgrim. 'I have your daughter. What do you say to that? Will you come out now?'

I could hear panic-filled voices inside the house. I felt so guilty for having allowed myself to be caught. I would have given anything at that moment to be back inside the house with them all.

'Don't give in, father!' I shouted. Halfgrim clapped his hand over my mouth. It stank of sweat, horse, and damp leather and I retched.

'What are your terms?' I heard my father's voice call.

'No terms. You come out and face justice, bringing all your treasure with you, and we'll let the rest go. Or the girl is mine to do as I please with and we burn the house with everyone in it.'

'How do I know I can trust you?' demanded my father.

There was a pause. My heart was hammering in fear. What was going through Halfgrim's mind? Was there nothing I could do?

'You don't know,' he said. 'You can't be sure. You can't trust me any more than my father could trust you. Perhaps I'll enslave all your women and claim the farm for my own. You can only hope that I'm an honourable man. More honourable than you were.'

I squirmed in the tight hold, but I couldn't move. I could only listen helplessly.

'You hide like the cowardly slave you are!' shouted my captor. 'But if you doubt my word, here's a taste of what's coming to you.'

Halfgrim wheeled his horse round and shouted orders to set the stable alight. I felt a spasm of fear that Ingvar might still be in there. Was he hiding, watching, or had he gone back down to the others in the tunnel? I watched, desperate, as three men rode up to the stable and then thrust their torches into the straw inside. They emerged coughing, and rode back down to us. I saw flames flickering inside the building. Smoke gushed out through the doorway and the gaps in the walls and roof, as all the remaining bedding and feed from last winter went up in flames. Soon the fire was licking the outside of the building.

'Please Freya and Eir and all the gods and goddesses, protect Ingvar,' I prayed silently. 'Let him have gone back into the tunnel.' I felt a sharp stab of guilt and anger at myself for failing to reach Helgi, for allowing myself to be captured.

As the stable turned into a shimmering tower of flame, cracking and roaring in the intensity of its own heat, I knew that even in the secret tunnel, my friends wouldn't be safe. The heat and smoke must be pouring into it, funnelled through the passageway. They would all be forced back into the house to take their chances with the same fate there. I felt sick with dread.

Our lives were in the hands of a cruel madman. I truly believed he wouldn't hesitate to burn us all alive. My wise and beautiful mother, my gentle and kindly father, my brother, my friends, and Ingvar, the friend of my childhood. Almost everyone I knew and loved in the world was inside that house.

'I've had enough of this,' I heard Halfgrim say impatiently. 'He's not coming out. Block the door and fire the house.'

'No!' I begged, desperately. 'Don't. Please.'

'Shut up,' said Halfgrim fiercely. 'You're my slave now, and you'll obey me.'

I watched appalled as men tore planks from the smithy and nailed them across the door of the farm. I didn't want to show my fear, but I couldn't bear it. I imagined the farm nothing but a burnt-out shell, still smoking, everyone burnt to ashes inside.

'Please, spare them,' I begged again, all pride deserting me. 'I'll do anything.'

'You have nothing I could possibly want,' sneered Halfgrim. 'And it's obvious your father cares nothing for you either, or he'd have come out by now.'

I knew this wasn't true. I could think of several reasons why my father hadn't rushed out to rescue me, and none of them were because he didn't care. I was in less danger out here than he was inside the house.

'Set fire to it,' ordered Halfgrim. Four men rode towards the house, their torches held aloft. Terror froze me and I choked on all the pleas I wanted to utter.

'It's a terrible waste,' said one of Halfgrim's companions. 'You won't find timber like this in Iceland again. It has to be brought from Norway. And there'll be treasure and weapons in there too.'

'Silence!' ordered Halfgrim. 'This is about honour and vengeance, not just loot. My father must be avenged. All these years, his soul hasn't been able to rest.'

His men had reached the house now. They spread out to the four corners, torches at the ready.

'Now,' nodded Halfgrim. But as he spoke the word, two of the torchbearers fell from their horses, arrows in their arms. Another screamed, and dropped his torch on the ground, as an arrow caught him in the leg. Their horses squealed and scattered. Only the fourth man threw his torch onto the roof where it lay smouldering.

'I suggest you all keep very still,' spoke Helgi's familiar and very welcome voice from somewhere behind me. I went limp with relief. He'd heard my cries for help after all.

There was silence except for the restless movement of frightened horses, quickly checked. Halfgrim was motionless, his arm tight around my waist.

'Who are you, and what do you want?' he asked.

'I'm a neighbour, and I want an end to this at once.'

'I have the right to vengeance,' said Halfgrim. 'The man who calls himself Bjorn Svanson is an impostor and killed my father.'

'Your father?'

'The real Bjorn Svanson. He was murdered nearly twenty winters ago in Norway, his ships and goods stolen. The impostor brought them all here and married one of my father's slaves. I don't know what happened to my kin who came here before to avenge his death. But they failed, and I won't.'

'You're mistaken,' said Helgi. 'All that will happen today is that you and your friends will ride away.'

Halfgrim made a sudden move behind me, and

something cold pressed into my neck. I froze. 'Either the impostor or his ill-begotten spawn dies today,' said Halfgrim, and turned his horse round slightly so Helgi could see the knife at my throat. The movement jarred the knife which pressed harder against me. I could hardly breathe for fear it would slice into me at any second.

'We can negotiate,' said Helgi quickly. 'But I only have your word for it that the man's an impostor. His daughter is certainly not to blame for any misunderstanding. If you hurt her, you make an enemy of me.' Helgi's hands were tense on his reins, and his horse was fretting as he spoke.

'We're at an impasse,' said Halfgrim. 'Because if you attack us, by Thor, the girl dies and the house will be burned. You won't be able to defeat us in time to save it or the people in it.'

My heart was hammering in my chest and my hands were sweating. For a moment it had seemed that Helgi had saved us, but now we were no better off than before. Our lives still hung in the balance. And the lighted torch still lay smouldering on our roof. At any moment it could catch and the house would burn.

'As I said: we talk,' said Helgi. 'I'm the *godi* for this region, so I'm the right person to negotiate a settlement between the two of you. I'm sure you'll find Svanson generous, as befits a former chieftain. He'll forgive your mistake and recompense you for your trouble.'

'That man was never a chieftain,' shouted Halfgrim furiously. 'My father was tall and red-haired like me, not small and dark like a slave. There are men here who knew him.'

'Bjorn Svanson was my kin too,' said one of Halfgrim's men. 'He's not the man who's bearing that name now. I saw him and confronted him at the summer market.'

I swallowed with difficulty for the knife was still pressing into my throat. My father *not* the real chieftain? That had been the mysterious incident at the market? I couldn't take it in. Had my whole life been based on a lie?

'As I said,' said Helgi with a calmness that was belied by his nervous horse. 'Let's negotiate.'

CHAPTER SEVEN

I was allowed down from Halfgrim's horse but closely guarded by two men. A knife was kept at the ready, but not against my throat. I could breathe again, but had no idea whether this was a brief respite only. I sat down on the damp grass, shaking from head to foot.

Helgi sent men to unblock the door, to pour water onto the smouldering roof of our longhouse, and to tend to Halfgrim's wounded men. It was lucky the summer had been so wet, or the fire would have caught far more quickly. Then Helgi and Halfgrim sat down to discuss terms. I couldn't hear what they were saying, and my stomach was churning with fear, wondering what the outcome would be. I kept trying to grasp that my father had lied to me. How many times had I heard and retold the story of how he came to Iceland? Was a single word of it true? The thought was hurtful and bewildering. Had he lied to everyone or just to me?

Several times Helgi walked down to the house to speak to my father: the negotiations seemed to go on for ever. I grew bitterly cold sitting on the open hillside in the wind. The warmth from the frantic ride to Helgi's had left me long ago. Once Halfgrim jumped to his feet, fists clenched. 'NO!' he yelled, lashing out at Helgi. His friends restrained him and they talked on.

At last they shook hands. Suddenly there was activity around us. Our people emerged from the house, bundles and clothing in their arms. Barrels too, and a sack of provisions. They made their way to our ship, their faces drawn and sad. Asgerd cast a frightened glance at me and mouthed something: I couldn't catch what. Surely we weren't leaving? Running away from our beautiful home, the crops sown in the fields, the horses, sheep, and cattle out at pasture?

Besides, the ship wasn't nearly big enough for us all. Years ago, when I was just a little girl, father had traded our *knorr*, the big cargo ship that had brought our household, young animals, and timber from Norway, for a faster ship that was more manoeuvrable. It was better suited to fishing, trading, and shorter journeys than the old ship, but it was much smaller. So what was happening?

I tried to get up, wanting to ask someone, but was pulled back down and the man who was guarding me threatened me with the knife. At last my father came out of the house, surrounded by a number of men. Ingvar was one of them, my brother Asgrim was another. Ingvar's eyes sought mine at once, and held them, a look of such sadness in his face that fear surged up in me once more.

The men kept close around my father as he made his way down to the ship. I could see that they were armed; they were my father's shield, preventing any of Halfgrim's men from attacking him, or worse still, picking him off with an arrow. My confusion and sense of loss grew.

My father climbed aboard the ship, and some of his men joined him. My brother Asgrim was among them. Others fell back, staying on land, watchful of the enemy behind them. Then Ingvar made his way over to me, his sword at his side. 'Come, Sigrun,' he said, stretching down a hand. 'It's time to go.'

'Go where?' I asked, taking his hand and letting him pull me to my feet. My limbs were chilled and cramped with sitting so long on the damp ground. Ingvar, seeing me struggle to walk, took my arm to support me.

'To the ship,' he said quietly. 'It was the best my father could do.'

'But . . .'

'Your father will explain it all to you on board.' Ingvar's voice was subdued, but also tense. 'Don't be afraid,' he added, pressing my arm reassuringly.

We reached the beach and crunched across the shingle down to the water's edge. Ingvar took me by the waist and lifted me onto the ship where my father pulled me into a bear hug.

'Sigrun, thank the gods you're safe,' he said, holding me close.

I hugged him tightly, dry-eyed and shocked. There was movement behind me and I realized we were making ready to cast off.

'Where are we going? What about mother?' I asked, horrified.

'She can't travel, Sigrun,' said my father, avoiding my eyes. 'And someone must mind the farm while we're gone.'

His voice was more choked up than I'd ever heard it.

63

'But . . . I haven't said goodbye. Gone where?' I asked. 'And why? What in Freya's name is happening?'

Father let go of me and moved abruptly away to take an oar. 'I'll tell you everything, Sigrun,' he said. 'But not now.'

I looked back to land, my home, which I'd never once left. Ingvar was standing just behind me and took my hand as I gazed out across the beloved green and brown slopes and the snow-capped mountains behind. It was impossible to take in that I was leaving them. I held Ingvar's hand tightly; it was the one fixed point in my whole world. The ropes had been cast off now and we were moving away from the beach out into the bay. The ship surged slightly as it moved out into deeper water.

'You're coming with us?' I asked Ingvar, bemused. 'I don't even know where we're going.'

Ingvar shook his head sadly. 'Alas, no, I can't go with you. Bjorn's only taking me across the bay to Ulf and Olvir, so I can tell them what's happened and beg their help. Father wouldn't give me permission to go further. He says he needs every hand now to get the harvest in. Yours as well as ours. And your household will need guarding too.'

'Guarding? Is there is still danger? Then why are we leaving? I don't understand.'

Ingvar's hand tightened reassuringly on mine. 'I don't think there's great danger. But Halfgrim has settled only a few days' ride along the coast, near where the market is held, and may take it into his head to cause more trouble. But your father and brother were his main targets, and they are safely away now.'

64

'My mother,' I said unsteadily, fighting to control the tears that threatened to escape. 'What if he attacks her? How can we be sure she'll be safe?'

'It wouldn't be honourable to attack a woman,' said Ingvar, his mouth set in a hard line. 'I promise you, Sigrun, I'll watch over her. For your sake.'

I looked up at him, and met his earnest blue eyes. 'I swear it to you,' he said.

My shyness, forgotten in all the fear and confusion, returned suddenly, and I dropped my gaze feeling the colour rise in my cheeks. 'Thank you,' I whispered.

Ingvar led me to the side of the ship, and drew me onto a bench near the prow of the boat where we were more private. Most of those on board were rowing and had their backs to us.

'You're going away from here for a while,' Ingvar explained. 'I have a farewell gift for you.' He smiled, looking a little embarrassed. 'I got it in Ireland and meant to give it to you before, but somehow there hasn't been an opportunity.' Reaching inside his tunic, he pulled out a piece of worked silver that was tied on to a long thin band of leather. He held it out to show me, and there, resting in the palm of his hand, was an amulet in the shape of a horse. It looked very old and very precious.

'The horse, for power and strength,' he explained. 'It's very ancient and I'm told it has magical properties.'

I reached out and touched it lightly as it lay in his palm, feeling the grooves of the engravings. 'It's beautiful,' I said reverently.

'I also chose it to remind you of all the work we've done together over the last few years,' said Ingvar. 'All those horses we've gentled. May I?'

So saying he reached out and put the amulet over my head. The leather became caught on my long hair, and he lifted it out of the way, allowing the necklace to settle around my neck. His hands lingered on my hair, stroking it gently back from my face. I could feel myself blushing.

To hide my embarrassment, I looked down at the silver horse that lay against the plain fabric of my kirtle, glinting in the sun. 'Thank you,' I said softly.

'I've been waiting for the right moment to give it to you,' said Ingvar. 'Wear it and don't forget me while you're away.'

'I'll wear it always,' I assured him earnestly. 'And I couldn't possibly forget you. Must I really leave? I don't want to.'

'Your father needs you,' said Ingvar. He slid his arms around me, pulled me close to him, and kissed me on the lips. The kiss left me startled and breathless. New feelings rushed through me: tenderness, affection, excitement. I understood for the first time how deeply I cared for Ingvar and it seemed he must care for me too, to give me such a precious gift and to kiss me in that way.

As I realized the state of my heart, the world seemed to rock slightly. Or was it just the motion of the boat? I didn't think so. It was a momentous realization which changed everything, and I wondered at myself for not having recognized it before. Strangest of all, I could *feel* Ingvar's tenderness towards me almost as if it was my own. I was confused for a moment. But then Ingvar was speaking again: 'Three years is a long time. I hardly dare ask you to wait so long for me.'

'Three *years*?' I exclaimed, startled. 'No!'

'I'm so sorry. That's how long Bjorn has sworn to stay away from Iceland,' said Ingvar. 'And now we're almost at Ulf's, and I must leave you.'

'Wait!' I cried, holding his hand tight. 'Three *years*? Won't I see you again? Why does father have to stay away? Is it true what Halfgrim said about him?'

Ingvar silenced me with another kiss. We embraced, holding each other tight, and I breathed in his scent of leather, wool, and sun-warmed skin, trying to hold it fast in my mind. I could sense sadness from outside myself, and somehow knew it was Ingvar's grief at parting, which was as deep as my own.

Ingvar let me go. He stood, raised his hand briefly to my father at the other end of the ship, and then jumped off the side onto the rocks at the edge of the bay. I watched him run up the first few roughly-hewn steps leading to Ulf's house on the barren mountainside that rose sheer out of the sea. Our ship manoeuvred back away from the shore, and headed out into the bay again, this time towards the open sea. Ingvar turned and stood waving to me. I waved back frantically, leaning over the side of the ship. His words went through my mind again and I realized he'd been asking for a promise.

'I'll wait for you,' I called to him. The wind whipped my words away, and I wasn't sure if he'd heard me over the surging of the sea against the rocks.

We rounded the watery foot of the next mountain and Ingvar was lost to sight. I sank back onto the narrow wooden bench feeling more alone than I'd ever felt before.

CHAPTER EIGHT

How could I exist away from my home for three long years? That was the anguished question that occupied my thoughts as the ship slid out of the huge bay into the open sea, tiny and unstable in such a vast expanse of unruly water. How could I bear to be parted from Ingvar for so long? And from my mother? In three years' time I would be *old*; I would be eighteen winters. I tried to imagine spending such a stretch of time away from my home, amongst strangers, and I couldn't. I touched the horse amulet, remembering how Ingvar had kissed me and felt my heart quicken. For some reason I couldn't explain to myself, I tucked the amulet inside my kirtle. It was Ingvar's gift to me, and I didn't want anyone else to see it.

I looked at my father and brother who were busy setting the huge sail. What did they feel about this exile? The answer came to me with unsettling clarity. My father was in a state of shock and grief and my brother was furious. How did I know that with such certainty?

I'd never sensed anyone's mood before this. My mother had tried to teach me to read auras, but I'd never become adept at it. I struggled to even see them unless I concentrated hard, and their swirls of colours were an impossible language. But this . . . Where had it come from? What had changed in me? My thoughts turned to the amulet. Ingvar had said it had powers.

I looked around the ship and focused on the different men on board. To my amazement, I could sense fear, dread, anger, excitement all around me. Erik and Geirmund were distressed about leaving their loved ones; the other men were excited at the prospect of travel. In a rush, I turned back the way we had come, reaching out to see if I could feel Ingvar's mood again, as I had earlier, longing to sense him one more time, but there was only emptiness there. Perhaps we were already too far away.

I knew my mother would scorn the notion that the amulet could bring me new abilities. She had no time for magic, believing it was used too often instead of sound medicines and good nursing. All gifts came straight from the gods, she said. But I wondered . . . I decided I had done right to hide the amulet. It would be my secret.

My thoughts were distracted from my new-found ability by my father's voice calling me. I went to him, unsteady on the heaving deck that seemed in one moment to drop away beneath my feet and at another to rise up hard to meet them, making me stagger.

'Sigrun,' father said, 'I'm putting you in charge of the food stores. Will you familiarize yourself with what we have brought, and be in charge of handing out rations twice a day, please.'

It was an order not a request. To my dismay, I realized I was the only female on board. 'Father,' I said. He was already walking away from me, but he paused.

'Please, father,' I said. 'Why are we leaving? Where are we going?'

'Not now, Sigrun,' said my father firmly.

I soon learned that one day at sea is very much like another: too many waves, too much wind, and too vast an expanse of salt water for comfort. The only variation was in whether we were scorched by the sun or drenched by rain. Neither was pleasant. And all the time, the relentless never-ending motion of the ship in the swell.

I prepared and served the food, endured the cold and the rain, and watched my father. He stayed busy and as far away from me as the small space on the boat would allow, avoiding my eyes. At night he wrapped himself in his cloak and in his misery and pretended to sleep. There was so much I wanted to ask him, but he didn't give me the chance. Whenever I tried, he turned abruptly away from me. I felt hurt and shut out, and wished he could share his unhappiness with me.

My brother was surly and bad-tempered. He spoke to me roughly, finding fault with the food and with the strength of the ale. Eventually I gave up trying to speak to either of them. I wrapped myself in my own thoughts and watched the coast of Iceland slip by. Tall rocky cliffs and headlands filled with bird colonies gave way occasionally to bays and beaches. At times, expanses of farmland or pasture, and the occasional longhouse, were visible from the ship; at others the land seemed hostile and forbidding. I realized this must be the route my parents had taken as settlers almost twenty years before, and I wondered what they had made of it all that time ago. I wondered yet again if it was true that my father had killed and stolen to get the ship. I wished with all my heart he'd explain it to me.

When we put the last southern headland to our stern and headed out into the open sea, I felt a wrench in my heart. This was the final farewell, the absolute parting from my home. There was no turning back now.

We sailed southwards for days on a vast, empty grey sea, the ship rolling and plunging in the heavy swell.

'Land! Land!' shouted Erik in great excitement one morning, from his lookout in the prow.

'The Faeroe Islands,' cried Asgrim. 'Can we make a stop?'

My father stood silently on deck, watching as the single mountain resolved into a green island, rising steeply from the water. The island became a cluster as we drew closer, each one green in the damp air, clouds hanging low over them. Abruptly my father shook his head. 'We don't stop,' he said curtly. There was an outcry.

'We need water,' I said timidly, adding my voice to the others.

'We don't stop,' Bjorn repeated angrily. 'We'll take on fresh water at the Shetlands.' So saying, he went aft, took over the tiller and steered the boat well clear of the islands.

We were all disappointed, but it was so unusual to hear my father raise his voice in anger that no one protested aloud. Asgrim flung himself onto a bench beside me, however, and began muttering angry complaints under his breath.

'As if it's not bad enough that he drags us with him into this disgrace,' he complained, 'he has to throw his weight around and forbid us shore leave as well. We could have lit a fire and roasted some meat tonight.' Asgrim glanced at me from under frowning brows: 'Have you tried asking him what we're doing here?' he asked. I could feel anger and resentment rolling off him in waves.

I shook my head. 'He won't talk to me,' I said sadly.

'He hasn't spoken to either of us,' Asgrim continued, his voice rising. 'We don't have a clue where we're going, or even why. He's treating us like slaves who have to obey orders.'

'Your father has a very good reason for not stopping here,' said Erik's familiar voice beside me. I jumped, not having seen him.

'He does?' I asked, curious.

'We stopped here once before,' Erik told me. 'On our way to the new land. We were unlucky and the visit had dreadful consequences. Your father won't risk that again.'

'What happened?' I asked, eager to hear more. I knew Erik had accompanied my parents to Iceland, and probably knew their whole story. But he was shaking his head.

'It's for your father to tell you,' he said. 'I'm just saying you should trust him.'

I looked over at my father and felt his deep sadness. I understood he couldn't bear to speak of what had happened because he was fighting his own misery. Erik had always been like a second father to me, helping me out of scrapes and keeping some of my transgressions hidden from my parents. I was inclined to be guided by him, but

Asgrim was not so easily satisfied. He snorted impatiently, got up and walked off. He leaned against the side of the ship, looking out to sea, his shoulders hunched in anger.

We reached the Shetlands two days later, and this time there were no arguments about whether or not to break our journey. We slipped past the low-lying, windswept islands until we found a beach where we could pull up our ship, and rowed onto it. The men shipped their oars, leaped into the shallow surf and hauled the boat above the high tide mark. I went with a few others to gather driftwood for a fire, though there was little enough to be found. We came back with a meagre armful, and would need to supplement it with what we had brought from home.

As I climbed into the ship to fetch extra firewood, father was unlocking a chest under the bench in the stern of the ship. I saw him take out a heavy purse, one of several, and tie it round his neck. Then he turned and saw me.

'I just came to fetch wood,' I said quickly, not wanting him to think I'd been spying on him. 'There was very little to be found . . . '

'Very well,' father replied calmly. 'Use it sparingly. Erik and I will trade for some fresh meat.'

Father vaulted over the side of the ship onto the sand, and called to Erik. I noticed they both had their swords buckled to their belts as they disappeared into the dunes at the back of the beach. We were in a foreign land, and the sight reminded me danger might await us here.

When I'd picked the firewood, I turned and saw my brother. He was standing on the other side of the ship, looking not at me, but at the chest father had unlocked. I could see his eyes glisten, and with a shock, I felt his greed. He wanted the money for himself.

When Asgrim saw me looking at him, he turned abruptly and walked away. Feeling uneasy, I threw the firewood onto the beach before jumping down myself. I almost wished I hadn't developed this unsettling ability to read moods and thoughts. It was uncomfortably like spying. I touched the amulet lightly and wondered again if that was where this unexpected ability had come from. It seemed the only explanation.

The fire soon crackled and flickered, casting a glow of dancing light on the men's faces as they gathered around the fire. The light was fading and the air was raw. Father returned carrying a whole sheep for roasting and everyone cheered. There was more than enough to feed the twelve hungry mouths that craved freshly-cooked food.

After the feast, once everyone was full and basking in the glow of the embers, father withdrew and walked down to the sea. I got up and followed him, feeling the cold air swirling unpleasantly about me after the heat of the fire. Father was picking up shells and pebbles, casting them into the water one by one. He didn't notice me until I paused beside him. He started a little.

'Father, where are we going?' I asked him softly.

He didn't answer at first; instead throwing another shell into the water. A small wave broke at our feet, staining the sand with wetness.

'I don't know,' he said at last. 'There was no time to

make plans. There was barely time even to consult your mother.'

'It doesn't seem fair,' I said tentatively, 'that we should have to flee our home like outlaws . . . '

'Yes, well, leave that for now,' said my father abruptly. 'I've told you I don't want to discuss that yet. I thought perhaps we could make for Hedeby first of all. It's a busy market town in the Mark, where we can trade the calf-skins I've brought.'

I nodded in silence, shocked that my father had so little idea of where we were going and what we would be doing. I steeled myself to ask another question.

'Is it really true, what Ingvar said, that we have to stay away three years?' I held my breath, dreading the answer.

'Those were the terms,' said my father in a low voice. His sadness mingled with mine, a fog of loneliness and unhappiness.

I didn't ask any more; I didn't think he would answer if I did. Instead we remained silent, side by side in the darkness until I began to shiver, and father ordered me to go and wrap up and get some sleep. I obeyed him, finding a spot close to the fire, but sleep was elusive.

My brother asked me about my conversation with father the next morning once we were out at sea again. He was furious that I'd found out so little.

'Did he admit he was once a slave?' he demanded.

'He didn't want to talk about it.'

'So you just let it be?' Asgrim's tone was scathing.

'Why don't you ask him yourself?' I said, stung by his harshness.

'I will,' said my brother, and beckoned to my father who had finished with the sail for the time being. Father came towards us, looking from me to Asgrim, a questioning lift to his brows. He knew what we wanted and was reluctant.

'Where are we going?' Asgrim asked brusquely. 'I think you should tell us. And how shall we live? We can't just drift around for three years.'

'Do you have any suggestions?' asked my father defensively.

'You should have the ideas,' snarled Asgrim angrily. 'This is all your fault.'

There was an appalled silence.

'Bjorn,' called Erik, unaware of the argument. 'There's a good-sized settlement ahead. Do you want to stop and trade?'

Father turned from us, with relief it seemed. I couldn't blame him. I shot Asgrim a reproachful look, which he answered with a sneer. I hardly recognized my brother in this angry and unpleasant young man. 'What's the matter with you?' I asked him.

'Don't you see?' he asked impatiently. 'If it's true, and father really is an escaped slave, and mother was a slave too, then we're nothing. I'm not the son of a chieftain. We have no lineage. We're merely empty impostors. Everything we've been told is a lie. It makes our whole lives meaningless.'

Asgrim left me, moving away to look ahead. I stared at the land, hardly seeing it, my mind full of my brother's words. Most of what he said didn't resonate with me. I didn't much care whether or not I was the daughter

76

of a chieftain. It took some adjustment, but ultimately I wasn't deeply concerned. The situation it had led us into now was far worse, and the fact that our parents had lied to us ran through my veins like poison.

I looked over at my father. He sighed as he squinted into the sun, looking at the settlement ahead, the creases around his eyes pronounced. This was the kind and loving father I'd always known; the father and husband who would do anything for his family. I tried to match this image with the lying, murdering, cheating ex-slave Halfgrim had made him out to be. It made no sense.

Whom was I inclined to trust? My own gentle, honourable father, or Halfgrim; a rogue if ever I saw one? There could be no doubt. With an effort, I pushed the painful thoughts aside. I *had* to trust father until he explained.

We sailed in towards a grey shingle beach near a collection of what looked like stalls or booths, about which many people were gathered, and in the background, a scattering of houses, farm buildings, and workshops.

The men jumped out of the ship in the shallows. Father lifted me out and carried me through the waves, putting me down on the dry shingle before returning to help haul the boat out of the water. He asked a few men to keep watch on the ship and the rest of us headed for the stalls. I followed father closely, but Asgrim made off on his own.

Together, we walked among the booths, which varied from simple trestle tables with wares laid out, to tents and rough buildings. A blacksmith was hard at work shaping a ploughshare while a lad around my age worked the bellows for him. I could feel the blast of heat as we walked past. An old man sat behind a table with

77

all manner of bone whistles laid out for sale. When he saw us, he picked one up and began to play, a haunting, mournful tune. A thin woman in a long green kirtle, her head wrapped in a scarf, called to me to come into her tent and have my fortune read. I shook my head, feeling afraid, and took my father's arm. I didn't want to know my future. I'd had enough of prophecies.

I'd never been in a place where so many people were gathered together. What was even more confusing was feeling all their moods. I knew the man with the bone whistles was desperate for money and the blacksmith was angry about something. Their emotions crowded in on me, and I had to fight to keep them at a distance, separate from my own.

Father had stopped to look at some bolts of cloth laid out in front of a booth, when two passers-by paused next to us. I felt the older man's curiosity. 'Bjorn?' he asked. We both looked up. A tall, burly man with a weathered, lined face and a bushy grey beard stood looking intently at my father. As he got a good look at his face, his questioning look turned into a broad smile. 'By Thor!' he exclaimed. 'It *is* you, Bjorn! Do you remember me, or have I grown too old and wizened?'

'Odin's beard!' replied my father in astonishment, and a smile lit his face. 'Well met, old friend!'

The two men embraced, clapped each other on the back, both talking and laughing at once. Then my father turned to me. 'This is my daughter, Sigrun,' he told the stranger, who turned an interested gaze on me. 'Sigrun, this is my very good friend, Thrang.'

CHAPTER NINE

'What are you doing here?' asked my father.

'I was going to ask you the same question,' said Thrang. 'Jarlshof, of all places in the world to meet! I'm here on business. I work as a carrier of goods.'

'Does it pay well? Do you live here?'

'Yes it does and no, I live further south. You're still in Iceland, Bjorn? How's Thora?'

The two men were obviously delighted to see each other. I stood a little apart watching them, and saw a shadow fall over my father's face as he said Thora had suffered a broken leg. Thrang must wonder at us leaving her at such a time, I thought suddenly. But Thrang turned to me. 'You are your father's daughter, I see, Sigrun,' he remarked. 'I see little of your mother in you.'

'That's true,' I agreed, thinking not only of my dark hair and brown eyes, but of my failure to excel at the skills she'd taught me.

'This is my son, Leif,' said Thrang, pulling his young companion forward. Leif was a broad, strong-looking young man with wiry hair like his father's, only flaxen instead of grey. I shook his hand politely and decided he must be about my age or a bit older.

'Bjorn, what do you say to sharing an ale and exchanging news?' Thrang asked. 'We've got a lot of years to catch up on.'

'Yes, of course,' said my father. He looked happier than I'd seen him since his return from the summer market.

'Here, Sigrun,' he said, thrusting his heavy purse into my hand. 'Buy us some fresh meat for nightmeal, and some fuel; firewood or peat or whatever they have here and anything you'd like for yourself too. It's a rare opportunity for you.'

I froze in shock, the heavy purse clutched in my hand. I had no idea how to do what he asked of me. Already the two friends were turning away to go.

'Father, wait!' I begged, catching hold of his sleeve. 'I can't! I've never used money . . . '

Father paused and grinned ruefully. 'I've neglected your education!' he said.

'In more ways than one,' I couldn't help adding. Then I felt bad as I watched his face close up and his new cheerfulness fall away from him.

'Leif will help you,' Thrang said, unwittingly smoothing over the awkward moment. 'He always drives a good bargain.'

The problem solved to their satisfaction, the two men turned and walked off together. I was left facing a stranger, an unfamiliar purse in my hand. I felt horribly alone. The fact that I could see our ship from here was little comfort.

'I'm . . . sorry if it's a nuisance,' I said to Leif.

'Not at all,' he said politely, but I could tell he was awkward about being left in my company too.

As I turned, the man selling the cloth caught my eye and started talking, telling me what quality his goods were, and how pleased I'd be with them. He picked up a bolt of blue wool and held it out for me to touch.

'Look how fine it would look on you!' the man was saying, holding it up against me. 'It would only cost you a few coins from your full purse!'

He touched my purse as he spoke, his hand brushing mine, and I backed away, suddenly frightened, clutching the money tightly.

'No, thank you,' I said, shaking my head. The greed in his eyes reminded me unpleasantly of what I'd seen in my brother's.

The money in this purse had to last us a long time. We had no horses to sell, no barley crop to harvest. Besides, I was living on board a ship. What occasion would I have to wear a fine dress? That belonged to the world I had left behind me, the world where I would like Ingvar to see me dressed like the summer sky.

'The lady doesn't want your cloth,' Leif told the man firmly, and ushered me away from him. I gave him a grateful look. Holding tight to the purse, I followed Leif to a farmhouse on the outskirts of the little settlement, where a man in a bloody apron agreed to sell us a whole sheep, a barrel of ale, and some peat for a fire and deliver them to our ship. I didn't like the speculative way he eyed me and the purse, but he quickly realized it was Leif he had to drive a bargain with and the two men haggled fiercely.

'Is it true you robbed him?' I asked Leif as we left. 'He seemed very upset with the price you agreed.'

Leif laughed; a cheerful, carefree sound. 'No, indeed I didn't,' he said. 'Traders always say that, even if they've sold you rotten offal at the price of the best cuts of beef!'

I blushed, feeling naïve and stupid. I had so much to learn.

It was evening before my father returned with Thrang, and there was still no sign of my brother. Erik and I had lit a fire on the beach, in sight of the ship, and had roasted the meat. My father called for the ale to be opened and for drinking horns. He sat with Thrang, Leif, and our men around the fire and talked. I listened curiously to Thrang telling my father about where he lived.

'It's become a great city,' he said, 'since the Norse took it over. It's one of the greatest trading centres in the northern world. There's nothing you can't buy there. Iron goods, leather, exquisite jewellery, silk, cloth and slaves. There's a constant coming and going of ships, bustle in the streets, and plenty of business for a man like me. Everyone needs their goods moved from one place to another, and few have their own ships. You should come and stay the winter with me, Bjorn. You'd be settled and I'd have help. We'd both benefit.'

'What do you think, Sigrun?' asked father, turning to me. 'Should we go and stay with Thrang for the winter, and see these sights?'

'Where is it you live, sir?' I asked Thrang politely.

I thought from what he'd said, the answer might be Dublin, where Ingvar had been last winter. But he named a place I couldn't remember having heard of before.

'My home is in Jorvik, Sigrun,' he said. 'It's in Northumbria, but it's a Viking city, where Vikings and Saxons live and work side by side. I'm sure you'd feel at home there.'

'We'll come if Sigrun agrees,' said my father. I nodded, thinking one place was much like another when we couldn't go home, and there was a buzz of excitement among the men. It was a popular decision. There would be plenty of new people to meet and lots to see. Very different to our quiet bay at home, where one or two passing ships in summer were the only variety. I felt everyone's excitement affect me, my nerves thrilling at the thought of seeing a city for the first time in my life.

'I suppose Jorvik will be bigger than this place?' I wondered aloud.

Several men guffawed with laughter at my ignorance and I blushed deeply.

'It's a very big city, Sigrun,' said Thrang gravely. 'When you've seen it, you'll realize that Jarlshof is to Jorvik, what a cowshed is to a big farm. There is no comparison.'

I felt my blush fade again as Thrang took my question seriously. And indeed, why should I know anything of Jorvik? I didn't remember ever hearing a single tale about it, living in the far north as we did.

We sat late, exchanging stories. Father didn't speak of the circumstances under which we'd left Iceland, and I guessed he'd done that privately when he was speaking to Thrang alone. Whether he'd told him the truth or some lie, I had no way of knowing.

At last the sun went down, the fire died, and the night turned cold. Thrang returned to his own ship for the

83

night, promising to speak to us in the morning. We all climbed aboard and huddled in furs and cloaks to sleep. I could hear voices around me still talking of Jorvik and the winter ahead. Gradually they grew quieter and then faded away altogether. The silence of night closed in and I drifted into an uneasy sleep, aware that my brother still hadn't returned. I knew my father had noticed it too, though he'd said nothing.

I was woken deep in the night by the sound of vomiting, and saw a dark shape leaning over the ship's rail. I couldn't think who it was until I heard my father's voice, low but firm: 'I don't expect you to return at this hour in such a disgraceful condition again, Asgrim.'

'May Thor smite me with his hammer if I care for the orders of a slave,' muttered Asgrim in a slurred voice. His body heaved again, and I heard the sound of his sick splattering into the water. The smell of it drifted to me on the breeze and I felt nauseous myself.

'You don't know what you say, Asgrim,' said father. 'You should be ashamed of yourself. You'd do better to keep a sober head and a still tongue. Only the fool seeks wisdom and courage in a goblet of ale.'

I realized Asgrim was drunk again, and was shocked. Both our household and Helgi's were moderate in their drinking, and this wasn't something I'd seen before, though I'd heard tales of drunkenness. Only wastrels who neglected their farms and beat their women drank themselves stupid. So why was my brother doing it?

Father said nothing more, and Asgrim eventually lay down with a groan and began to snore. I drifted slowly back to sleep.

I awoke to feel the rain on my face, the air raw and cold. I shivered and burrowed under my furs, but couldn't recapture sleep. The rain had woken everyone, and they were stirring, stretching, beginning to talk. I sat up, tousled and uncomfortable. It had been such a long time since I'd had a bath and at that moment, I'd have given almost anything for a soak in our pool at home, where the water ran hot from the mountainside even in the coldest winter. My mother called it a blessing from the goddess.

Thrang appeared with Leif as we were making the ship ready to depart.

'I have to go on to the Orkneys from here,' said Thrang. 'There's little point in you following. I'm delivering timber and then heading back down to Jorvik. If you'll lend me a man in exchange for Leif, he can accompany you to Jorvik, and make you welcome until my return.'

My father agreed, Geirmund went off with Thrang and Leif came aboard. Meanwhile, my father nudged my brother awake with his foot. 'Drinking yourself stupid is no excuse for shirking your share of work,' he said. 'Lend a hand!'

Asgrim sat up, muttering and cursing, and rolled up his furs. As he got to his feet he stumbled and rushed for the side, green in the face. I turned away, ashamed, hoping Leif wouldn't notice.

We made a good distance that day with fair winds and sunshine. Asgrim recovered, but his mood remained surly. I avoided him and father avoided both of us. How sad mother would be if she was here to see it, I thought. But if she'd been here, mother would never have allowed these estrangements to grow. Thinking of her made me resolve to approach my father, not to let him shut me out as he was doing.

'So, father,' I asked, approaching him at the stern of the ship, where he sat, tiller in hand, squinting into the sun, 'how do you know Thrang?'

'How do I know Thrang? Ah, now there's a tale,' my father said, and something like a smile touched his lips. He became lost in thought for a few moments, and then his brow clouded with less pleasant memories. I could feel the shift in his mood as well as see it.

'I'd like to hear it,' I prompted him gently when he remained silent.

Father looked at me for a moment, and I could tell he was deciding how much to tell me. Or perhaps even whether to tell me the truth.

'Thrang was our captain on our voyage to Iceland,' said my father at last. 'He's a good man and utterly trustworthy.'

I waited expectantly for more, but it didn't come. 'That's a very short tale,' I remarked.

'I'll tell it to you sometime, my daughter,' said father, with a sigh. 'Not all of it is edifying.'

I wanted to ask more, and to explain that both Asgrim and I would understand better if he trusted us, but my father prevented me by shaking his head at me and calling Erik to his side to discuss the route along the coast ahead. I sighed and moved away, sad and disappointed that I couldn't reach him.

CHAPTER TEN

The coast of Scotland was bleak, and for three days it rained in torrents. We huddled under our cloaks on deck by day, battling contrary winds and choppy seas. By night we slept under makeshift shelters of animal skins. They leaked around the edges and even when they didn't, the dampness penetrated everything. I was more homesick than I could ever have imagined possible.

I thought of the three long years that must pass before we could turn homewards once more, and ached with sorrow. They were like a vast ocean of time that I could see no way of crossing. Three summers when there would be foals to gentle and to train and I wouldn't be there to help. Three years of babies that my mother would have to deliver without her apprentice. How was her leg healing? It would be so long till I knew.

I thought of waiting all that time to discover whether Ingvar loved me, and sighed with longing. In three years I'd be almost too old to be married. I touched the horse amulet, my constant reminder of him. I'd have exchanged all the wealth in my father's purse to be back in our own cosy, fire-lit longhouse instead of being out at sea in the rain.

On the fourth day the rain eased at last. The sun came

out and everyone's clothing steamed. I felt damp and dirty, my skin raw and chapped from exposure to the salt wind and the wet weather.

'Father, can't we stop?' I begged. 'We need to bathe, even if it's only in a cold stream. And we need to dry out by a fire.'

My father smiled kindly at me. 'Very well, Sigrun. Will this bay do for you?' He pointed inland to a sandy beach backed by woodland.

'Yes, it will,' I agreed at once, relieved.

We beached the ship on the sand and looked around us. I'd never seen such huge trees before. They towered over me like giants, and I was half afraid to go in among them. Tentatively, I walked up to the nearest one and put my hand against its rough bark. I looked up and felt dizzy for a moment. It was as tall as four or five men at least.

'Why do they grow so tall?' I asked my brother. He shrugged and pushed his way past me.

'They just do. Help us find some firewood.'

I followed him in nervously, and found everything soggy with the rain. My feet squelched in mud which gave off unfamiliar scents of rich earth and rotting vegetation. The trees stood silent around me like waiting warriors, still for now but full of power. They had a tangible presence.

I found some damp branches lying on the ground and pulled them back onto the beach with me only to find that Asgrim and Erik had found a whole tree, long fallen and brittle. I left them breaking it up with an axe, picked up a cloth, a cake of soap, and a clean kirtle and looked for the nearest stream.

I found a sparkling brook, and followed it back into the woods, climbing alongside it up a hill. I wanted to be sure of privacy. When I came to a small pool, the water swirling as it tumbled in from a short fall above, I stopped and looked around. I could see and hear nothing but the birdsong in the trees, so I relaxed and stripped my filthy clothes off. The water was so cold I gasped as I submerged myself. Shivering, I scrubbed myself clean, the rough soap scratching my skin. Then I shook my long hair out of its plaits and scrubbed at that too, rubbing the roots with the soap.

I was just rinsing the last soap from my hair when a rustling in the trees and a flash of red spooked me suddenly. I became aware how alone I was and fled from the pool, splashing and stumbling in my hurry. Shivering, I rubbed myself dry with my cloth, dressing quickly, in case it was a spirit of the pool that I'd disturbed. I dragged on my clean clothes and hurried back along the stream. Not far below my pool, I found my father, his back to me, his sword at his side. He turned as I crashed through the undergrowth towards him.

'Father?' I asked, surprised.

'I was standing guard,' he explained. 'We don't know if there are people nearby or whether they're friendly.'

I flung myself at him in relief and hugged him, still shaking from the cold and the strange encounter.

'What's the matter?' he asked. 'Did something frighten you? It wasn't wise to go off alone.'

'I'm sorry. It was just some spirit or creature that startled me,' I confessed. 'And I'm afraid of the trees too.'

'Really?' he asked, sounding surprised. He started

walking back down towards the beach and I followed. 'Well, I suppose you've never seen them before . . . I miss them at home. Woodland like this is beautiful. Peaceful.'

'It's a place of power,' I said. 'I haven't worked out whether it's good or menacing yet.'

Father smiled. 'You are more like your mother than you know,' he told me. I felt a wave of his sadness, and realized he was missing her just as I was.

'Father,' I said hesitantly, 'why did you leave mother quite alone? Wouldn't it have been better to leave either Asgrim or me to care for her?'

'I couldn't leave Asgrim,' said my father at once. 'He was in nearly as great danger as I was from that man.'

'You mean Halfgrim?' I asked timidly.

Father nodded. 'I was going to leave you with Thora. Only she foresaw that I needed you.'

I felt confused. 'But, father, I can't protect you with visions like she can.'

'She seemed to think that you would help me in some way,' he replied.

I touched my horse amulet and wondered what, exactly, my mother had seen. What role did I have to play? We were nearly back at the beach now. I could see the sea ahead of us between the trees. I could also glimpse the men bathing naked in the stream where it ran down out of the wood.

'I'd better not go and embarrass them,' I said, drawing my father to a huge fallen tree trunk. 'And I want to talk to you about the things Halfgrim said. Father, is any of it true? It would help so much if you'd explain.'

I held my breath, half expecting him to get up and

leave me, to avoid my questions as usual. But he didn't. Instead he leaned his elbows on his knees and sank his head forward onto his hands, hiding his face.

'Oh, Sigrun,' he groaned. 'How hard your mother and I have worked to protect you from this knowledge, so you could grow up without the shadow of fear hanging over you.'

A slow, sick feeling grew in my stomach. So this was it, after all. My father was an impostor. I dreaded to hear it, but I had to know. 'So . . . Halfgrim *was* telling the truth?' Every nerve in my body longed for my father to deny it. I was scarcely breathing; I was so tense, waiting for his words.

'He was telling the truth he knows,' said my father at last. 'The truth he was told. But there are many truths, Sigrun, and few of them are absolute.'

'Please, father,' I begged. 'No riddles.'

My father took a deep breath, and I could sense the pain in him. He didn't want to talk about this. Perhaps I was being selfish, insisting on hearing. But I needed to know what my parents had done to get us the life we had lived for all of my fifteen years. Most of all, I needed to understand.

'Well then. It's true that I killed a chieftain called Bjorn Svanson and made off with his ship. I've borne his name since that date, so I'm indeed an impostor, Sigrun.'

I caught my breath, horrified and fascinated at the same time. I didn't speak, waiting for my father to continue.

'But so much lies behind a simple tale like that, my daughter. So many blighted lives, so much pain and suffering. It's not as simple as it might seem at first glance.

I was much younger than you are now when I was captured and forced into slavery. You can't imagine . . . I'm not denying my guilt. Many would call it a crime. But there were circumstances that made it seem quite different at the time. Even now, I regret nothing, especially when I think what could have been, had I acted differently.'

Father looked at me earnestly, asking for my understanding. I nodded faintly. My thoughts were in a whirl of confusion, trying to see my father in this new light.

'And was my mother a slave too?' I asked.

'No, Sigrun,' he said, shaking his head. 'Not that it makes a difference: slave or master, it's all a matter of chance. It doesn't make you a better or worse person. But no, your mother was a prosperous farmer's daughter. My sword, Foe Biter, belonged to her father, who had been a warrior in his younger days. I met him, briefly. Svanson stole Thora from her family the same day he took me from my master in place of tribute,' my father told me. 'He needed a healer to take to Iceland. But the first thing he did to both of us was tie us . . . '

'Bjorn!' shouted Erik's voice from the beach.

'No!' I exclaimed, frustrated. After weeks of silence, a lifetime of silence, in fact, my father was finally relaxed and speaking freely.

'I'm busy!' father called. 'Can't it wait?'

Erik was coming towards us. 'I'm sorry,' he said, casting an apologetic look at me. 'But there are locals on the beach. I *think* they're friendly . . . '

My father leapt to his feet at once and reached out a hand to pull me up too.

'Come, Sigrun,' he said. 'Let's see what they want. Stay close.'

I followed him, afraid that more danger awaited us. The men were small, broad, and dark haired. They were barefoot, and wore homespun cloth that any Viking woman would be ashamed to dress her man in. It was shabby and dirty, and badly woven. They carried no visible weapons however, and when they spoke, my father seemed to understand what they said, though I could not.

'They're speaking Saxon,' said Leif quietly to me, noticing my puzzled looks. 'They've come to make sure we aren't going to be attacking their village, I expect.'

I turned a horrified look on him. 'Do . . . ?' I began and didn't know how to continue.

'Oh yes, it's a Norse pastime to raid the villages on this coast,' said Leif. 'No one from Jorvik would prey on this country, of course, but the ships from Norway and Denmark do.'

I remembered Ingvar's dreadful tale and shuddered. 'Then they're very brave to approach us,' I said.

'I suppose seeing us bathing reassured them,' said Leif with a grin. 'You can't do much pillaging with your clothes off.'

I saw that all our men bore signs of having dressed hastily, their hair still dripping, and laughed a little.

'Ah, what wouldn't I give to take part in another raid,' said my brother coming to stand on my other side. 'Think of the glory and riches I could win!'

I looked up at him, taken aback, and saw a far-away look in his eyes. I recalled Ingvar's tale and remembered that Asgrim had been with him on the raid he'd described to me. How could Asgrim have been a part of that and yet still want to commit such acts? This wasn't the brother I thought I knew.

'I went all the way to Dublin and back last year,' he told Leif over my head. 'We passed endless settlements but only once did we stop and plunder. Helgi had the courage and ambition of an old woman. If it hadn't been for the pirates attacking us on the way back, we'd hardly have seen any decent action all year.'

I was shocked to hear my brother speak so rudely about Helgi who'd always been so good to us, but I bit my tongue, knowing it would make him furious to be criticized by his little sister.

My father finished speaking to the strangers and turned to Erik, clearly pleased. 'Let's get a fire going, shall we? I think we should invite our guests to eat with us.'

There was a bustle at once, as the men lit the fire and I began to prepare the supper. I could see there would be no opportunity to learn more from father tonight, and was bitterly disappointed.

CHAPTER ELEVEN

The mouth of the river Ouse was bristling with ships. Huge cargo vessels, letting down vast sails as they swung into the narrow channel, smaller boats that looked as if they'd been out fishing, and a warship under oar, its sides lined with colourful shields. I stared in amazement. There were smaller craft too, manned by one or two men, hugging the shore out of the way of the larger ships. We slid past some and followed others away from the sea, inland past tall trees, tended fields, and marshy plants.

I pushed my damp hair back off my face and sighed with the heat. Now we'd left the open sea behind us, it had intensified unbearably. It was like a shimmer in the air, making it thick and heavy to breathe, and causing the perspiration to break out on my skin.

'It can't be natural that it's so hot, surely?' I remarked to my brother. He scowled at me.

'Don't be so ignorant, Sigrun,' he said. 'The summer is far hotter in the south than at home.'

I felt stupid and wished I hadn't spoken. My brother never seemed to have a kind word for me these days. But then he seemed to relent. I saw a rare flash of the old, friendly Asgrim, as he said more mildly: 'This heat is nothing to high summer. Wait and see.'

High summer. Sun month. That was almost a year away. I didn't want this painful reminder that it would be so long till I saw my home again. I could only bear it if I didn't think about it.

The men rowed up the river in the heat all day, and I was kept busy taking drinks to them. One young man passed out at the oar. I revived him with a cloth dipped in cool water and persuaded him to lie down in the shade in the bottom of the boat. I'd never truly appreciated the climate of my home country before.

At last the city was in sight. A vast number of buildings stretching into the distance; more than I'd imagined could exist in the whole world. Around them, a huge rampart of earth with a timbered wall atop it, the wooden posts sharpened to vicious-looking points.

'Is that Jorvik?' I asked Leif wonderingly.

'It is!' he said. His eyes shone, and I could feel his pleasure at arriving home. It rolled off him in a joyful cloud.

'What's that . . . wall thing?' I asked, afraid of revealing my ignorance again, but curious to know.

'Those are our city defences,' said Leif. 'Not everyone welcomes the Norse presence in Jorvik. King Alfred of Wessex, for example, would be glad to drive us out.'

There were shouts ahead. Several craft guarded the entrance to the city, and one was heading straight for us, a man in the prow signalling us to pull over.

'You're approaching the city of Jorvik!' he called. 'State your business if you want to proceed.'

'It's nothing to worry about,' Leif assured my father, who was looking surprised. 'They know me.'

The other ship, full of armed men, came abreast of us and three men jumped aboard. 'Your business in Jorvik?' the first man asked.

Leif stepped forward, spoke to the guards and I felt the atmosphere relax. As Leif had said, the guards knew him.

'Trader?' the man asked, before he left, with a glance around the ship.

'I have goods to trade,' acknowledged my father. 'But my main purpose is to visit my friend.'

'Where are you from?' asked the Jorvik man. 'Norway?'

'Iceland.'

After a cursory search of the ship, we were permitted to pass on into the city, though my father had to pay a tax to 'King Siefred of Jorvik'.

'Why do we pay a tax to their king?' I asked.

'That's the way with kings,' father said. 'They organize defences and soldiers so everybody feels safe to work and trade here, but they all have to be paid for. And of course the king lives high on the money too.'

As we drew closer, I stared at the Jorvik houses. They were not very like our houses at home, nor yet like the stone dwellings on the Shetlands. They were a mixture of timber, plank, and what looked like sticks and mud. The smell was powerful. Mixed with the stench rising up from the filthy water of the river, was a fug of stink from the town itself: latrines, animals, droppings, cooking, and smoke. I put a hand over my nose, fighting the urge to cough and splutter.

'Breathe deep, little sister,' said my brother with a wicked grin. 'This is city living for you, in all its glory.'

'How can you bear it?' I asked, my whole face creased with disgust.

'By closer acquaintance with all its pleasures,' he replied.

I assumed he was talking about the drinking habits he'd learned in Dublin, so I didn't ask him any more.

We rowed towards a quay of hewed stone where many ships were already moored and it took all the men's concentration to manoeuvre our boat into a narrow berth. Once the boat was safely moored, my father organized stowing the oars, refolding the sail, and gave Erik instructions to clean the ship.

'We'll need to keep at least four of us aboard at all times,' father said to Erik. 'All of them sober. There'll be plenty of thieves and tricksters around in a city this size. Do you mind taking first watch? I'll relieve you later.'

Erik agreed, and my father beckoned Asgrim and me to follow him ashore. And so we entered the great city of Jorvik.

Houses were built back to back, side to side. Between them ran narrow, dusty streets crammed with people walking, trading, talking, and arguing. There were dirty children running about, and men on horseback. I saw a woman leading a goat on a rope and a lad driving a pig with a stick. I was surrounded by people brushing past me, by ear-blasting noise and offensive smells. Their emotions crowded in on me unpleasantly and I fought hard to hold them at a distance.

'How many people live here?' I asked, appalled, as we were caught in a crowd almost as soon as we'd left the ship.

'I don't know,' my father answered, hurrying to keep up with Leif who was threading his way confidently through the streets. 'I would guess many thousands.'

I felt the unfamiliar press of humanity around me, so many people packed into this defended, bustling, noisy place, and did something I hadn't done for years. I reached for my father's hand and held it tight, dreading that I might lose him in this terrifying place. He gripped my hand comfortingly in return and gave me a quick, reassuring smile.

Thrang's house was down a side street, part of a long row, facing another line of houses just across the road.

'Why do they build them so close together?' I asked bewildered. I'd been wondering the same thing all the way through these stinking, overfilled streets. 'Where do people grow their food and keep their animals?'

Asgrim rolled his eyes but father answered gently. 'Most people here do neither, Sigrun. They are crafts-people who sell their goods or trade them for food with farmers from the surrounding area. If they spread out more, the city would be too sprawling to defend.'

'Oh,' I said in a small voice, feeling humiliated by my own ignorance. I'd heard of cities, but I'd had no picture in my mind that matched this. How did they fare in times of bad harvest, these city people? When food was scarce, and I could certainly remember winters when it had been at home, where did they turn?

We passed a house in front of which a man seemed to be squatting behind a sort of fence. I glanced curiously at him and then hurriedly looked away. It looked almost as if he . . . No, he couldn't be. I glanced one more time, just in time to see him stand up and casually tug his tunic back down over his bare backside. Oh, by the goddess, he'd been relieving himself out in the busy street.

Before I'd recovered from the shock, we'd arrived. Leif was throwing open the door of a large part-timbered house and inviting us inside.

'Welcome to Jorvik!' he said.

Thrang's house was very different to our longhouse at home. Our house was one large room filled with people, cooking fire, looms and other work tools. In contrast, this house felt cold and empty. We entered at street level, into a room which was bare save for some tables and benches.

To my surprise, Leif led us straight through this room and on down a dark, narrow staircase. The nearest thing I'd seen to it was our secret tunnel at home: the dank, earthy smell reminded me of that frightening time when our house was surrounded by enemies.

But down the stairs we found a large room, lit by a fire and oil lamps. It seemed very bare with no loom, no butter churn, and no fishing nets hanging up, but there were cooking pots, a large table, and barrels of food stored. A few chickens scratched in the earth floor and clucked softly in mild indignation as the four of us arrived. At first I thought there was no one here at all, but then I saw an elderly woman crouched by the fire, stirring something in a pot. I looked around me and tried to imagine living here. It was going to be very strange.

CHAPTER TWELVE

The first night in Jorvik was long and sleepless. I'd looked forward to having a roof over my head once more, but now that I did, I found the cellar room airless and stuffy. I listened to all the men snoring in the darkness and wondered how it could be so hot at night-time. I longed to go outside to breathe fresh air, but that would have meant going out into the street, and I didn't dare. It was noisy too. The city didn't seem to rest. I could hear voices calling out and laughter way into the small hours.

At breakfast the next morning, Leif offered to show us Jorvik and my father, who'd returned from a night watch on the ship, agreed. My brother brightened at the prospect of going into the city.

The centre of Jorvik took my breath away. It was like nothing I'd ever seen or imagined; like the market at Jarlshof multiplied a hundred or a thousand times. All those people and stalls and goods crowded into restricted spaces between the many houses. I felt penned in and breathless. I took hold of my amulet, and held it tight for a moment, trying to draw strength from its magic and protection.

'This is a bigger place than either of us has ever seen before,' said my father, looking down at me with a smile.

I nodded dumbly and took the hand he held out, holding it tightly as we made our way through the crowded streets. I hated walking among so many people.

'It's no bigger than Dublin,' said my brother, walking with a nonchalant self-assurance which bordered on a swagger. 'I like city life. It beats scratching a living out of the dirt.'

My father frowned, but said nothing. I too made an effort to hold my tongue, but I couldn't believe Asgrim was speaking about our precious farm like this. Especially knowing how hard my parents had worked to build it up from nothing. It was stupid as well. After all, Asgrim had no trade that would enable him to make a living in a city.

We walked down one street where they were making cups, bowls, plates, and other things out of wood. In another they all seemed to be making ropes of different sizes and materials. There were stalls of leather goods, with the most amazing shoes and helmets. We turned a corner and came to a street full of food. Some vendors were selling vegetables I'd never seen before. I recognized carrots, but nothing else. The colour and freshness appealed to my eye and palate at once. Another was selling fruit; berries larger and juicier than any I'd seen.

'Look!' I exclaimed, tugging my father's hand so he turned to look. 'I've never seen these berries before. They're so big. What are they?'

'Blackberries,' said Leif with a smile. 'And those are apples. Don't you know them?' I shook my head, and Leif pulled a purse from his pocket and exchanged part of a silver coin for some of the fruit which he offered us. The blackberries were large, juicy and astonishingly sweet. Leif held an apple out to me next. It was huge and I had no idea how it should be eaten so I shook my head nervously. My brother however, bit with relish through its green skin and deep into the white flesh beneath. I watched as a trickle of juice ran down his chin and he wiped it away with the back of his hand. I decided I'd try one the next time I had the chance.

The next street was lined with stalls selling fabrics. There were woollens of all descriptions. Some raw and untreated, some dyed and woven into fantastic shades and patterns. I'd rarely seen such skilled workmanship.

Some stalls had a fabric I'd never seen before, and I was drawn to touch it. To my surprise it was thin, soft, and delicate. I gasped slightly at the rich feel of it under my fingertips.

'What is it?' I asked the stallholder wonderingly.

'Finest silk,' he told me. 'All the way from China. And just the right shade to compliment your dark hair,' he added as I reached out to touch a cloth in a deep, rich shade of blue.

'Silk is the latest fashion for the women who can afford it,' Leif explained. 'It tells everyone you are well-to-do. I've heard it's much more comfortable than wool, especially in summer.'

'In that case, Sigrun should certainly have some,' said my father with a grin. 'I can't have her looking like a rustic here in Jorvik.'

Before I could say a word he began to bargain with the vendor. I tugged on his sleeve. 'Please, father,' I whispered. 'I really don't need . . . '

But he shook his head at me and insisted. In only a

few moments I was the owner of a folded piece of the beautiful blue cloth, and was quite speechless. I hugged it to me as we began to make our way back.

It was a few minutes before I noticed that my brother was no longer with us.

'Oh,' I exclaimed, looking around. 'Where . . . ?'

'He slipped away while you were buying the cloth,' said Leif apologetically. 'I wasn't sure if I should say.'

My father made no comment, but a deep frown furrowed his brow.

When we reached the house again, it was to find Thrang had returned home. 'Thrang!' exclaimed my father. 'We only beat you here by a day!'

'I know the best ways and the swiftest currents, my friend,' replied Thrang, clapping my father on the shoulder. 'Come, let's have some mead. Erik, Leif, come and join us!'

I had nothing to do but sit and listen to the merriment of the men who weren't guarding the ship. At home I would have helped get the meal or talked to the other women, but Thrang's servant frowned at me and shook her head when I offered to help, which surprised me. I sat disconsolately by the fire and stared into the flickering flames wondering what I was going to find to do with myself, shut in this house in the city.

It was late before my brother returned. The door had been locked for the night, so he had to knock. As soon as the servant had let him in, Asgrim demanded to be let out again. I could hear him retching out in the street, and shuddered. What had happened to my brother? What was making him behave like this?

My father went up to him. There was a fiercely whispered exchange at the top of the stairs, which I couldn't help overhearing.

'What do you mean by coming back in this state again?' I heard my father hiss. 'You are a guest in Thrang's house. You owe him your duty, not drunken foolishness and mess. The whole house stinks now.'

'Don't tell me what to do,' said my brother rudely, his words slurred and his voice loud in the relative stillness of the night. 'I don't take orders from a slave!'

I caught my breath and scrunched up tight under my covers, clutching my amulet in horror at the disrespect. I could feel the anger of both men like a wave of poison seeping into the house.

There was the sound of an angry exclamation, quickly stifled, and then my father spoke low but full of suppressed rage. 'Keep your voice down! Would you throw my past in my face? You should be glad I've given you a different life. At least I know how to behave as a guest. Clean yourself up and get some rest. There's work to be done in the morning.'

My father's footsteps, quick and firm, came down the stairs and crossed the room. I heard him fling himself onto his furs. My brother's footsteps soon followed, unsteady and faltering. He tripped, swore, and fumbled with his bedding.

Once the servant had locked the door again, the house fell silent, the stillness broken only by my brother's drunken snores. Father didn't snore, and I suspected that, like me, he was lying awake, unhappy. My brother's behaviour was upsetting him. And perhaps he was thinking of my mother, left alone and injured at home. Well, not completely alone, of course. Asgerd would look after her and the others would run the farm and house. But I wished we could be there with her. I thought of her many times in every day, and worried constantly about the fact that Halfgrim lived only two days' ride away.

I thought of Ingvar too. In the cover of darkness, I touched my amulet to my lips. I remembered his farewell kiss. I'd thought of it so many times since, that I no longer knew what was real and what was imagined. I longed to see him again, to watch the way his fair hair caught the light and glowed, and the way his blue eyes flashed when he was enthusiastic about something. Was he sleeping now, as I was trying to do? Did he think of me?

I eventually fell asleep with the wide bay and the broad mountains of Iceland stretching out in the empty spaces of my mind, their shimmering grandeur a dazzling contrast to the overfilled city I now found myself in.

CHAPTER THIRTEEN

My brother was surly at breakfast. Having been rudely awakened by my father, he sat silent and grim faced, wincing at loud sounds. Thrang and Leif politely ignored him and continued to chat with father. After breakfast father took Asgrim aside.

'This can't go on, Asgrim,' father said. 'You're a grown man and must behave like one. You've been taught manners and decent standards of behaviour. I want you to remember them.'

'Decent standards?' sneered Asgrim. 'What, like killing and stealing? Very well, I'll be happy to learn those from you.'

Father's lips tightened as he fought to control his temper: his shoulders were tense and his hands twitched into fists. However, after a moment's silence he spoke again and his voice was controlled.

'Thrang needs a crew for his ship from tomorrow. I've volunteered to go and you'll accompany us. Sober. Is that clear?'

'What are we doing working as labourers when we have our own ship?' asked Asgrim angrily. 'We could sail out and take plunder and win glory in our own right, not skulk here as though we don't know any better. There are fighting men aplenty in Jorvik who would go with us for the chance of booty.'

'Never!' exclaimed my father, raising his voice. 'I won't prey on innocent families. We'll do honest work to repay Thrang for our keep. You'll accompany me tomorrow.'

'Of course,' said Asgrim, but his voice and bearing showed no remorse. Father turned away, but I saw the sly look which Asgrim threw at his back and felt uneasy. I watched for an opportunity to speak to father privately, but it didn't come. He said he, Thrang, and Asgrim had work to do, and sent me to market with Unn, their slave woman, to help carry home the food she bought. I hated the experience. Unn was unfriendly, and the crowds terrified me. I came home longing to speak to father, but he'd already gone out again with Thrang. By the time I could tell him my fears, Asgrim had disappeared.

When the following morning came, Asgrim had still not come back from whatever haunts he frequented at night. Father was forced to sail without him, taking four of our other crew members from home, and leaving his most trusted man, Erik, with a handful of younger men to guard our boat.

'Take care, Sigrun,' he said, kissing me on the forehead. 'I'm very sorry to leave you alone here so soon, and with your brother misbehaving too. But you'll be more comfortable here than on the ship. Leif has said he will look out for you while we are gone, and Erik will too, of course. Take care.'

I hugged my father tight. I was sick with fear for my brother and dreaded being left alone. I had to bite my lip to stop myself begging father not to leave me.

Leif went to the quay to help ready the ship. I followed them all to the end of the street, watched until they were out of sight and then went back into the empty house. Thrang's two servants were out and I was all alone for almost the first time in my life. I sank down on the floor beside the empty fireplace and felt the loneliness fill me, draining away all my strength and purpose.

I was still sitting there, outwardly idle, but inwardly seething with emotion, when Leif returned. He came into the room and stood awkwardly by the door, shifting from one foot to the other. I summoned up a wan smile.

'So . . . it's just the two of us, then,' Leif said.

'Yes.' I nodded. I felt embarrassed, and so did Leif.

He cleared his throat. 'I'll be out a great deal . . . on business, I'm afraid,' he said. 'That's why I stayed behind and why my father was grateful for Bjorn's help. But I'm free this morning, if you would like to . . . Bjorn said you might like to look at the stalls with . . . with medicinal plants.'

'That's kind of you, but you must have a great deal to do,' I said quickly. It occurred to me that my father had left me no money at all.

'Then what will you do this morning?' asked Leif, troubled at my refusal.

'I . . . ' I paused, unable to think what I might find to do. I had no mending to occupy myself with, there was no loom in Thrang's house. I had the new fabric but no needles or thread to make it up. There were no animals to tend.

'I really have no idea,' I confessed, trying to hide my

sudden desire to cry. 'I know no one and my usual occu-
pations are the chores of a farm.'

Leif smiled. 'Come with me then,' he said. 'If you buy
some plants, you can busy yourself preparing them.
Your father has given me a purse of money for you: he'd
meant to give it to you himself but forgot.'

'Oh, in that case . . . Thank you! I need needles and
threads to make my new dress too,' I admitted. I got to
my feet, glad after all not to be left alone all day. 'Will
you help me bargain?'

'Of course,' said Leif cheerfully. 'I'll get you the best
prices anyone could.'

We stepped out into the busy streets and the heat,
dust, and smells of the city enveloped me like a cloud.
Every fibre of my being longed for the fresh, clean air
of home. That feeling lasted all the way through the
crowded, noisy streets. This was the fourth time I had
walked along them and I felt that no matter how long I
stayed in this place, they would never become comfortable or familiar.

The herb market, however, put all such thoughts out
of my mind. The stalls were crowded, but when I saw the
wares they had on offer, I lost all my shyness and fear in
excitement. 'Cloves!' I gasped. 'Mother used her last over
a year ago and no one has brought any so far north!' I
rushed forward to touch the prickly brown sticks. 'And
ginger! And here is . . . oh, it must be lavender, and . . .
rosemary!'

I heard Leif chuckle beside me, and realized I was
behaving like an over-excited child. I smiled and blushed.
'How much money did father leave for me?'

'Enough to buy several stalls full of goods, I imagine,' he replied. Overhearing this, the trader became very attentive, and ignored all other customers to serve me.

I missed my mother now. There were many plants and roots that were unfamiliar to me that she might have known. I was used to gathering and drying the native plants, but I'd never seen such variety as this. I began selecting items, listening to the advice and suggestions of the trader.

'This is valerian,' he said, offering me a shrivelled-looking root. 'You'll want some of this.'

Valerian, for inducing sleep. I'd heard of it, but never seen it till now. I added it to my growing pile. Elder and willow bark too, for reducing fever. I also chose garlic, which smelled unpleasantly strong, but I was told was a good purge and tonic, as well as beneficial in fighting infection. I added hollyhock: a cure for coughs, or so the trader said.

When my selection was complete, Leif began to bargain. He haggled fiercely, but so did the trader. The sums of money meant nothing to me. I watched Leif count out several coins, at last, and a couple of pieces that looked as though they were parts of coins. Then the treasure trove of medicinal plants was mine, wrapped into a parcel and tied neatly for me to carry home. I knew my mother would give a great deal for these; she'd felt the lack of many of them in recent years.

I looked up at Leif as we walked away. 'Did that cost a great deal?'

'A little more than I expected,' said Leif with a grin. 'But you aren't yet bankrupt.'

We bought needles and threads and then headed home by a different route. One street we walked down had a very different kind of sale going on: groups of men, women, and children tied by the wrists and ankles being looked over by Norse men and Saxons. I caught my breath. Helgi kept a few slaves: I'd known them all my life and they were part of his family. But I'd never seen this trade in human beings. There was a look of hopelessness in their eyes that cut me deeply. Worse than that was the fear and sadness I felt from them. I tried to shut it out, but it was too strong. It came over me in waves, weighing me down.

Everything my father criticized in the practice of keeping slaves came back to me. It all made sense when I saw this. The humiliation of having your mouth forced open and your teeth examined, as if you were a cow or a horse. One little boy was crying as he was looked over. I wondered where his parents were. Had he been snatched away from them? Had my father once been sold in the busy street like these poor souls? His story, so recently revealed to me, made this sight unbearably poignant; far more so than it would have been just a few short months ago. As I watched, money changed hands, and the boy was led away. The man who took him looked ordinary enough, and I prayed he'd be kind.

If only I could buy them all myself, and set them free. But there were so many. And most were probably out of reach of their homeland, without friends or family in Jorvik. What would they do? My steps lagged, as I watched. I felt desperately guilty I was doing nothing.

'Are you thinking of buying a slave?' asked Leif as he

noticed the direction of my gaze. I shook my head in silence, and stared at my feet, ashamed of my own inability to help.

Around the next corner was a tight press of people. We moved more and more slowly and eventually came to a halt, our way forward blocked by the crowd.

'What's going on?' I asked Leif, who was standing on his toes, looking over the crowd. I wasn't tall enough to see a thing.

'I can't quite see, oh . . . it looks like a fight,' said Leif.

'A fight?' I asked, taken aback. 'In the street? Isn't someone going to stop it?'

Leif shrugged. 'Most people will see it as good entertainment. It could have been a bet or a challenge.'

'I see,' I said uneasily. I could hear shouting and whistling in the crowd and realized some were cheering the combatants on.

'This could take a long time to clear,' said Leif, after waiting impatiently for some moments, as the shouting and cheering grew louder. 'Follow me.' So saying, he began to weave through the crowd, bearing across to the right hand side of the street. I tried to follow, but I wasn't used to pushing through crowds.

I got further and further behind, and began to be afraid that I would lose Leif altogether. Just then the crowd surged back, and I was almost knocked off my feet in the press. I began to panic, feeling I couldn't breathe. Some of the men and women around me smelled so bad, I couldn't imagine when they had last taken a bath. It was obvious that they neither observed the weekly washing day, nor took care of their teeth. To my relief, Leif reappeared just ahead of me. He reached out and grasped my hand, pulling me through the crowd after him. I hurried as best I could, for even I, inexperienced in city life as I was, could tell the mood around us was growing ugly.

Clinging tightly to Leif's hand, I felt the press of people lessen. The air was cooler, I could breathe again, and then we were out of the crowd, making our way down an almost empty alley between two lines of tall dwelling houses. Leif knew the city well and had found a way that avoided crowds.

'Thank the gods,' I exclaimed, drawing deep breaths of air into my lungs.

'You hate the crowds, don't you?' said Leif.

I thought how very kind and understanding his smile was. 'I've never experienced them before,' I said by way of excuse. 'I never went to market with my father. He took my brother sometimes, but never me.'

'Didn't you go anywhere at all?' asked Leif curiously. We were walking swiftly now. I realized that he was still holding my hand, and withdrew it from his with a blush.

'No. I'd never left our bay until now, except to nurse a neighbouring family or deliver a baby. We're very spread out. Each family needs a lot of space to farm. The soil is thin and the climate very harsh. It's not warm like here.'

'You don't make it sound very appealing,' said Leif.

'Oh, but it is,' I hastened to assure him. 'It's wonderful, it's—'

At that moment a horse burst out of a side street, much too fast, narrowly missing us. It was sweating and rolling its eyes, its hooves pounding the street. I cried out with fright and ducked. The horse wheeled sharply to avoid us and for a moment everything was noise and confusion. Then a slight, dark-haired girl fell heavily to the ground beside me. With a cry, I rushed to help her. She lay in the dust, barefoot and dressed in rags, her face streaked with dirt and tears and a livid bruise across one cheekbone.

'Are you hurt?' I asked, dropping to my knees beside her.

To my horror I saw why she'd fallen: she was bound tightly by the wrists. My eyes followed the rope to see the other end was held by the man on the horse: a stocky man with a huge, neglected beard and long, dirty hair. He yanked hard on the rope, dragging the girl upright. She struggled to her feet and stood trembling and swaying.

'Damn you, Maria!' the man shouted, and to my horror, he raised a stick he held in one hand to strike her.

'Don't!' I cried, scrambling up and throwing myself between them. The stick whistled through the air right by me, narrowly missing my arm.

'Get out of my way, girl!' shouted the man angrily. 'Unless you want a beating too!'

'You mustn't strike her!' I cried, beside myself, putting my arms around the girl. She was so thin, I could feel all her bones. 'She's already hurt!'

'She's a troublesome, runaway slave! I can do what I like,' he shouted angrily. 'I can kill her if I choose. How dare you interfere?'

'Sigrun,' said Leif urgently. He was trying to draw me away, one hand on my sleeve. I pulled away. I'd walked past the other slaves helplessly, but this was too much. I looked at the girl. There was such a heart-rending look in her dark, liquid eyes; a surge of her helplessness and despair swept across me. But I sensed the man's mood too; he was angry and vicious. He started upbraiding me in a coarse but unfamiliar tongue. I understood enough to know he was insulting me, but couldn't catch the words. I felt his cruelty, and knew that the girl was going to be made to suffer.

'Sigrun, you can't interfere,' said Leif again. 'She's his slave. Don't anger him.'

I felt rage at Leif's cowardice. He should support me, not advise me to look the other way. I knew my father wouldn't do so, and nor, I was certain, would Ingvar. I shrugged Leif's hand off my arm for the second time.

'If she's a troublesome slave, then perhaps she's for sale?' I asked the horseman.

A crafty look crept into the man's eyes. My heart sank as I sensed his greed outpace his anger. 'She cost me a great deal of money,' he told me in heavily-accented Norse. 'She was a gift for my niece.'

'Sigrun, please come away,' Leif begged. 'You're making a scene.'

'I want nine silver marks for her,' said the horseman. 'Or I'll be sorely out of pocket.'

I looked at Leif. 'How much is left in my father's purse?'

Leif gasped with shock. 'Nowhere near that much! She's not worth it either.'

I felt daunted. The man was dirty and unkempt, but he wasn't poor. The fabric of his tunic was good quality, and he was astride a fine horse. He was probably used to driving a hard bargain.

I held out my hand for my father's purse, and reluctantly, Leif gave it to me.

'This is what I have. No more, no less. Will you take it?'

The man took the purse from me, weighed it briefly in a hand with ragged filthy fingernails, loosened the drawstring and glanced inside. Then he threw it in the dirt in front of me.

'You're wasting my time, Viking wench,' he said angrily. He kicked his horse on, yanking at the rope that bound the girl, even though I stood barring his way.

I felt the girl's despair. She didn't say a word, nor did she look at me, but her anguish cut me like a knife. Did I have nothing else on me of any value? I had to save her from this fate.

'Wait!' I cried, catching the horse's bridle and halting it again.

I only owned one item of value and it meant more to me than anyone could imagine. It had given me new powers, a new confidence. And it carried the precious memory of Ingvar. But was any talisman worth more than a life? With a wrench that tore at my heart, I unfastened my secret amulet from my neck. I held it out, the polished silver catching the summer sun. I prayed Ingvar would understand what I was doing and forgive me.

'This is a powerful and valuable amulet,' I said. 'Will you take this in exchange for the girl?'

I had his attention now, I could tell. But before he could speak, Leif interrupted.

'No,' he said, firmly.

'Please, Leif,' I begged. 'Don't make this more difficult . . .'

'I'll pay for the girl,' Leif interrupted me, speaking to

117

the horseman. 'But you'll not get nine marks of silver.'

'Don't I know you?' asked the stranger.

To my surprise, Leif blushed deeply. 'Yes, I'm Leif Thrangsson,' he said, less confidently than usual.

The stranger nodded. The name meant something to him. He switched to his own language and began to bargain. I followed little of it, but finally Leif handed over some coins from his own purse. The stranger palmed them and roughly thrust the rope binding the girl into my hands. 'She's mute,' he said. 'A fine quality in a woman. Watch her, or she'll run off.' With that, he rode off without a backward glance.

I was left face to face with my new possession; a bruised and frightened human being.

CHAPTER FOURTEEN

I tugged at the knots that bound Maria's wrists. 'Don't be afraid,' I said to her softly. 'We aren't going to hurt you.' I had no idea whether she understood, but I hoped my tone was reassuring.

'Don't be a fool, Sigrun,' said Leif, placing his hand over mine as I struggled with the knots. 'You can't untie her here in the open street. You heard what Eadred said. She's a runaway.'

'Eadred?' I asked. 'You *know* that . . . brute?'

'Come, Sigrun, please,' said Leif, clearly uncomfortable. 'Can we go home and discuss this in private?'

It was not until he said this that I noticed that the previously deserted alleyway was now quite full of people, staring at us openly. I blushed to realize I'd caused such a scene, and submitted to Leif taking the rope from my hands, and leading the girl. He took my hand in his free one, and hurried us both home.

'Unn?' called Leif as we went down the stairs. 'We need some food and drink, please! And would you start to heat water for washing?'

'You left the house empty and unlocked,' Unn complained as she stoked the fire and fetched a jug of whey. 'I was at the market.'

'Well, there's nothing missing is there?' asked Leif impatiently. And as Unn shook her head, he added, 'No harm done then.'

'My father will pay you back the money you spent,' I told Leif, as I wrestled once more with the tight knots around the girl's wrists.

'There's no need,' said Leif. 'Consider her a gift, to seal the friendship between our families.'

'Thank you,' I said, restraining myself from pointing out that the word *gift* still made the girl sound like a possession.

'You're welcome. As long as you don't let her run off.'

The ropes fell away at last, revealing chafed and bleeding wrists. I murmured my sympathy, and touched Maria's hands gently. 'That must hurt you very much,' I said.

She looked away, neither answering nor meeting my eyes.

'She doesn't speak, don't forget,' said Leif. 'She might not even understand Norse. Eadred's household is Saxon.' He tried speaking to her in the Saxon tongue, but got no more response than I had. He shrugged. 'A recent slave, or a stubborn one,' he said.

Unn brought goblets of whey, and I held one out to the girl. She hesitated, but then took it, and sipped a little of the sharp, sour liquid. I could see her hands were shaking.

'Have some bread,' I said holding some out. 'Look, you can dip it in the whey.' She seemed to understand, because she did as I suggested.

When the water was hot, Unn poured it into the

wooden tub in the partitioned-off area of the downstairs room we all used for bathing and changing. I added a handful of the healing herbs I'd bought in the market, and then led Maria to the water. She stood there, unmoving, not looking at it. She must want a bath though; she smelled as though she'd slept in a midden. She'd been on the run, so perhaps she had.

'You need to bathe,' I told her slowly and clearly, pointing at the water. I helped her peel off her dirty garments, pulling her ragged tunic carefully over her head. She submitted, standing miserably, head down, as both Unn and I gasped over her injuries. Her back and legs were laced with cuts and bruises. She'd been beaten often. Tears of sympathy pricked my eyes.

'The poor girl,' muttered Unn.

We both helped Maria wash, tipping pans of warm water over her head, scrubbing her lice-infested hair clean with soap and combing it. I used a soft cloth to cleanse the many wounds on her body and wipe her face clean of dirt.

After the bath, we wrapped her in a clean, dry cloth and I smeared healing ointment on her many hurts. She winced, catching her breath as I touched the broken skin on her wrists, pulling her hand away.

'I know it hurts,' I said gently, 'and I'm sorry, but it will stop infection. It's important. Will you trust me?' I looked up into Maria's dark eyes, and sensed her fear and confusion. 'I want to help you,' I told her. 'You're safe here.'

Hesitantly, she held out her hands once more.

'I'm Sigrun,' I said, carefully spreading ointment over

the lacerations. There was a long silence. Then she nodded slowly.

'She'll be gone by morning, if you don't bind her,' Leif
said to me over the remains of nightmeal. The long late-
summer day was fading outside and the room was lit by
the glow of the cooking fire. Unn and Ivan, Thrang's two
slaves, sat by the fire on the far side of the room. Erik
and the other men were on the ship, and Asgrim was
still out somewhere, so the house was quiet. Maria was
curled up asleep on a pile of furs, her cheek resting on
one hand, her dark lashes closed over her eyes. I looked
across at her.

'She won't run away if I treat her kindly. And in any
case, would you honestly be able to bind a rough cord
onto those injured wrists?'

'You could tie her ankles,' Leif suggested seriously. He
picked up another piece of beef and sank his teeth into it.

I looked at him reproachfully, setting down my empty
goblet. 'They're nearly as bad.'

'I'm just trying to protect my investment,' he said.
'What's the point of paying for a slave you don't keep?'

'She won't be a slave,' I said, annoyed with him.
'Father would never allow me to own a slave, and I
wouldn't want to. But I hope I can persuade her to stay
and be a companion to me. I can't gain her trust by tying
her up.'

Leif looked puzzled. 'Everyone has slaves,' he said,
ignoring my point about trust. 'How does your father
farm?'

'He pays his workers,' I said, unwilling to discuss the real reason for my father's principle. I changed the subject: 'Where do you think Maria's from?' I asked.

Leif shrugged. 'Could be anywhere,' he said. 'But I'd guess from the south somewhere. Maria isn't a name I've heard before. She has dusky skin and black hair, and she's more delicately built than the peoples from the east.'

'Thank you for rescuing her,' I said to Leif. 'I didn't think you wanted to help.'

'I didn't,' he admitted. 'We'd have done better to leave be. Eadred is a powerful man.'

'He's certainly a cruel one. What made you change your mind?'

'I couldn't let you trade that amulet,' said Leif unexpectedly. 'I think it means a lot to you.'

I was startled and must have shown it.

'I've seen your hand go to your throat often when you're unhappy or frightened,' said Leif. 'I hadn't seen the amulet until today, but I guessed you wore something important.'

'It means the world to me,' I admitted. 'I thought I'd kept it a secret.'

Leif smiled and was about to speak when there was an urgent knocking on the door upstairs.

'I'll get it,' said Leif, getting to his feet.

I stared idly into the glow of the small fire, thinking about Maria. Voices drifted from upstairs and then two sets of feet hurried down. Leif came first, closely followed by Erik, who wore a worried frown.

'Sigrun,' he said, out of breath, 'have you seen your brother at all?'

I half stood up, fear gripping me. 'Not since yesterday,' I said. 'Is he in trouble?'

'The ship's disappeared,' said Erik. 'I left four men on board, but when I came back, it had sailed. I've asked people on the nearby ships: the man who was in charge answers to Asgrim's description. Sigrun, I fear your brother has stolen our ship.'

CHAPTER FIFTEEN

'Asgrim must have needed to take the boat for a short trip somewhere,' I said, my voice shaking.

Erik sat down heavily on a bench and rubbed his face. He looked grey. Leif quietly poured a goblet of mead and put it into his hand. 'Thank you,' muttered Erik, but his hand shook so much he had to put the goblet down on the table. 'Apparently, Asgrim hired new crew members and carried supplies on board,' he told me. 'It sounds like he's taken on some of the raff and scaff of Jorvik. He must have talked our younger men into going adventuring with him.'

'Surely not,' I faltered. I sat down beside Erik on the bench, my knees weak and trembling. 'There has to be some mistake.'

Erik shook his head. 'I fear not. Asgrim's taken this business of your father's very badly. And it's come at an age when he's got more courage than sense.' Erik put his work-worn hand over mine and clasped it tight. 'I'm sorry, Sigrun. I've let you and your father down.'

'No, no, Erik, *you* haven't,' I said distractedly, returning the pressure of his hand. 'You've always been like a second father to us. Has he really gone? It couldn't be a mistake?'

Erik shook his head. 'I'm afraid not.'

'If you ask me, Asgrim's been desperate to go adventuring all along,' said Leif quietly. 'He talks of little else, out of his father's hearing.'

I knew he was right and somehow Leif's words made my brother's desertion real.

'Oh, how will we get home?' I cried. My stomach twisted with panic at the thought that we were stranded here. 'How could he do this to us?'

Leif put a hand on my shoulder. 'If only we had our ship here,' he said, 'I could have pursued him.'

Erik snorted. 'I suspect he thought all that through,' he said angrily. 'He's timed this well. As if Bjorn hasn't got enough to worry him. Asgrim is a spoiled, greedy, heedless young fool, mad for glory and riches. He has no idea what he'll have to do to get them.'

'I think he does know,' I said reluctantly, remembering Ingvar's dreadful tale, 'but I don't think he cares.' I didn't like to think so badly of Asgrim: until recently he'd been the best brother I could have wished for. But right now the very thought of him filled me with shame and anger.

I awoke the following morning having slept badly, a sense of deep dread inside me, and my head aching. It took me only a moment to recall that my brother had betrayed us and left us without a ship in this strange city. I rolled over and had a second shock. The sleeping furs next to me were empty. Maria had gone.

Sick with disappointment, I sat up. The room was empty. Tears of misery filled my eyes and spilled over.

How could she run off? It was hard to remember I'd led an ordinary, happy life until a couple of months ago. Now my father was an outlaw, my mother injured, Asgrim a traitor, Maria had run away, and I was exiled from my home and from Ingvar. How could I even face another day?

A light tread on the stairs interrupted my self-pity. A slight figure came into view, almost tripping over a kirtle that was much too large, the sleeves rolled back clumsily. 'Maria!' I exclaimed, hastily wiping my eyes, embarrassed to be caught crying. The realization that she hadn't fled in the night filled me with relief. Maria bowed her head, acknowledging me, and crouched by the fire, stirring some porridge. I could smell its creamy, comforting scent from where I sat.

Leif appeared over breakfast. Ladling himself a brimming bowl of porridge, he joined us at the table. 'Erik's begged passage on a boat downriver to hunt for Asgrim,' he said. 'I told him he's wasting his time, but he feels he owes it to Bjorn.'

I nodded, ashamed that Erik, who was no longer a young man, should have so much trouble and worry over my heedless brother.

Leif glanced at Maria, then at me. 'You were right and I was wrong,' he said. 'She's still here.'

'Yes.' I smiled faintly. 'I'm glad of it.'

'She needs clothes of her own though,' Leif said with a grin. 'Yours are too big for her.'

I spent the next two days quietly indoors with Maria,

trying not to let my fears about my brother overpower me. We sewed a new kirtle that fitted Maria properly, and made up my own overdress from the blue silk father had bought me. I cut a leftover scrap into the shape of a flower and stitched it to the front of Maria's new kirtle.

'This is a sign that you're a freed woman,' I explained to her. 'You're no longer a slave. Do you understand?'

Maria looked at me, but gave no sign of understanding. I took her hands in mine.

'I free you,' I said again, slowly and carefully. 'I'd like you to stay here and be my friend, if you're willing.'

Maria looked down, and a little colour crept into her face and neck, but I still wasn't sure if she understood.

We laid out my new herbs and medicinal plants, tying the ones that needed drying into bundles and fastening them to the rafters. I chatted to Maria, relieved to have companionship through the long, lonely days. She seemed to listen although she didn't reply. Sometimes she looked intently at me, or frowned. Once she smiled. I was especially glad of Maria's company as Leif was mainly out, busy in the city. Erik didn't come back and I began to worry about him.

I longed constantly for father to return, but when I finally heard the longed-for sounds of his arrival above stairs several days later, I froze, feeling dread gather in me like ice. How would I break the news? Father swept into the room, ruddy and wind-blown from days at sea, Thrang close behind him.

'Well, Sigrun!' exclaimed my father cheerfully. 'We concluded Thrang's business well, and brought him back a richer man.' He embraced me, lifting me right off my feet and holding me close. I smelled sea and fresh air on his tunic. 'How did you manage in our absence?' he asked.

'I have bad news,' I said abruptly.

My father paled at once. 'From home?' he asked hoarsely.

'No.' I shook my head. 'It's not mother. But Asgrim has left, and taken the ship.'

'What?' My father's voice was thunderous. His rage grew as I related the tale. His words of fury were interrupted by Thrang who was listening quietly from the bottom of the stairs.

'Have you checked the store?' he asked.

'Store?' I turned to him, confused. He was looking very serious.

'Surely not,' said my father in a voice that wasn't quite his own.

'Sigrun, did you and Leif leave the house unattended at any time before he left?' asked Thrang.

'No, I . . . ' I remembered the trip to the market. 'Yes, we did.'

Thrang had already crossed the room and was dragging a pile of furs from one corner, levering up a trapdoor that had been concealed under them. He grasped a taper, lit it at the fire and descended a short ladder into the space under the floor. When he emerged again, his face was sober.

'Well?' demanded father harshly.

'My goods are still there,' said Thrang heavily. 'Yours are gone.'

'Even the chest?' asked father.

'Even the chest,' confirmed Thrang.

I remembered my father's money chest and Asgrim's greed as he'd looked at it.

'It was hidden down there?' I asked. My hands were as cold as ice, and I didn't feel steady on my feet. 'That was the work you did before you went away?'

Before father could reply, we heard the door opening upstairs and the heavy tread of many footsteps overhead. Thrang slammed down the trapdoor and pulled the rugs across it. 'That's our crew coming for a meal,' he said. 'We'll talk more of this later.'

Unn had so much work to do preparing food for so many that she let Maria and me lay bread, meat, and fruit on the tables upstairs and pour the ale. I worked in a daze, unable to think straight. The men had been at sea for days. They were in high spirits, knowing they were about to be paid, and ate and drank heartily, filling the room with their loud, cheerful voices. Only my father sat shocked and silent, hardly touching either food or drink. When the crew had gone at last, I sat down beside him, put my arms around him and leaned my head against his shoulder.

'What was in the store, father?' I asked him softly.

'Everything of value,' said my father with a groan. 'Money, calfskins, wool; everything I was going to trade. Thrang offered it to me as a place of safe-keeping. I couldn't leave goods of such value aboard ship. We entrusted the secret only to Asgrim, who helped us carry everything here.'

The true depth of my brother's betrayal struck me. He'd knowingly robbed us of everything we had, leaving us not only stranded here, but penniless too. How would we live? 'Have we nothing left?' I asked.

My father pulled a purse from his tunic. 'This is full. But it's all I have.'

'Oh, and I stupidly spent money on medicines,' I said. 'If only I hadn't!'

My father waved that aside. 'It was only a small sum,' he said.

'And there's an extra mouth to feed,' I confessed. 'Father, I haven't introduced you to Maria yet.' Nervously, I beckoned Maria forward, and she came to stand shyly in front of us. 'She was being badly treated,' I explained awkwardly. 'So Leif paid for her, and I've freed her. I hope . . . that's . . . that you don't mind . . . ' Of course my father wouldn't be angry with me. But it was such a bad time to include an extra person in our household. My father's courtesy didn't fail him for a second. He held out his hand to Maria, and she tentatively put her own into it.

'Welcome, Maria,' father said gravely. 'I hope you'll be happy with us, and I'm sorry that you've caught us at such a bad moment.'

Maria nodded and then retreated hastily to the fireside.

'Don't despair, my friend,' said Thrang. 'This is a misfortune, indeed, and that headstrong lad of yours needs a whipping, but you're among friends. You won't starve. My home is your home, for as long as you need it.'

'Thank you, Thrang,' my father replied, his voice heavy. 'I'm grateful to you. But I don't choose to be a burden on anyone. I've become used to being a man of wealth and standing, you see.' He gave a short, rueful laugh. 'And I would prefer to think better of my son than I do right now,' he added sadly.

'Father, how will we get home?' I asked, voicing my main fear.

My father hugged me. 'I'm afraid that day is a long way off, Sigrun, my dearest,' he said. 'Asgrim will surely have returned by then.'

'If he returns at all,' I said fearfully. 'Erik said he hired some desperate men. He's gone after them.'

'We must hope he'll return; that they'll both return safely,' said father.

'And if the worst comes to the worst, we'll take you home ourselves,' Thrang promised. 'I'd love to see Iceland again, and pay my respects to Thora too.'

'Thank you,' we both said gratefully. Thrang made the long, arduous, and dangerous journey sound like a short ride to a feast with neighbours. But the offer, generous as it was, didn't solve how we would get through three long years with no ship and no money.

CHAPTER SIXTEEN

✳

We were all still sunk in gloom when Leif returned home towards evening. As soon as he'd embraced his father, and welcomed him back, we told him of the robbing of the storeroom. Leif was sympathetic but abstracted, and seemed to have troubles of his own on his mind.

'Did your business not prosper today?' I asked him as I brought him ale.

'What?' Leif asked. 'Oh, yes, that went well enough.'

He then sank deep into thought once more, sipping his ale without seeming to taste it. I could sense he was worried. I wondered for a moment if he was thinking about our troubles, but I recalled he'd worn a worried frown when he'd walked into the room. I sat beside Leif at supper and found him an absent-minded host. He broke off mid-conversation and stared into the distance.

'Is something troubling you?' I asked him at last.

'Oh . . . nothing you need worry about,' he replied. 'You have more than enough on your mind.'

'Leif, you rescued Maria for me, and cared for us both while father was away. I'd like to help,' I told him. 'Sometimes just talking about a problem can lighten it.'

Leif sighed. 'I'm as helpless in this as you are in your troubles,' he said and rubbed his hand across his face.

'There's a young woman I know,' he said self-consciously. 'She's ill.'

'I'm sorry,' I said, my sympathy stirred. 'What's wrong with her?'

'As to that . . . I don't know exactly,' said Leif. 'Her maid told me she has a fever and can't see anyone.'

'Has she seen . . . ' I began tentatively, 'anyone who can help? A healer?'

'Yes, the best that Jorvik has to offer. Her uncle is a wealthy man and close to the king himself. She's in good hands.'

'That's good,' I said. 'I shall pray to Eir for her too.'

Leif covered my hand briefly with his. 'Thank you,' he said softly. 'And I'm sorry to hear the latest news about your brother. I had no idea that my father had let Bjorn use our secret store. Otherwise I'd have checked sooner.'

'It would have made no difference,' I said sadly. 'It was already too late by then.'

My father and I went for a walk together on the following day. We kept to the quieter streets, avoiding the market stalls.

'Tell me the story of how you came by Maria,' he asked. I told him, dwelling on the cruelty of the man on the horse, but omitting mention of my offer to swap my amulet for her.

'She was being dragged behind a horse, you say?' my father asked.

'That's right. She fell and hurt herself. It was the cruellest thing I'd ever seen.'

134

'The first time I saw your mother, she was being dragged along behind a horse,' said my father.

This brought my head up in shock, to stare at him. 'No!' I exclaimed. 'My *mother*? How could anyone treat her like that?'

'It's true,' father told me. 'If you think Halfgrim is evil, you wouldn't want to have met his father. I was being dragged too, and the pace was punishing. I helped Thora up the first time she fell. The second time I couldn't reach her. That's how I came to kill the chieftain whose name I stole. I'd already made up my mind to do so when he killed my sister earlier that day.'

I gasped. 'No,' I whispered, appalled. 'Your sister . . . ?'

'Yes. She was with child and couldn't run behind the horse. It was the worst day of my life. Even worse than the day I was first captured. It haunts me still.'

I was dumbfounded. My mind recreated a picture of how it might have been; my mother dragged along the ground, bruised and hurt, my father unable to help, already driven mad with grief for his sister, so full of anger and pain that he was moved to kill. I shuddered. This was a very different view of his motivation. A different story to any I had imagined up to now. It was tragic, honourable, and it moved me deeply.

'And then you decided to steal the ships?' I asked hoping he wouldn't shy away, close up as he had done up to now.

'That was your mother's idea. We had King Harald's army on our heels, pursuing the man I'd killed. Your mother had a vision of us sailing away on the ships, and . . . er . . . persuaded me we should take that escape route.'

'So you ran away together, even though you'd only just met?' I asked curiously. 'That must have been so strange.'

'Very strange. But we were in so much immediate danger that perhaps the strangeness didn't strike us until later.'

'Why did you never tell us?' I asked him. 'Why keep it such a secret? Told like this, it's nothing to be ashamed of.'

'Don't you see? Our safety depended on people believing that Svanson had sailed to Iceland and settled there. Your mother chose a location away from the main trade and travel routes from Norway. We hoped to remain peacefully there, far out of the way of anyone who'd known him. If I'd told the real tale, it might have spread and reached his kin. We especially couldn't risk you or Asgrim knowing the truth. Children are apt to blurt things out to strangers, no matter how carefully you warn them.'

'But not now that we're older,' I objected. 'You can trust me now.'

Father nodded and sighed a little. 'We always meant to,' he said. 'But how do you find a good moment to reveal such a secret? We put it off from year to year.'

Father took my hand and drew it through his arm. I leaned on him as we walked. There was a moment's peace between us as we each thought about what had been said.

'I think you might have won Asgrim's loyalty better if you'd taken him into your confidence,' I said instead. 'On the journey here, perhaps.'

'It's possible,' my father admitted. 'But I'm not sure

136

he'd have listened. The temptations of adventure and easy wealth had too strong an appeal to such a hot-headed young man.'

I stayed silent, burning to criticize my brother's conduct.

'I don't know what we can do about the situation he's left us in,' said my father. 'I can accept Thrang's hospitality; he offers it freely and I, Erik, and the others can work for him. I've been generous to him in the past. But we'll need money living in a city like this. We can't make a purse last one year, let alone three. It's troubling me.'

'Three years here!' I gave an involuntary groan.

'Are you very unhappy?' my father asked. 'Did I do wrong to bring you with me?'

I felt guilty at once, remembering that he didn't want to be here either, and that he'd brought me because my mother had foreseen he'd need me. He needed help now, and I couldn't see that I was any use at all.

'Perhaps I'll get used to it,' I said. 'But it feels very enclosed. If I could at least walk out of the city, it would be easier to bear. But the defences keep us all crammed inside.'

'Yes, it's a strange way to live, when you're used to roaming the open landscapes we have at home,' agreed father. 'But you seem to have found some consolation. You're getting on well with Leif, aren't you?'

I became aware of my father's close scrutiny and felt myself blush.

'He's . . . he seems very nice,' I said self-consciously.

'I couldn't help noticing you holding hands last night,' father said.

'We weren't,' I said, half confused, half indignant. 'It's not like that.'

'Really?' asked father. 'Thrang wanted to marry your mother, you know. He was one of her most devoted suitors. It would be very fitting if you married his son. And you'd be so much safer here in Jorvik than in Iceland. Away from all our family trouble.'

'Please, don't,' I begged, the heat burning in my face now. 'It's out of the question. You know that I—' I stopped suddenly, not knowing whether father *did* know of my feelings for Ingvar. Had he seen our farewell on the ship, or had he been too busy sailing it? I was in doubt, and the thought of telling him my secret feelings and longings was acutely embarrassing.

To my relief, father dropped the subject. Instead we talked of home and of the coming winter until the heat faded from my face and we reached Thrang's house again. There Leif awaited me impatiently.

'Sigrun, thank Thor you are back!' he exclaimed as soon as I entered the house. My father raised his brows. Leif didn't notice and drew me aside, speaking in a low voice: 'I need a healer. Can you come with me? It's urgent.'

CHAPTER SEVENTEEN

✴

My heart sank. He needed a healer. I was sure I'd be completely useless. 'I'm not very . . . experienced,' I faltered, panicking. How would I manage without my mother to guide me?

'What's this?' asked father curiously.

'An acquaintance is very sick,' Leif told him. 'I need your daughter's help. I'll take good care of her, I promise.'

'Of course,' said my father at once, knowing nothing of my agonizing self doubts. 'Don't keep Leif waiting, Sigrun.'

Unable to voice my fears, I ran reluctantly downstairs to collect my bag of medicines. I would have to try. Perhaps if I was very lucky, it would be some condition I recognized.

Maria was sitting sewing by the fire. When she saw me preparing to go straight out again, she looked disappointed.

'Would you like to come with us?' I asked her. 'We're going to tend a sick lady.' Maria nodded, threw her sewing aside and jumped to her feet. It was the first time she'd shown clearly that she understood me. It would be good to have someone with me at this ordeal.

Leif poured out his tale as the three of us hurried through the streets together.

'She's called Leola,' he explained to me. 'She's the girl I told you about . . .'

Maria stopped dead in her tracks. I looked round, surprised.

'What's wrong?' I asked her.

Maria was shaking her head, backing away. Before I could stop her, she turned and hurried back to the house.

'What . . . ?' I asked Leif bewildered.

'She won't want to come,' said Leif, looking uncomfortable. 'I forgot. You see, Leola is Eadred's niece. She's living in his house.'

I froze, torn between wanting to help and a reluctance to go near Maria's cruel master again.

'Please, Sigrun,' Leif begged. 'Leola's nothing like her uncle. She's a beautiful, sweet-natured girl. And she's so very ill. Her usual healer hasn't been able to help her. Now her maid is afraid she'll die. They've agreed to let you try what you can do. I'm depending on you. Please, please don't fail me.'

I felt a churning of nerves and dread. Leif was relying on me. Someone's life hung in the balance. I'd never treated serious illness without my mother present. I might kill rather than cure her.

'Is there no one else?' I asked Leif.

'She's seen the most respected healer in the city and she failed to help her,' said Leif, anguish in his voice. 'You're my last hope, Sigrun.'

I tried to conquer my nerves, and nodded. I could at least examine the poor girl.

The house was one of the largest I'd seen, close to the centre of the city. Leif hammered on the door and it was opened quickly by a frightened-looking girl in a plain kirtle that spoke the slave or lowly servant.

'This is the healer I promised to bring,' Leif said, pushing me forward. I was ushered in at once, the door was closed behind me, shutting Leif out.

The slave girl led me into a stuffy, darkened room where the smell of unwashed body and sickness prevailed. That wasn't the only smell either. Something strange, something I couldn't quite identify, lingered in the air. I knelt down beside the pale-faced figure wrapped in furs. It was hard to see in the gloom, but as I tentatively touched her face, it was slick with sweat.

'Who are you?' whispered the figure in a voice so faint I could scarcely hear it.

'I'm Sigrun, Leif's friend,' I said. 'I've come to see if I can help you get better. Can you tell me what's wrong, or should I speak to your . . . servant?'

A hand, bony and as cold as death, reached out from under the covers and gripped my wrist. It gave me a shock, and I almost pulled back. But the girl was trying to speak. I leaned forward trying to catch her words.

'A sudden sickness,' she whispered. 'I don't know what caused it.'

Her breath smelled strange, like the room, of strong but unfamiliar medicines.

'What have you taken?' I asked. 'What did the last healer give you?'

Slowly, as though every movement was an effort, the girl reached inside her tunic and pulled out a shell,

141

threaded onto a narrow strip of leather. There were a couple of small bones attached and a bead.

'What's this?' I asked.

'A charm,' she whispered. 'To bring the blessing of the goddess.'

'That's it?' I asked, dumbfounded. 'What medicine did she give you? What did she say was wrong?'

'None. She said it was a curse.' She looked away and closed her eyes as she whispered this.

I bit back my indignation. Such ignorance! But it wouldn't do to criticize another healer's methods. 'It's important to invoke the goddess,' I agreed as calmly as I could. 'But in your case you may need some medicine as well. Do you have any pain anywhere? A stomach ache or tooth ache?'

Leola shook her head. I checked for fever, but there was none. I examined my patient. She was thin, but not emaciated. I could find little wrong apart from a tender belly, which could simply be her time of month. It wasn't taut with disease or disturbance. She seemed unwilling or unable to answer my questions.

The slave reappeared with an oil lamp. By its flickering light, I could see how pale Leola was. But I still had no idea what was wrong. In desperation, I got out my bag of runes. I wasn't even sure why; they'd never spoken to me yet. But I didn't know what else to try. I touched my amulet for luck and courage. It helped me read people's moods, so perhaps it would help with this.

Nervously I unlaced the leather that tied the small pouch, and dipped my fingertips in among the small pebbles as my mother had taught me. I waited for the sign, the tingling in the fingers that she said would come when I touched the rune that could help me. I'd failed to sense it so many times. But this time I had a small hope that the amulet might guide me.

I stirred the stones with my fingertips, feeling their smooth coldness, stilling my mind, opening it, and suddenly a pebble tingled against my skin, asking to be picked out. I grasped and withdrew it, my eyes shut. Twice more I repeated the process, and then I opened my eyes and cast the three pebbles onto the small sheepskin I'd laid out. The first stone: fertility. The desire to be wanted. I looked at the sick girl beside me. She looked anything but fertile. As usual, the runes made no sense to me.

I looked at the second stone: the power that is difficult to master. Was that a message to me? I thought of the power of the runes, which I could never read. The power of the medicines and plants I carried with me, but found so difficult to use; to judge which would be most effective and what dose to give.

I was useless: a fraud. I should apologize, get up and leave. I couldn't even read the runes, how could I cure anyone? How could I be so bad at this when my mother had spent so many years teaching me?

Leola groaned and curled into a ball. It looked as if she had some kind of belly cramp. I panicked. Was she going to die, right now? I had to do something.

I looked at the third pebble. I'd picked the empty rune; the hardest of all to read. Everything and nothing. The turning point. Emptiness.

How could emptiness, fertility, and sickness go together?

I closed my eyes, trying desperately to still my mind, and held my amulet tightly. 'Freya, guide me, help me see the truth,' I prayed under my breath. Suddenly, it all snapped into place in my mind with an almost frightening clarity. Leola *had* been fertile. She had been with child. But now there was emptiness. She'd lost it.

'You've miscarried,' I said abruptly. 'Why didn't you tell me?'

'No, no,' whispered Leola. 'That's not possible. I'm not married.'

I thought of Hild at home, and disregarded her words. In any case, I was a farmer's daughter. I wasn't so stupid as to think babies only came when you were married. But there was a missing link. Something I still didn't know. I looked back at the second rune, searching for its message, and this time it came to me: the power that's difficult to control. I'd been on the right track after all, but the message wasn't about me. Leola had taken some medicine or poison.

'You took some potion to get rid of it. Didn't you? That's what I can smell and that's what's made you so ill.' It all made sense to me now. I could hardly believe it. For a moment I didn't dwell on the fact that I still might not be able to cure Leola, but was simply intoxicated that the goddess had spoken to me at last. Then a dreadful thought struck me.

'It wasn't Leif's baby, was it?'

The claw-like fingers grasped my wrist again. 'NO! Don't tell,' she whispered frantically. 'I don't know how you know about the baby, but you mustn't tell. Swear it!'

'Of course I won't,' I said. 'I promise you.'

'Swear it on your heathen goddess. She's the one who betrayed me to you!'

'Healers never tell the secrets of those they treat,' I said, for a moment feeling like a fraud again. 'But if it will comfort you, I swear on the goddess Eir, not to tell.'

The girl fell back on her sleeping furs, exhausted and out of breath after her outburst. She began to weep in a quiet, desperate way.

'If I'm to help you, you need to tell me what you took to kill the baby,' I told her.

'I don't know what it was. My maid bought it for me at the market. From someone who didn't know us. An old woman.' She paused to sob helplessly again.

'Did you lose much blood?' I asked.

'Some, but not much worse than the usual monthly courses,' said the girl through her tears.

It seemed her distress, held in until now by fear of what she'd done to herself, had completely overcome her.

I'd never seen a case like this. Where I lived, babies came when they would and if a couple weren't married before, they married when they knew. In our small community, babies were welcomed as a blessing.

'Listen,' I told her, shaking her gently. 'It's difficult to treat you without knowing what you took. But I'll do my best. All right? I'll give you some medicines that will act to purify your body of the poison you took. And tonics, to help you get strong again. You must drink lots too, that's important. I'll make up some angelica tea. And you should eat berries. Do you understand?' Leola nodded, but didn't stop crying.

I got up and went to find her maid who was hovering outside the room.

'What was it?' I asked sternly. 'Rue? Yarrow? Juniper?'

The maid looked at the ground, her cheeks flushing. She shook her head. 'I don't know,' she whispered.

'You shouldn't give your mistress unknown substances,' I scolded. 'You could have killed her. I'll bring some medicine. Meanwhile keep her warm and try to get her to stop crying.'

The maid nodded and then hurried to the door to let me out. I was proud of myself as I stepped out into the sunshine of the street. I'd diagnosed a patient, despite being lied to. Completely by myself. The runes had responded to my touch for the first time and the goddess had guided me. Whether I could cure her was another matter.

Leif was waiting for me outside the door. 'Will she be all right? What's wrong with her?' he asked as soon as he saw me.

'She's very sick,' I said, remembering my promise to Leola. 'She thinks it's a curse. I believe she's inadvertently taken something poisonous.'

Leif gasped with shock. 'Can you help her?'

'I'll try,' I promised. I wanted to ask Leif how well he knew Leola, why he'd waited outside the house and not come in, but I didn't know where to start, so I said nothing.

I attended Leola twice a day. I prepared decoctions of stone bramble and brewed angelica. And when Leif heard that I'd recommended berries, he took blackberries to the house every morning.

It took many days, but at last Leola began to grow stronger again. I was amazed at my success and began to feel a completely new confidence.

'How's Leola?' was Leif's first question when he returned from the city each day.

'She has a cough that troubles her,' I said on the eighth day. 'I think she developed it because she was so weak. But she was sitting up today, having her hair combed and choosing a fabric for a new dress.'

'Thank Thor!' exclaimed Leif devoutly.

I felt I was deceiving him. I didn't need the powers of my amulet to guess he was in love with her, and I wondered how shocked he'd be if he knew she'd been with child. But I'd promised to keep her secret.

I caught Maria's eye as I looked away and saw something there. I sensed anger and dislike in her. Not towards me, nor Leif. I hadn't forgotten she'd been a slave in Eadred's household, and wished she could tell me about it.

Leif was among the first to be allowed to visit Leola and receive her thanks for finding her a healer who could cure her.

'She says you saved her life,' he told me afterwards. 'You must have very powerful magic.'

I shook my head. 'It's not magic, just a matter of finding the right treatment,' I said.

The next day when I arrived at Leola's, Eadred was there waiting for me. He looked surprised when he saw my face. 'You're the Viking girl,' he said. 'Do you still have that slave or did she run off?'

'She's still with me, but no longer a slave,' I said stiffly.

I remembered the cuts and bruises on Maria's body and had to force myself to be polite.

'I believe I owe you thanks for saving my niece's life,' Eadred said. He held out a small purse. 'Please accept this as payment.'

My first impulse was to throw it in his face. I wanted to tell him I would accept nothing from a man who would beat a defenceless girl. But just in time I remembered my father's pressing need for money, and swallowed my pride. At least this purse won't go towards buying a new slave, I thought, tucking it into my bag.

'Here you are, father,' I said, when I got home, and put the purse of Jorvik coins into his hand. 'Will this help our situation a little?'

My father stared at the coins in silent astonishment.

'That was for helping Leif's friend get better,' I told him.

Father hugged me. 'This will last us for many weeks,' he said gratefully. 'Your mother was right. Now we know why she sent you with me.'

'I don't suppose it'll happen again,' I said cautiously. But I was wrong. Leif and Leola both told the story of her recovery to their acquaintance. Within a week, I was summoned to another household to treat a sick child. To my relief, I cured her and word spread. Soon someone was calling for me nearly every day.

CHAPTER EIGHTEEN

Time passed. Soon it was *Gormánuður*, slaughtering month, but there was no slaughtering in Thrang's house, because in the city we bought meat from the market. Erik had returned with no news of Asgrim. We knew he'd sailed out of the Ouse, but we had no idea where he was now, or how he was planning to spend the winter.

We were meanwhile gradually becoming known in the city and one autumn evening we were invited to a banquet held in honour of the king himself.

'Eadred's giving the banquet for King Siefred,' Leif explained. 'It's a great honour that we should have been invited; I think we owe it to Leola. And to your skills, of course.'

I was surprised. We'd lived quietly in Jorvik until now. Thrang and father worked and talked together, Leif had his own set of friends he visited, and I'd become used to our quiet fireside in the evenings and Maria's silent but pleasant company. To be invited out among the nobles of the city was a great change. I felt shy and awkward and didn't want to go, especially not to Eadred's house. I looked to my father, pleading silently to be left behind.

'I don't want to go either, Sigrun,' said Thrang, seeing

my look. 'I can't stand the family. But refusal would give offence.'

'It'll do you good to meet some new people,' said my father. 'You can wear that silk overdress we paid so much for!'

'I meet many people, father,' I objected. 'I go into new families several times a week.'

'That's different,' said my father. 'Tonight you'll be an honoured guest.'

I always am, I thought. I was welcomed into every household I visited with reverence and hope, and I hadn't yet grown used to it.

'Honour and Eadred aren't words that belong in the same sentence,' said Thrang in a surly tone. 'He's none too particular in matters of business, I can tell you.'

'Father, he's one of the king's closest friends and a man of great standing in Jorvik!' exclaimed Leif, annoyed.

'And don't think I don't know you're defending him because he's got a pretty niece,' snarled Thrang. 'Don't bother with your best dress, Sigrun,' he added. 'Or with bathing before we go. They're dirty, hairy Saxons and don't wash from one end of the year to the next.'

My father laughed a little. 'You're very harsh!' he commented. 'Why do we go, if it will be that dreadful?'

'As I said, it won't do to offend the king,' said Thrang. 'And it may just put some business my way.'

'Two good reasons,' agreed my father with a smile.

'It wouldn't surprise me to hear we've been invited because the king wants to meet an Icelandic chieftain,' said Thrang, effectively wiping the smile off my father's face.

'I'm no chieftain,' he said, his cheeks losing a little of their colour. 'We have neither kings nor chieftains in Iceland. It was my intention to lie low in Jorvik, not to draw attention to myself.'

'Too late,' said Thrang gruffly. 'Your daughter's done that for you. Everywhere I go these days, I'm asked if it's my house the new healer's staying in.'

'I'm sorry,' I said to my father, conscience stricken. But I couldn't help but be flattered at how sought-after I'd become. At first I'd thought people would discover I didn't know what I was doing. But as I helped more and more people and the runes spoke clearly to me, I'd begun slowly to believe a little in my skills. I began to understand how well my mother had taught me. I still missed my home with an ache that never seemed to lessen, but my confidence was growing day by day.

I was also being paid for much of the work I did, sometimes in coin which I gave to father and sometimes in gifts of food which I presented to Thrang. I never asked anyone for a fee, but people gave what they could afford. We no longer had any immediate money worries. I was fulfilling my mother's prediction, looking after father, and the thought pleased me.

'Well, I for one am delighted with this invitation,' said Leif, interrupting my thoughts. 'We live together in Jorvik; Saxon and Viking side by side. I don't like to hear them insulted.'

'Then they should wash!' said Thrang, exasperated. 'I can smell a Saxon half a street away, and it offends my nose.'

I remembered the smell in Eadred's house and couldn't resist a grin.

'You see!' said Thrang triumphantly. 'Sigrun agrees with me!'

I shook my head, not wanting to upset Leif, who was clearly expecting an evening of great enjoyment.

'Leola's the daughter of the former Northumbrian king,' said Leif. 'She's a princess.'

'She's trouble, whatever else she is,' growled Thrang. 'Don't think you can turn up here with her on your arm one day, because I won't have her for a daughter-in-law.'

'That's not your choice,' said Leif angrily. 'When the time comes, I'll marry to please myself, not you.'

Thrang gave a gruff bark of laughter. 'Of course you will,' he said more mildly. 'But not that girl if you have any sense.'

Still arguing, the four of us washed, changed, and walked to Eadred's house. There was a crowd gathered, a mixture of Norse and Saxon as Leif had predicted. The smell of unwashed bodies and clothes was stronger than the smell of roasting meat in the house, and I wondered at Leif, choosing to fall in love with a Saxon girl. He was so clean and neat himself. But when Leola came gracefully towards us, she smelled fresh and perfumed, unlike her kin. She looked very pretty, dressed, as I was, in a silken overdress over her woollen kirtle, her dark hair neatly plaited. Rich jewellery gleamed at her throat and wrists, and beautiful brooches pinned her dress.

Leif didn't try and hide his admiration for her. It was written on his face, in his eyes; it oozed from every pore of his body. Leola bestowed a particularly sweet smile on him, and allowed him to hold her hand a little longer than was necessary, casting down her eyes as she did so, as though overcome with shyness and modesty. But I sensed no shyness in her; only excitement. She was enjoying herself, surrounded by admiring guests; the centre of attention. It was a part she was playing. I reminded myself she'd already been with child, so she wasn't as virtuous or innocent as she was pretending.

I was seated between a Norse woman and a young man at table. The woman ignored me, talking and flirting loudly with her neighbour on her other side. The young man sat silently. He was fair and handsome, but looked arrogant and disdainful too. He was so busy watching Leola that he had no attention to spare for me. Leif had secured a place beside her, and looked very happy whispering in her ear. She was smiling, clearly pleased by his words. She turned aside for a moment to cough, and I frowned, my professional interest aroused. That cough still lingered, though in every other way she seemed well. I wondered about the hollyhock I'd bought but not yet tried. Perhaps that would help her.

I saw Leif half put his arm around Leola asking if she was quite well. I sensed jealousy and anger beside me. I looked at my neighbour and saw him glaring at Leif. I searched my mind for something I could say to the young man, to distract his attention from Leif and break the uncomfortable silence between us.

'Do you live here in Jorvik?' I asked him at last.

He looked round at me as though he'd only just noticed I was there. 'What?'

Feeling stupid, I repeated my pointless question.

'Of course I do,' he replied impatiently. 'I'm the king's son.'

'Oh, I see,' I said, feeling even more stupid. 'Sorry, I didn't know. I'm a visitor here. My name's Sigrun.'

'Mmm,' said the young man, sounding bored, looking away again, his eyes seeking Leola once more.

I knew that I shouldn't feel embarrassed, because it was he that was rude and ill-mannered, not me, but I couldn't help it. Seated as I was, I had nothing to do but eat, watch, and listen. It was a long, dull meal, and I longed to be at home with Maria. She must feel betrayed tonight, knowing we were dining in the house of her former masters. It was an uncomfortable thought.

We were served oysters, mussels and other shell-fish, platters of roasted beef, ducks and golden plovers stuffed with walnuts and berries, as well as a wide selection of vegetables, including leeks, carrots, and parsnips. I'd never seen such a spread, but felt too nervous and uncomfortable in my surroundings to do more than sample a few of the delicacies. At long last the dishes were cleared and an expectant buzz filled the room. Unexpectedly, my neighbour spoke to me.

'Well, let's hope the entertainment will be good tonight. Eadred's going all out to impress my father, I see.'

'It was a fine feast,' I agreed, not knowing what else to say.

He snorted slightly under his breath and I took it to mean he didn't agree with me but wasn't going to say so.

'So which is your father?' I asked him. I'd been trying to work it out all evening. I'd imagined a king would be someone so important that I'd be able to pick him out in a crowd, but I'd been wrong.

'He's sitting on Eadred's right,' said my neighbour, pointing out a wiry, fierce-looking man, dressed modestly. When I looked closely, I could see something powerful about him. He wouldn't be a man to cross.

'And will you be king after him?' I asked curiously.

I realized at once that this was a tactless question. Of course I shouldn't mention his father's death so casually. But I didn't get the reaction I expected. My neighbour scowled darkly.

'I will not be, unless my brother Thorvald dies of the sickness that's currently plaguing him, or by some other lucky chance,' he replied.

I was speechless. How could he speak of his brother like that?

At that moment, a hush fell on the crowded room as the entertainment began. A man played a haunting tune on the panpipes, which gave me goose bumps down my arms, it was so beautiful. Another recited poetry: some contained words of wisdom, others were outrageous insults about a man called Alfred who was married to a goat and wore women's dresses. I'd never heard of him, but the poem made everyone roar with laughter. The king laughed louder than any.

'Who's this Alfred?' I asked my neighbour.

'He calls himself the King of Wessex,' he said briefly. 'He's a Saxon.'

When the poetry was over, a woman told, very dramatically, the story of the conquest of Jorvik. I listened avidly, for I knew little of the history of the city. The woman finished the tale with a recital of the current King Siefred's brave deeds, to which the king listened with obvious pleasure. After the story, Eadred whispered to the king, and then turned to my father.

'The king would very much like to hear about your country of Iceland,' he said. 'Would you be willing to speak a few words?'

I knew my father's reluctance to tell stories and felt a moment's panic on his behalf. But there was no need. He was bowing with all his usual good manners and agreeing to speak. I watched as he straightened himself, refused a horn of wine, and took a moment to gather his thoughts.

'I live in a land in the far north,' he began, 'an island surrounded by icy sea, with the frozen wasteland of the gods just a few days' sail to the north. Even on our island there are vast tracts of ice that would take a man many days to cross. And yet in places it is a warm land, a land of many wonders. Springs run hot out of the ground, so we never need to heat water for bathing. And we have mountains that are alive and at times spew fire and ash into the sky and make the ground shake and quiver beneath our feet.'

His audience was enthralled at once. I was aware that there wasn't a sound in this crowded room, as the guests almost held their breath, afraid of missing a word of his tale. It couldn't be completely new to any of them. Other Icelanders must have visited Jorvik, but my father made our land sound mysterious, both blessed and cursed by the gods. He wove a kind of magic in the room while he spoke, and no one interrupted.

When father finished, there was tremendous applause, exclamations and questions. Before we left, he'd been presented with a pair of fine silver brooches by the king as a mark of honour for the story, and had been showered with further invitations. I'd been mentioned to the king as a skilled healer, and engaged to visit his eldest son, Thorvald, who was ailing. I felt a surge of butterflies in my belly at the request. The king's son was an important patient. What if my new-found skills should suddenly desert me?

The young man sitting next to me looked taken aback when he heard who I was. 'You're the healer who cured Leola?' he asked.

'I am,' I agreed.

'I see. Please don't feel under any obligation to cure my brother,' he said, once more depriving me of the power of speech.

As we walked home through the dark streets, I took my father's arm. 'So much for lying low in Jorvik,' I said.

'Indeed,' said my father, and his teeth flashed white in the darkness as he smiled.

'You always were a fine storyteller, Bjorn,' said Thrang. 'You'll be invited everywhere once they get to know how many tales you can recount. As many suppers as you can eat.'

'I've never sought that kind of renown,' sighed my father. 'You see, Sigrun, it was my duty before, in my life of captivity, to entertain with stories. So I've wished to leave it behind me.'

'That's a great pity,' said Leif. 'To let such a gift go to waste.'

Father chuckled a little. 'Very well, I'll embrace it,' he said. 'I have little choice for the time being.'

'You'll be well paid too,' said Thrang. 'As you were tonight.'

'Then I shan't need to rely so heavily on Sigrun,' said my father. 'That would be a good thing. Here, Sigrun, I'd like you to have these.'

So saying, my father handed me the silver brooches he'd been given by the king.

'They're too precious for me to wear,' I gasped.

'Nonsense,' said all the men at once.

'Wear them for my sake,' said my father. 'Unless we need to sell or trade them, they're yours. They'll suit that fine silk dress better than those homemade ones you're wearing now.'

He began to question Thrang about the various families in the city, so I fell behind and walked beside Leif for the last two streets, holding the valuable new brooches in my hand.

'Did you enjoy the evening, Sigrun?' Leif asked.

'The entertainment, I did,' I said. 'The music especially was wonderful.'

'It was, wasn't it? And what did you think of Leola, seeing her in company?'

'She's very pretty, very graceful,' I agreed cautiously. I had grave misgivings about the girl's character.

'I hope to make her my wife, whatever father says,' said Leif in a low voice. 'I'm sure he'll see her worth once he gets to know her.'

I couldn't feel that Leola would make Leif a good wife, and I wished I could warn him, but it was impossible for me to divulge her story. I remembered the king's son, and the way he had eyed Leola during the evening, and shivered slightly. Leif was not the only young man in love with her.

'What's the name of the king's younger son?' I asked Leif.

'Knut,' said Leif. 'Didn't he tell you?'

'I had very little speech with him,' I said briefly.

'Arrogant so-and-so, isn't he?' said Leif. 'He's been paying Leola attentions, the dog, but luckily for me she can't stand him.'

I wasn't so sure he was right.

Maria was pleased to see us come home. She'd waited up for us, keeping a glow in the fire, and a lamp or two lit, so we could see to get into our furs for the night. The nights were cooling at last now winter was here.

As I lay down beside Maria, I was aware she was restless, as though something was bothering her.

'We've been in the house of your enemy, haven't we?' I whispered. 'I feel as though I've betrayed you somehow. Do you forgive me?'

In the darkness, Maria took my hand and squeezed it reassuringly.

'That's a relief,' I whispered. 'I couldn't do without you. They treated you abominably at Eadred's, didn't they?'

A nod in the semi darkness. Another thought struck me.

'Did Leola treat you badly too?'

A very vigorous nod.

'That doesn't surprise me,' I whispered soberly.

CHAPTER NINETEEN

Two days later, Thrang, Leif, and Bjorn all left to sail some goods north along the coast before winter set in. They took our remaining men with them.

'Isn't sailing dangerous at this time of the year?' I asked anxiously.

'We won't go out of sight of the coast,' said my father, giving me a farewell hug. 'And Thrang is the most skilled captain I've ever known. I'm glad for your sake you have Maria to keep you company. Otherwise it would be so lonely for you here.'

'She's a very good friend,' I agreed. 'But I'll miss you.' I hugged him tight and then stood back and waved them off, standing at the front door of the house.

I wandered forlornly down the stairs. A week stretched ahead of me with only Thrang's two surly slaves and Maria for company. After the excitement of the party, it felt very flat. I sat down listlessly beside the fire where Maria was pounding grain into flour. Unn was out and the house was quiet. The only sounds were the distant noises of the city outside our walls.

'Would you like me to take a turn with that, Maria?' I asked at last, feeling I ought to shake off the lethargy that had come over me.

'No, I like to help,' said Maria.

For a second or two, I didn't react. Then it hit me: Maria had spoken. My heart gave a great leap of excitement.

'What . . . what did you say?' I asked her breathlessly.

She smiled but didn't repeat her words. But I'd heard her. She'd spoken Norse, with an accent, it is true, but I'd understood.

'I thought you couldn't speak our language,' I said at last. 'That you couldn't speak at all.'

'I couldn't speak,' she said in a soft voice. 'A long time, I couldn't.' She spoke slowly, hesitatingly, and with a lisp. 'After they took me. When words come back again, I stay quiet. I speak only to other slaves, never to enemies.'

'But I'm not your enemy, am I?' I asked her.

'No. You help me,' said Maria. 'Treat me well.'

'And you've been a good friend to me,' I said. 'I'm so grateful for your company. Especially going out to so many strange households in the city.'

Maria smiled a little. I'd told her before how glad I was of her presence.

'I don't know how much you've heard and understood,' I said. 'But my father was enslaved as a child too.'

Maria nodded. 'People not mind what they say near me,' she explained. 'They think I can't tell their secrets.'

I smiled ruefully. I'd had the same thought. 'So where did you learn to speak Norse?' I asked her.

'I speak bad,' she said. 'I listen. And speak with other slaves. We all from different places. We have to speak Norse or Saxon.'

I reached out and put my hand on her shoulder,

pressing it affectionately. 'Will you tell me about yourself?' I asked her.

Maria bent her head over the grain. After a moment's silence, she took a deep breath and looked up. 'I tell you,' she said. She put the mortar and pestle aside and sat up straight, clearly bracing herself. 'I grow up by sea, in a country far south of here. Many weeks' sailing. The summers hot there and winter short. I live with my brother, parents, grandparents. We farm, my father fish. We poor, but life . . . good.

'When I ten, raiders come,' she said. She sighed deeply, looking into the distance, reliving scenes from long ago. 'No one attack us before. But now they sail right up onto beach. Big, yellow-hair men. No mercy. They cut down my father with swords so his blood runs like river in dust. My grandfather too. They take everything. Burn our home with big fire. My mother she beg them not to take us, my brother and me, when she understand what they want. So they . . . they . . .'

She faltered and stopped, choked with emotion.

'You don't have to tell me,' I said, horrified. 'If it's too distressing.' I felt sick, listening to her tale. I thought of my father. Was this how he'd been taken too? His family killed while he watched, helpless?

Maria wiped her eyes fiercely with the back of her hand and cleared her throat.

'I have not words for what they do to my mother,' she said, her voice shaking. 'It make me not speak for long, long time. In the end, they kill her too. I want to die. My heart breaking. Everything—everything I love is gone. But they tie us and put us on their stinking ship. There were others. All young. We sail for weeks. Some die of a fever, my brother too. The men threw them in the sea.' Maria paused to wipe tears from her cheeks. 'They do more raids, take more children. They bring us here.'

I sat quite still, chilled by her story. 'Here to Jorvik?' I whispered. I wanted to ask her if she knew the men who'd done this to her, if they lived here still, but I didn't know how to get the words out. Perhaps I was too afraid of what I might hear.

'Yes, Jorvik. We sold, all of us.'

'To Eadred?' I asked.

'No,' Maria spoke more freely now that she had finished telling me about her family. 'To Norse woman first. She made me work hard. I run away. Once, two times. More. So, after two years, she sell me. To Eadred.'

I shuddered. 'Did he work you hard too?'

'Not so bad. They are rich. Have many slaves. But he . . . the master . . . I don't like him. He is cruel man, like Leola. I run away again. Lots. But couldn't get out of city. So he catch me every time. Beat me.'

'I'm so sorry,' I said. I knew my words were inadequate. How can anyone express sympathy for such a life with mere words? Such cruelty, such unnecessary pain. And all so some men could earn a little money. I wondered fearfully whether my brother was committing such shameful acts, and then pushed the painful thought away again.

'Not your fault,' Maria said. 'You give me better place to live. You kind.'

'But I can't give you back your home or your family, can I?' I asked her, cut to the quick by this realization.

'I thought I was so noble rescuing you, but what good is that when my people have destroyed your life? I'm ashamed.'

'You done nothing to be ashamed,' Maria said. 'You help people who are sick. That is good way.'

'There is always more one can do. There ought to be.'

Maria smiled a weary smile. 'Perhaps,' she said.

'How old are you?' I asked her.

'Fourteen, fifteen. I not sure.'

'The same as me. So you've spent four years in captivity? It's a long time.'

Maria agreed, nodded. 'Sometimes I want to remember, but I've forgotten so much. It's faded. They even take away my memories.'

I felt deeply sad. For Maria herself and for all the lives torn apart by slavery. I felt sadness for my father's life, and for mine too, now also shattered by the aftermath of his escape.

'Were you trying to go back home?' I asked. 'The times you ran away?'

Maria shrugged. 'What I go back to? Everyone killed. My village burned. Nothing. No one. No, I not run to anywhere. Just run to escape beating with stick.'

'You've escaped now,' I told her. 'You're free, for what that is worth. Perhaps it is worth nothing when you have nowhere to go.'

'It is worth much. Very much. I not forget it,' said Maria.

We sat in silence. I could think of nothing to say that wouldn't sound utterly trivial. At length, Maria picked up the grain and began to pound it again.

'Now I tell of Leola,' she said. 'She not a good girl. Leif shouldn't marry her.'

'I knew it!' I exclaimed, both relieved to have my suspicions confirmed and alarmed for Leif's sake. 'Please, tell me what you know.'

Maria shook her head with a dark look. 'First of all, she is cruel girl. Not because she stupid. Because she like it. You saw many hurts on me when I come here?'

'You know I did,' I agreed, wincing at the memory of the terrible bruises and cuts I'd helped to heal. 'I assumed that it was Eadred who . . . ' I paused, horrified. 'You mean it wasn't Eadred who beat you? It was Leola?'

'Both,' Maria told me, her voice hard as she remembered that time. 'But Eadred, he get angry and hit. Then he stop. Not so bad. Leola, she also tie me and hurt me. Pull here,' Maria held up a few strands of her hair and mimed it being yanked hard from her head. 'One time she cut me with knife.' Maria pulled up her sleeve, revealing a jagged scar on the tender skin of her forearm.

I gasped with shock. 'Why?' I asked.

'She in bad mood,' said Maria simply.

It was as though the temperature in the room had dropped. I shivered, imagining what Maria's life had been like at the hands of Leola and her uncle.

'And she greedy girl,' said Maria. She leaned forward, an earnest look in her eyes. 'She want dresses, jewellery, pretty things. She want to be rich.'

'I thought she already was,' I said. 'Isn't she a Saxon princess?'

'Yes,' Maria agreed, 'but she want more. She come to Jorvik to find rich husband.'

'That makes sense,' I agreed. 'I wonder who she has her eye on? Not Leif if she's after great wealth or position.'

'I not know,' Maria shrugged. 'She see many men, get presents, listen to sweet words. But one special one. She meet him secretly.'

'But you don't know who?' I asked curiously. I thought if Maria knew that, we might have the identity of the father of her child. But to my disappointment, Maria shook her head.

That piece of information was likely to remain secret, I reflected. And after all, it was none of my concern.

CHAPTER TWENTY

I slept badly that night. My dreams were haunted by Maria's stories of terror and violence. I tossed and turned and couldn't settle. Morning took a long time to come. I must have dozed at last, because I woke to daylight peeping dimly into the cellar and Unn raking and building up the cooking fire.

Maria was silent at breakfast. I wondered if she regretted taking me into her confidence. Or perhaps the telling and reliving of her traumatic experiences had upset her yesterday. But when I caught her eye she smiled at me.

'It's strange being here with all the men away, isn't it?' I asked her.

'Quiet,' Maria agreed with a nod.

'When they return . . . are you happy for them to know that you can speak?' I asked tentatively.

Maria looked thoughtful for a moment and then nodded. 'Yes,' she said at last. I smiled, thinking now I had a real friend, one to talk to. And it didn't need to be a secret.

Before we'd finished eating, there was a loud knock on the door. I started, spilling my porridge. I put down my bowl with a clatter and hurried up the stairs to answer the door. A tall man stood outside. 'You are Sigrun Bjornsdottir?' he asked me.

'I am.'

'The king has sent me to take you to see his son.'

The summons I'd been dreading. When the king had asked me to heal his son, I had thought and half hoped he would forget about it again, but clearly he hadn't.

'Will you come with me?' I asked Maria. Her presence always made it so much easier to go into new houses, and I needed that courage more than ever today.

'Of course,' she said with a quick smile.

The slave waited while Maria and I readied ourselves. I washed my face, scrubbed quickly at my teeth, combed my hair and tied it in a scarf. I put on a clean apron dress, pinning it with my new silver brooches as I'd given my old ones to Maria.

The king's house was the largest I'd seen in Jorvik. It reminded me of home in its layout and design; I felt a pang as I entered it. There was a large central long-fire, and trestle tables standing at the top of the hall. The king's table was marked by his very grand, ornate high seat, presently unoccupied.

The slave showed us to a bench and told me his master would be with us shortly.

'Do you think he means the king's son or the king himself?' I whispered nervously to Maria. She shrugged, looking around her.

'Have you been here before?' I asked.

Maria nodded. She knew the grand people of Jorvik far better than I did. As a silent slave she had seen and heard far more than her masters imagined. To them, she was an almost invisible being with no feelings.

'What's he like, the king's son?' I asked.

'He's here,' Maria replied with a warning nudge. I jumped and scrambled to my feet as a tall, powerfully-built young man came across the room towards us. He resembled his younger brother: confident and used to having his own way. But I could see at once that he was in poor health. He looked pale and wasted, with an exhausted, washed-out look, and his attempt to walk without a limp didn't fool me. He was in pain: I could see it in the way he moved and the amulet helped me feel it too.

'You're the healer my father thinks I should see?' he asked, in a tone that clearly suggested I was wasting his time.

'Yes. My name's Sigrun,' I said. 'How can I help you?'

'I doubt very much that you can,' he said disparagingly, taking a seat near me. 'I don't intend to discuss my intimate body functions with a young woman.'

I felt flustered. Why was he so rude? Was that the way of kings' sons? 'I may be able to treat you,' I pointed out. 'And then you'll feel better. Is it a stomach disorder that ails you?'

It was a guess, but a fairly safe one. Stomach disorders were rife in the city, and he had the look of it.

'What if it is? I'm sure it will clear in time without any charms or spells of yours.' His tone was deliberately offensive.

I rose to my feet, stung. I always offered my help freely if it was requested, and I'd never been ridiculed or treated rudely. 'I'm sorry to have troubled you,' I said. 'You clearly don't want my advice. We'll go now.' I glanced over at Maria who had risen too, and we both began to walk towards the door. I felt humiliated, but was determined to retain my dignity.

'Oh, come back, come back,' cried Thorvald. 'My father will never let me hear the last of it if I send you away!'

'I only treat people who want my help,' I said, pausing, and glancing back. 'You clearly don't.'

Thorvald got to his feet with an effort and walked towards us, grimacing fractionally as he put weight on his right leg. 'Oh very well, I'll admit, I'm worn out with this flux,' he said.

I hesitated. I was still tempted to leave, king's orders or not. I wasn't convinced Thorvald was going to take me seriously.

'I'll behave myself, I promise,' said Thorvald with a sigh. 'For Odin's sake, girl, let's get this over with.'

Reluctantly I returned to where he threw himself back onto the bench with a half groan. I was tempted to point out that his tone was still not respectful, but decided to give him one more chance.

'It probably *will* clear without medicine,' I said, returning to his former remark. 'But I may be able to shorten your suffering.'

'Then for Odin's sake do so,' he muttered.

I asked him some questions about the nature of the disorder, which he answered reluctantly, about his general diet, and about how long he'd been suffering. He'd been unwell, it seemed, for a long time. It was clearly one of those illnesses that lodges in the gut and won't shift.

I left my runes in my bag, sensing that consulting the goddess would provoke Thorvald. After all, the treatment was straightforward enough.

'There are two ways to treat this condition,' I told him. 'They are best done together. One is to avoid very rich foods for a time: less meat, butter, and wine. Simple foods like milk products, grain, and vegetables will be easier on the stomach.'

'So now I'm to eat pap like a baby, am I?' demanded Thorvald.

I ignored him. 'I can also brew you a decoction,' I said. 'If you send a servant to me tomorrow, I'll have it ready.'

Thorvald rolled his eyes and I sensed his impatience. 'And don't you have some magic seashells or beads I should wear, too?' he asked. 'For a large fee, of course.'

I bit back the retort that rose to my lips. 'No, I don't. And there will be no charge for my help,' I added recklessly, determined to prove I was no quack turning a quick profit. 'But I think, whilst I'm here, that I should take a look at that leg as well, don't you?'

Thorvald stared at me, taken aback. 'How did you know?' he demanded. 'Not even my molly-coddling father has noticed that.'

'He doesn't look at you with a healer's eyes,' I said, cautious not to betray the part my amulet played in my powers of detecting emotion, mood, and pain. It was a sense that seemed to grow more acute with each passing day.

After a moment's hesitation, Thorvald bent forward and rolled up his legging to reveal a nasty gash in his calf. He winced as the fabric brushed his swollen skin. It was obvious the injury was causing him a lot of pain.

'A wound from a rebel's sword from my last trip outside the city,' he said. 'So, will the leg have to come off?'

He spoke lightly, as though jesting, but I sensed that this was his real fear.

I examined it carefully. The gash was badly inflamed, yellow with pus and very hot to the touch. No rot had yet set in, though it looked as if it might at any moment.

'I think I can treat this,' I said. I reached into my bag for a salve I kept there and began to smear a little on the wound. I felt Thorvald tense and take a sharp breath as even my light touch caused him pain. He shivered too: the wound was infected. If I didn't work quickly, a fever would begin.

'I'll come back this afternoon with a more potent salve,' I promised him. 'I'll bring the decoction at the same time. I hope we can avoid amputation and perhaps even cauterizing, but I won't know for sure until I see how it responds to the treatment. You've neglected this too long.'

'I know, I know,' said Thorvald, visibly shaken by my words. 'But then I've not met a healer before who appeared to know what she's doing. It's all charms and spells and rubbish that doesn't work. I usually think time is the best medicine.'

'That's often true, but not always,' I said, rising to go. 'I'll see you again later.'

Thorvald nodded and we left him. The guards at the door straightened themselves as we passed, and threw the door open for us. I was relieved as we stepped out into the street, and gulped the cooler air, ignoring the light rain that had started to fall.

'Is he that rude to everyone?' I asked Maria. 'Or is it just women?'

'Just women,' said Maria, drawing the hood of her cloak up against the rain. 'Unless he wants their favours.'

I looked at her sharply. 'Is he another of Leola's suitors?' I asked.

'I think yes,' said Maria.

I sighed. 'Well, I'm not looking forward to going back,' I said. 'He's not the most grateful of my patients.'

We turned the corner, and lounging against the side of the building, his clothing peppered with raindrops, was Knut. I wondered why he was standing around in the street in such weather, but was about to pass him without greeting, assuming he wouldn't recognize me. I was very surprised when he straightened up, came forward and fell into step beside me.

'Hello, healer,' he said.

'Hello, king's son,' I replied. If he couldn't be bothered to remember or use my name, then why should I use his?

He chuckled. 'Very well, I've forgotten your name,' he said. 'Remind me!'

'I'm Sigrun. And this is Maria.'

'Ah, Sigrun, is it?' he said, ignoring Maria. 'How strange I should have no memory of your name at all. And do you need reminding of mine, or was that merely to put me in my place?'

'You're Knut,' I said. I wondered why he had this sudden interest in me when he'd barely bothered last time we'd met.

'You've been to see my brother?' he asked.

'Yes,' I said surprised. 'How did you . . . ?' A sudden suspicion struck me: 'Were you waiting for me?'

'Just friendly family concern. How is he?'

'Why don't you ask your brother himself how he is?' I asked, bewildered. 'Why ask me?'

'Ah well, you see, in our family, we don't always talk as much as you might think. And when we do, we don't always hear the truth. So tell me, is he likely to die, or am I hoping too much?'

The memory of his previous remarks about his brother came back to me. 'Have you really been waiting here in the rain, in the hope that I'll tell you your brother's dying?' I asked, shocked.

'Well, that would be putting it very bluntly. As I said, I prefer to say that I'm merely enquiring after his health. I don't live with him and my father, you see. We found we clashed rather too often for anyone's comfort so I found a house of my own nearby. But I like to know how they are.'

I was appalled by his callousness. What kind of a family was this? I would have liked to tell him what I thought of him, but I'd listened to a great deal of talk in Thrang's household about not offending the king. And unfortunately I suspected that rule probably extended to his sons.

'Your brother is well enough, thank you for your concern for him,' I said coldly. 'And now, if you don't mind, we have work to do.'

Knut bowed slightly, and let us walk on without him. I couldn't help glancing around once to see if he was following us. He wasn't, but he was standing watching us go and lifted his hand in a brief wave. 'See you again, Sigrun,' he said.

CHAPTER TWENTY-ONE

'As if I would tell him anything!' I said angrily to Maria once we were safely back in Thrang's house. 'Even if he'd been the most caring brother in the world, a patient's symptoms are between me and the goddess.'

'What goddess?' asked Maria.

'Eir. She's the goddess of healing. She teaches us the secret power of herbs. We must never betray her secrets to a man, nor speak of people's illnesses unnecessarily.'

Maria nodded, pounding the bark, leaning over it, using all her weight to grind it into fine powder.

'Thorvald may be rude and ungrateful, but I'll do my best to cure him,' I muttered, crumbling some dried leaves into a pot of hot water.

Maria glanced up at me looking amused by my indignation. 'It's king's family,' she said mildly. 'They not like us. They fight each other for power.'

By the time Leif, Thrang, and my father returned, Thorvald's wound was healing, and his stomach settled. His father Siefred thanked me personally and promised honour and respect to my family as long as we stayed in Jorvik. Thorvald himself sent a fine gold bracelet with a servant who presented it to me with his master's compliments.

When he'd gone, Maria and I both bent over it to admire the workmanship.

'It's a snake,' said Maria. 'Eating itself.'

'It's the Midgaard Serpent,' I explained. 'It holds the whole world in its coils.'

'I never heard that. Norse have strange beliefs,' said Maria. She picked up the bracelet and weighed it in her hand and then sent me a wicked look. 'It cost lot of money. Thorvald must like you, oh much!'

'You know very well he doesn't!' I retorted. 'He's just grateful, I suppose. I probably saved his life treating that wound. In any case, a costly gift shows the giver in a good light. He's showing me he's wealthy as well as generous.'

Maria smiled. 'What you do with it?'

'We can wear it!' I said. I picked the bracelet up and turned it so that the gold caught the light. 'We have enough money for now. We're acquiring quite a collection of fine jewellery, aren't we?'

I laughed, delighted that despite Asgrim's treachery, we had more money than we needed. With the help of Ingvar's precious amulet, my skills had made our stay in Jorvik more comfortable, and I was very proud of myself.

'You'd better have first turn wearing this,' I said to Maria. I caught her hand and slid the heavy bracelet onto her wrist. 'I'm already starting to look too much like the fine ladies of Jorvik, and nothing like a farmer's daughter from Iceland. I don't recognize myself.'

* * *

176

A few days later I called on Leola with some hollyhock for her cough. I was pleased to find her almost back to full strength.

'I hear you go everywhere now, and have made a name for yourself,' she said.

'I've been fortunate to meet with trust and kindness,' I agreed. 'I'm grateful for your recommendations.'

'Oh, it was my uncle, mainly,' Leola said indifferently. 'Will you take a drink before you go?'

I was tired and thirsty after my long walk, so I agreed. Leola fetched a goblet for me and a jug of whey. As she reached forward to pour the grey-white liquid, a gold bangle slipped down her arm onto her wrist, peeping out from under the sleeve of her woollen kirtle.

'Oh, that's just like mine,' I said, struck by the coincidence. I pulled back my sleeve and held out my arm to show her the serpent which Maria had insisted it was my turn to wear today.

There was a clatter and the jug of whey spilled across the wooden table. 'I'm sorry,' said Leola loudly, jumping to her feet and running to fetch a cloth. 'I'm such a clumsy thing,' she added, as she wiped up the mess. There was a vivid flush in her cheeks, and she'd pushed the bangle back out of sight on her arm.

I opened my mouth to ask what the matter was, but Leola rushed to change the subject and chattered busily about anything and everything else for the remainder of my short visit.

I could tell how relieved she was to see me go. For some reason, she'd been completely thrown by the incident. I wasn't sure if it was because I'd seen her bracelet or because I had one the same. I'd assumed it was a coincidence, but her behaviour made me wonder if it was something more.

My father's return put all thoughts of Leola out of my mind, however. He was there when I got back and in the excitement of greeting him and hearing about the voyage, I forgot all about the bracelet.

The winter month of Ýlir came without any sign of my brother. I thought of home and wondered how my mother felt about spending the feast day of Yule without us all. I hoped her leg had healed now. I thought of Ingvar too, and wondered, if I had been there, whether there would have been any stolen kisses under the Yule boughs. His face came vividly into my mind, and I felt breathless at the thought. The longing for him and for home was an ache that I couldn't treat with any medicines I had.

We were invited to the king's for the Yule feast; a great honour. It couldn't compete with the thought of home, of course, but I was looking forward to it all the same. There would be good food and all manner of entertainments: music, stories, and games. My father was to be one of the storytellers, and had kept his chosen story a secret even from me.

I went out to see an old lady with arthritis first thing in the morning, followed by a visit to a boy in the poor quarter with rickets. I carried a portion of *skyr* for him, milk curds made from fresh milk using our Icelandic recipe. Milk in all its forms was always good for rickets, just as berries or sheep brains always cure winter sickness. Sometimes food is the best medicine there is.

Maria didn't go with me to my patient, as she was busy helping Unn prepare some Yule delicacies. Instead, Leif walked the first couple of streets with me.

'Where are you off to this morning?' I asked Leif. 'Not business on Yule day surely?'

'No, indeed,' said Leif, looking a little self-conscious. 'I'm visiting friends today.'

I suspected he was planning to call on Leola, and my heart sank a little. He still saw her frequently and his ardour for her didn't seem to have cooled in the least. I said nothing however. We parted, and I made my visits. They took considerably longer than expected, as both families pressed me to take refreshments and to drink each other's health in celebration of the feast day. It was well into the afternoon before I reached Thrang's house again.

My father and Thrang were engrossed in a noisy game of Fox and Geese, while Erik watched, a jug of spiced wine between them on the table. They were clearly all in a good mood. Maria and Unn were baking by the fire and the other men were out.

I noticed Leif sitting quietly in a dark corner of the room, well away from the fire.

'Did you find your friends well?' I asked, sitting down next to him. He turned to look at me, and I caught my breath when I saw the dark bruise discolouring one side of his face. 'What happened?' I asked.

'Officially, a beggar tried to rob me in the street,' he said quietly, nodding towards his father.

'I see,' I said. I got up and searched through my medicines, looking for my arnica salve. This was a new medicine I'd discovered in Jorvik for bruises and I intended to take lots home with me.

I brought the salve across to Leif and gently smeared it onto his cheek, pausing while he flinched and caught his breath with pain.

'And unofficially?' I asked.

'If I tell you, it must remain a complete secret,' begged Leif under his breath.

'I'm good at secrets,' I assured him.

'I visited Leola.'

I smoothed the last of the salve out across his cheekbone, and sat back. 'I guessed as much,' I said, disappointed.

'I found her alone, and in great distress. She's rarely alone, you know. She's very popular, and has a great many friends. But today she was sitting by herself, still and silent. I asked her what was wrong, and she said she couldn't tell me.'

I wager she couldn't, I thought. She probably had some affair of the heart to hide. But I said nothing, waiting for Leif to go on.

'She burst into tears. Sigrun, I couldn't bear it. That beautiful, innocent creature in distress and tears! I couldn't help myself.'

'What did you do?' I asked startled, forgetting to keep my voice low.

Leif hushed me, but his father had heard my voice and

looked round. 'Ah, Sigrun. You're treating that bruise, I see,' he said, seeing the pot of salve in my hand. 'Good girl, thank you. If I ever get my hands on the scoundrel that did this . . . !'

He ground his teeth angrily, but then my father called his attention back to the game.

'I didn't do much,' Leif whispered. 'I don't consider it wrong. I wanted to comfort her. I gathered her in my arms, held her close and swore that I'd do anything, anything at all I could to help. That I was hers for life. I told her again of my love.'

'And what did she say?' I asked.

'Nothing. She kept crying. But she clung to me, and it melted my heart. I . . . I kissed her. I swear I was only trying to comfort her.'

'Of course,' I agreed, wondering for the hundredth time what the young men all saw in Leola. 'Was she angry with you?'

'Leola? Angry? No! But then . . . just at that moment, her uncle walked into the room.'

Everything was now clear. Leif didn't need to tell me of Eadred's anger, his outrage, I could imagine it all.

'He had three of his men throw me out of the house,' Leif finished. 'I tried to tell him I wanted to marry her.'

'What did he say?' I asked curiously. Leif was not a bad match for the Saxon girl. He and his father had a successful business and were relatively wealthy.

'He said . . . well, he said, "Don't make me laugh",' repeated Leif bitterly.

'And what did Leola herself say?' I asked.

'She didn't have a chance to speak, with her uncle

ranting like that!' said Leif defensively. 'But she would have said yes, I'm sure.'

'Maria says Leola's very ambitious,' I said cautiously. 'You told me yourself she was born a princess.'

'She doesn't have a mercenary thought in her!' said Leif hotly. 'How can you say such a thing of her?' He put his head in his hands and groaned. 'I'm not going to the Yule feast with the king tonight. Eadred's sure to be there.'

'He can't hurt you at a feast,' I pointed out. 'I'm sure your father won't want you to offend the king by staying away.'

'I don't care,' said Leif. 'I'll not show myself in public with this bruise. It would be humiliating.'

'I'd offer to keep you company,' I said. 'But I don't think my father would allow it.' I'd been looking forward to the feast, but Leif was my friend and I wanted to support him.

'No, of course you must go,' said Leif at once. 'Don't worry about me.'

I sat with him a little longer and then began to get ready for the feast. Maria helped me heat water and pour it into the tin bath, and I shed my rough working kirtle and enjoyed the luxury of warm water and scrubbing myself clean of a week's city dirt.

I'd put on my best kirtle, woven of softest wool, and was pinning my silken apron dress over it when I heard the sounds of an arrival.

'Sigrun!' called my father. 'Have you finished?'

I stepped out into the main downstairs room, my long hair still wet from the bath, to see an agitated slave talking to my father. As soon as he saw me, father turned.

'Sigrun, you're needed at a birth,' he said. 'It sounds as if the woman is in great difficulty.'

'Please come with me right away,' the slave begged. 'My master is a chieftain and will pay very well. My mistress is in terrible pain.'

'Of course,' I said at once. 'Let me just get changed.'

I withdrew again and with a sigh I pulled off my fine clothes and dressed in my plain kirtle again instead. I'd been looking forward to tonight. If only the woman could have waited until tomorrow to have her baby.

'But you can't miss the Yule feast!' exclaimed Thrang, startled when I reappeared in my work clothes.

'How could I sit at a feast knowing that a mother and child might be dying for want of my help?' I asked him.

'Of course, I see,' said Thrang. 'When you put it like that, to be sure . . . we'll make your apologies to the king, of course.'

'And mine too, please, father,' said Leif. 'I'll walk Sigrun to this woman's house. The town will be rowdy tonight. Everyone's celebrating, most of them with drink.'

'Thank you,' I said, touched, as Leif put my cloak around my shoulders and fastened it for me with the pin.

'You're welcome,' he said, ignoring his father's grumblings. He smiled down at me, and then winced as it hurt his injured face. 'It's cold out,' he warned me.

I laughed up at him. 'Not by Icelandic standards,' I assured him.

'Will Maria go with you?' asked Leif.

I looked round at Maria. She'd been intending to spend the feast night at home with Thrang's servants and a couple of my father's men and I'd had the feeling she'd been looking forward to it. I felt bad about disrupting her evening, but she jumped to her feet at once.

'Of course I come,' she said at once. 'You need me.'

'I'm always glad of your help,' I told her gratefully. 'In fact, I don't know what I'd do without you.'

'You're a good girl, Maria,' said my father. 'Sigrun's very lucky to have your assistance.'

Maria rarely blushed, but this praise brought a deep colour to her cheeks.

CHAPTER TWENTY-TWO

The three of us hurried through the darkening streets. There were few people out in Ousegate and those that were, were cheerful and good-humoured. The commercial quarter through Pavement was unusually quiet. It was a cloudy evening with few stars and some wind and would probably be very dark later.

As we reached the large house we'd been called to in Fossgate, I could already hear screaming and crying. I felt a spasm of fear at the thought of the task ahead. I'd never handled a difficult birth without my mother's help. The babies I'd delivered so far in Jorvik had come easily into the world.

'It may be a long night,' I said nervously to my companions. Maria nodded, biting her lip.

'Would you like me to wait?' asked Leif. It was a courageous offer, but I knew how little men relished the fuss and pain of a birth.

'No, don't,' I said. 'They'll send someone back with us, or if you're worried, you can call for us later and ask how it's going.'

'I'll do that,' said Leif. He clapped us both on the shoulder for good luck, waited until we'd been let in, then walked off into the city.

'*You're* the midwife?' asked an angry-looking man, as I took off my cloak in the upstairs room of the house. I could see by his fine tunic that he must be the chieftain himself. 'You're just a child! What do you know about delivering babies?'

All my fears and doubts rushed back to me. What if he was right? Perhaps I wasn't experienced enough. The mother could die. For a few moments, my cowardice battled with my training and I wanted to turn tail and leave.

Then I remembered all the many births I'd helped my mother at. My hand went to my throat and I briefly touched the amulet hidden under my kirtle. It gave me the courage I needed to read that the man was more afraid than angry.

'I am not inexperienced, though I'm young,' I said to the chieftain as calmly as I could. 'If you'd prefer to call an older midwife, I'd be happy to work with her. Or I can leave now.'

'The usual midwife is sick with a fever,' he said, his voice desperate. 'The other is a drunk, and my wife refused to have her. She wants you. She's heard you are *supposed* to be something out of the ordinary.' He looked me up and down. 'May Odin protect her,' he muttered.

I remembered my mother telling me never to be upset at the things husbands say when their wives are in labour. 'They're usually terrified,' she'd said. 'Especially when it's their first child. They're afraid for their wives, for their unborn child, and afraid of the whole mystery of birth. They forget their manners.'

Remembering this comforted me. 'I promise you, I'll do my best,' I said.

His poor wife was in a dreadful state. Sweat-drenched and wild-eyed with pain and fear, she clung to my hand as though I was the goddess herself come to save her. Standing close to her, I could feel her agony like a wave breaking over me, threatening to drown me.

'Help me!' the woman begged over and over, as the pains racked her body.

For a moment I wished I didn't have the ability to feel what other people were feeling. I considered taking off the amulet to prevent myself being overcome. But I needed it to guide me. So instead, I tried to breathe deeply and concentrate. I longed for my mother's calm, confident presence and her skill. My hands were shaking as I examined the woman. I found the baby was breech and I was fairly certain it was too late to turn it. What should I do now?

I cast the runes, waiting for the goddess to guide me. The woman's screams were rending the air beside me, making it difficult to think. But to my relief, the message was clear: the baby would find his own way into the world. My task would be to ease the labour for the mother. I thought quickly about the various plants I'd brought with me, and went to find Maria.

'Mix up some powdered elder bark and some valerian, would you, Maria?' I asked urgently. 'She's in so much pain, poor woman.'

'You can help her?' asked Maria, shaken by the woman's screams. Her eyes were wide as she prepared the medicines for me.

'I pray that I can,' I said. But in truth I was afraid.

* * *

Leif had called for us twice and left again, and the new day had dawned before the baby was born. He was alive. I sent Maria to tell the father the good news while I tended to the new mother's hurts. Maria helped me wash the baby gently in warm water, while the mother lay utterly exhausted, unable even to look at her new son. When he was clean, I wrapped him in a soft woollen cloth, held him close and carried him about the room. He looked up at me out of huge, dark eyes, reproachful, as though this way of coming into the world was not what he'd expected at all. 'You were the wrong way round,' I whispered to him. 'A child born feet first is asking for trouble.'

He slept awhile in my arms while his mother slept too, then he woke, hungry. His cry woke his mother, and I showed her how to suckle the baby before I left them together, happy at last.

Maria was dozing by the fire, and Leif sat on a bench nearby, his head in his arms. The new father, the young chieftain, was awake, however, so I sent him in to greet his new son. Our voices woke the others. Maria stirred and stretched.

'You must be worn out,' said Leif sleepily, sitting up.

'I am,' I agreed wearily, sinking onto the bench beside him. 'I've never been so tired in my life.'

My midwife skills had been tested to the limit and beyond. I'd spent most of the night terrified that my patients might die, and working to prevent it. I was exhausted.

As Leif fetched our cloaks, I went to speak to the chieftain. He was cradling his new-born babe tenderly in his arms.

188

'I'm going to leave you now,' I told him, my voice faint. 'But I'll come back soon to check on the mother and child, if you are happy for me to do that.'

'Yes, please do,' he begged without a trace of his former hostility. 'I'm very grateful to you.'

As we stepped out into the street and the cold air hit me, I swayed on my feet. Leif caught me.

'Take my arm,' he said. 'Lean on me, Sigrun. You've worked yourself too hard. You need a long rest today.'

'I do,' I agreed, leaning on him as we walked slowly towards home. It seemed a far longer road than it had done when we walked it last night. I knew I should ask Leif whether he'd gone to the king's feast in the end, and I should thank him for taking care of us, but I was too tired to speak. All I could think of was my sleeping furs waiting for me, warm and comfortable, at our journey's end. My mind was already there, although my body still walked.

When we reached the house, Bjorn and Thrang were up breakfasting together over a jug of ale.

'Ah! Welcome home!' exclaimed Thrang as we all came down the stairs.

'Was it a hard night?' asked my father.

'A breech birth,' I said with a shudder. 'The first I've had to deal with alone. But they're both well. It's a boy.'

'The chieftain will be pleased to have a son,' said Thrang. 'A man needs a son.' He reached out and patted Leif on the back as he spoke. 'So you've been lingering with the womenfolk all night, eh, Leif, instead of attending the king's feast? Well, well, you're that age, I suppose. And so I think you'll be glad to hear our news. Come and sit down all of you. You too, Maria.'

'News, father?'

'My friend Bjorn and I had a long talk over the mead last night,' said Thrang. 'About the past, about the future, and about the importance of our families.'

'It sounds like you both got drunk and thoroughly sentimental,' said Leif with a grin at me. 'I thought it was a feast with entertainment, not a maudlin drinking party.'

'Behave yourself, lad, and hear what we have to say,' Thrang admonished him. 'We're thinking of your happiness, so don't scoff.'

'Now I'm really nervous,' said Leif, mock seriously, while his eyes still laughed. I couldn't help smiling too, weary as I was. But I sensed both our fathers were very much in earnest.

'Bjorn, you tell them,' said Thrang. 'Perhaps he'll listen more respectfully to you, the impudent dog.' So saying, he punched his son playfully on the arm.

'Well, as Thrang said, we've been talking about our lives and what made us happiest, and about what you young people have ahead of you. And the first thing I decided is that Maria belongs with us now, for as long as she wants to stay.'

Bjorn turned to Maria and held out his hand.

'As a mark of respect for what you've been through, Maria, and of gratitude for the help you've given Sigrun these last months, I'd like to offer to foster you as my daughter. You'll be a member of our family. That means Sigrun and my wife Thora will teach you all you need to know, and I'll give you a dowry when you marry.'

Maria sat silent, obviously at a loss for words. Twice she opened her mouth, but no sound came out.

My father glanced over at me, not knowing how to read Maria's silence. I could feel that Maria was moved. I went to sit beside her and hugged her tight. 'Welcome to the family,' I said. 'I've always wanted a sister.'

Father solemnly shook Maria's hand, and though she said nothing, we all saw how her beautiful dark eyes shone bright with unshed tears.

Then my father turned to me. 'The other thing concerns your happiness closely, Sigrun. It's a subject I've mentioned to you before.'

A presentiment of what might be coming suddenly wiped the smile from my face and the joy from my heart. The last of my strength drained out of me. I was so desperately tired. How could they do this to me now?

'I want you to . . . that is, Thrang and I thought that . . . '

He stumbled into silence and looked over at Thrang for help.

'That you and Leif should consider getting married,' said Thrang. 'It's our dearest wish.'

'*What?*' roared Leif, his good humour gone at a stroke.

I sank down onto a bench and leaned my head against one hand. 'No,' I said softly. I would never agree to live the rest of my life in Jorvik. I longed for home every day, and I longed for Ingvar too. I had no idea whether he wanted to marry me or not, but I had to find out.

'We've noticed how close you've become,' said my father quickly, 'and we thought it would further the happiness of you both.'

'Bjorn has promised a most generous dowry, Leif,' said Thrang.

'Sigrun, there is no greater blessing than a happy marriage,' my father assured me.

'Absolutely not,' said Leif loudly, trying to speak over both men's attempts to persuade us. 'I love Sigrun, but I love her . . . as a sister.' Leif smiled apologetically over at me. 'I think you'll find she regards me the same way.'

I nodded. 'Yes, that's right,' I agreed. 'Leif is like a brother to me.'

I knew I should tell them that both of us were in love with someone else, but I blushed to mention Ingvar to my father in case I had mistaken his feelings and intentions towards me. And I knew Thrang would be furious at the merest hint of Leola's name.

Thrang raised his hands for silence. 'There's no need to say anything now,' he said. 'All we ask is that you both consider it. Such warm liking is a very sound basis for a marriage. That's how I married in the end. I was very happy, and missed my wife sorely when she died. So please, just think about it.'

Both Leif and I were silent, avoiding each other's eye. I could feel his anger with his father seething beneath his calm exterior. For myself, I was deeply embarrassed. To think that one's father should make such plans, discuss such important matters behind one's back. I knew it was often done, but I hadn't expected it. Now things would be so uncomfortable between Leif and me, just when we had established such an easy friendship.

Suddenly, something disturbed my thoughts. Some intrusive emotion. It wasn't in the house, it was just outside.

'Someone's here,' I said abruptly, lifting my head to listen. 'They're angry.'

'What?' asked my father confused. 'What do you mean, Sigrun?'

Everyone was staring at me. My tiredness momentarily forgotten, I was suddenly afraid for my father. Had danger pursued him to Jorvik? Instinctively, I moved closer to him and took his arm.

Before anyone else could speak, there was a thunderous hammering at the front door upstairs. We all looked at each other. There was a short silence and then the banging started again.

'I'll answer it,' said Thrang, jumping to his feet. He pulled his sword down from the wall and buckled it to his belt. 'Best to be prepared,' he said.

My father fetched his sword Foe Biter and held it in his hand as we stood in watchful silence. Thrang disappeared up the stairs, and we strained to hear the voices as he opened the door. I wanted to tell my father to hide, to run away, but we all stood frozen.

There was a thump and Thrang's voice was raised in protest. Heavy footsteps thundered down the stairs and some seven or eight armed men burst upon us. Maria screamed, and I cried out in terror. Two of the men made, not for my father, but for Leif and pinioned him between them. My father drew his own sword and rushed to his defence, but the tallest man cried out: 'Put up your sword! We're the king's men, and any injuries will be punished!'

Father fell back, looking confused. 'What's going on?' he demanded.

'You have no business bursting into my house,' roared Thrang, running down the stairs after the men, sword in hand. 'What in Thor's name do you want with my son?'

The tall man moved to stand in front of Leif. I saw his face and recognized Thorvald, the king's eldest son. 'Leif Thrangsson,' he said, 'we've been sent to bring you before the king.'

I looked from Leif to Thorvald in confusion. What was going on? If the king wanted to see Leif, why did he not just send a message?

'And I tell you again, Leif had nothing to do with it,' shouted Thrang.

'To do with what?' asked Leif, looking as perplexed as I felt. 'What's the matter?'

'They're arresting you, Leif,' said Thrang. 'On the king's orders.'

'Arresting . . . ?' I murmured, not quite understanding. My father put a finger to my lips and I was quiet. He pulled me close, one arm tightly around my shoulders.

'Where were you last night, Leif Thrangsson?' asked Thorvald. 'Can you account for yourself?'

'I escorted these two ladies to Chieftain Thorhall's house in Fossgate,' said Leif slowly. 'The chieftain's wife was having a baby and Sigrun is a midwife.'

Thorvald looked round at me and bowed very slightly. 'I apologize for bursting in on you like this, Sigrun,' he said more quietly, 'but we have reason to believe . . . ' He left his sentence unfinished, and turned back to Leif. 'And you stayed there all night?' he asked, his voice hard again.

'No, I left them there, and went back to collect them later. What's this about?'

'And what did you do in the meantime?' continued Thorvald, ignoring his question.

'Wandered around, had a drink or two. It's really none of your business.'

'But you didn't come to the feast even though you'd been invited.'

'Would you show yourself at a feast with a face like this?' Leif asked him, indicating his bruise.

'And how did you get that?'

'I was attacked in the street,' muttered Leif. I could sense his discomfort, lying in front of all these people.

'That's not true, is it?' said Thorvald, perceiving the lie at once.

'I don't need to answer your questions until you answer mine,' said Leif angrily, trying to shake off the men who held him.

Thorvald smiled unpleasantly and folded his arms across his broad chest. In the middle of all the confusion and panic, I noticed that he was looking fully recovered from both his illness and his wound.

'You were given that bruise by Eadred, for trying to seduce his daughter, weren't you?' demanded Thorvald. 'And now she's disappeared, and you have no explanation of where you've been.'

'What do you mean she's disappeared?' demanded Leif. 'What's happened to her?'

'We're hoping you can tell us that,' said Thorvald. 'Eadred is with the king, and very angry. He's accused you of abducting her. The king is taking this seriously. If you're found guilty you'll be put to death.'

'No!' cried Thrang.

He rushed forward to protect his son, but two of the men held him back.

'Father!' I whispered, terrified, clutching his arm. 'We must do something!'

Had Leif really been with Leola last night? Even if he had, he didn't deserve death.

Leif was dragged away, still shouting and protesting his innocence. Thorvald paused beside me for a moment, looked as though he was going to say something, but then followed his men to the stairs.

'We will do something, Sigrun,' father said quietly. 'But I'm sure the king will hear him out and this will be resolved happily. There will be witnesses and people to speak for Leif.'

I wasn't so confident. A wave of nausea swept over me. I was terrified for Leif. I'd been afraid Leola would bring trouble on him, but there was no satisfaction in being proved right.

'Bjorn, I must follow them, and see what I can do to help,' said Thrang. His face was white, his voice hoarse. 'Will you come with me?'

'Of course,' said my father at once. He turned back to me. 'Sigrun, we'll do what we can. I promise.' He stroked my cheek briefly. 'You're exhausted, my dear child. Get some rest. We'll have Leif back here for you before you wake up.'

He gave me another hug, snatched up his cloak and followed Thrang from the house.

CHAPTER TWENTY-THREE

I tried to rest, but it was impossible to lie still with thoughts of Leif under suspicion, and in such danger. I had no experience of kings and their ideas of justice. Would he even listen to what Leif had to say? I sat up abruptly, a cold sweat breaking out all over my body.

'They won't execute him at once, will they?' I cried out.

Maria laid a soothing hand on my shoulder.

'No, Sigrun,' she said. 'Not today. You need rest, then maybe we can help him.'

I didn't know if she was right or not, but her words soothed me a little. I lay back down but tossed and turned while my body and head ached with tiredness and worry. Then, quite unexpectedly, I fell into a deep sleep. I didn't wake until the middle of the afternoon, and then started upright, feeling guilty. Maria was asleep beside me and my father was sitting quietly at a table on the other side of the room. I wondered if it was his arrival that had woken me.

'What did the king say?' I mumbled, the mists of slumber still curling around my brain. 'Where's Leif?'

Father crossed the room and crouched down beside me. 'Leif is detained,' he said. 'I'm sorry, Sigrun, the evidence looks very heavy against him.'

'Detained where?'

'The king has a prison.'

'I must see him. He was with Maria and me most of the night. If I could talk to him . . . '

'No one may visit him, Sigrun, it's forbidden.'

'But what will be done with him? Who will decide whether he's telling the truth?'

Bjorn shook his head. 'It's decided on the whim of the king. Thrang says some prisoners are left for months in the prison and then executed or released quite suddenly, according to his mood. But don't cry, Sigrun. All may yet be resolved.'

'I'm so afraid for him,' I said, wiping away hot tears.

There were footsteps on the stairs again, and Thrang appeared, looking haggard and weary.

'The king has gone out of Jorvik on business,' he said, sitting down heavily, unbuckling his sword and throwing it on the table with a clatter. Beside me, Maria awoke, and sat up, bleary eyed.

'And what comes to Leif meanwhile?' asked my father.

'He remains where he is until the king returns or he tells us where Leola is hidden. Meanwhile the king's son is in charge, and a more unpleasant fellow than Thorvald is hard to imagine.'

'But Leif doesn't know where she is!' I exclaimed. 'I'm sure of it.'

Even as I said this, a sneaking doubt made me squirm a little. I knew Leif was desperately in love. But so that he would steal Leola away? I truly didn't know what to believe.

'I've spoken to Eadred. He insists he caught them together just yesterday. Leif doesn't deny it. And then the girl vanished that very night.'

'Can Leif not say where he was?' I asked. 'He was at Thorhall's with us for several hours.'

'He's very vague, the young fool,' said Thrang. He laid his head in his arms and groaned aloud. I got up quietly and went to fetch him some ale. When I placed it beside him, he thanked me, but didn't manage a smile.

'I told the king that Leif had no intentions towards the Saxon girl,' said Thrang. 'That we'd been deciding his engagement to you at the very moment the soldiers came in. But he wouldn't listen.'

I wanted to object, strongly, to Thrang spreading the word of our engagement. Neither Leif nor I wanted it. But it was not the time to say so if it could help Leif to be freed. My insides twisted again with fear for my friend. I had to do something.

That night a half-forgotten memory began to trouble me. Something that connected Thorvald and Leola. What was it? I didn't remember until halfway through the night when I suddenly woke with the image of the golden bracelet in my mind. Leola had the same bracelet as Thorvald had given me. Had it been a gift from him? Was he her secret lover? I remembered his half-apologetic manner towards me as he took Leif, and wondered if I'd solved the riddle.

Early the next morning, I set out alone, wearing the golden bracelet, telling Maria I was going to see a neighbour with the gout and there was no need for her to come. Once out of the house, I hurried through the crowded streets to the jewellers' quarter. There were many stalls there to choose from, and I went from one to another, asking who'd sold the bracelet. None recognized it.

'That's not Jorvik made,' said one man at last, examining the working of the gold carefully. 'I've never seen that style, and I know all the goldsmiths working here. I'd say that was made in foreign parts: bought at Hedeby or Dublin perhaps.'

'Thank you. Thank you for your help,' I said to him.

I went to the king's house next. The guards stopped me at the door.

'I'm Sigrun, Thorvald's healer,' I told them with more confidence than I felt. 'I've come to check on his wound.'

The guards conferred together and asked someone inside the house. At last they let me in. I stepped nervously out of the cold into the warm, smoky hall.

I was kept waiting a long time, sitting on the benches near the fire, twisting my cloak restlessly in my hands, trying out in my head all the things I could say to Thorvald. Most of them sounded stupid and I dismissed them, growing steadily more uncomfortable the longer I waited. I began to wish I'd brought Maria with me after all.

At last I was called in to see Thorvald. He was sitting in his father's room receiving visitors and I could feel his keen enjoyment of being in charge. When I entered the room, he nodded to dismiss his attendants. I stood awkwardly before him as he lounged at his ease in the king's great carved chair.

'What is it, healer-girl?' he asked at last. 'My leg is quite recovered, as you well know.'

'I'm pleased to hear it,' I said and then hesitated.

Thorvald grinned. 'Let's not pretend. I know why you're here. It has to do with that scumbag merchant's son who's made off with Leola. Am I right?'

I frowned. I disliked how much Thorvald was enjoying this. I could feel the satisfaction and pleasure in him. 'I believe he's innocent,' I said.

'So you've come to plead his case? A betrothed maiden would always believe her man innocent, even if he's been seeing another woman. Why would I take your word?'

I took a deep breath to steady my nerves. 'No,' I said. 'I haven't come to plead for him. I've come to ask what *you* know about Leola's disappearance.'

'Me?' Thorvald looked astonished. 'Are you accusing *me* of making away with the wretched girl?'

'Perhaps,' I said. 'I have reason to believe there is some connection between the two of you.' I paused, aware that I needed to be cautious about what I said. I suspected that Thorvald was the father of Leola's baby, but I couldn't say so in case I was wrong.

Thorvald sat very still. 'What makes you say that?' he asked.

'I noticed that she wears the same bracelet that you gave me,' I told him. I shook back my sleeve to reveal the golden serpent. 'The Midgaard Serpent is a strange thing for a Saxon girl to be wearing, wouldn't you say?'

'Leola has many admirers,' Thorvald replied coolly. 'Any number of them are Norse. Why me?'

'You're right of course,' I agreed. 'But the thing is: these bracelets weren't made here in Jorvik. I asked the jewellers. They were bought abroad. By someone wealthy.'

'What are you saying?' demanded Thorvald.

'I'm not saying anything. I'm asking you. Do you know more than you are saying about Leola's disappearance? You can't let our friend lose his life for something he hasn't done.'

There was a long silence between us. We watched one another warily.

Then Thorvald leaned forward. 'Listen,' he said, 'I may have had a passing fancy for the girl once. I may even have visited her a few times. But I haven't seen her in months. I've no idea where she is now. For all I know, Eadred is right that it's Leif hiding her.'

There was a sincere note in his voice that couldn't be mistaken. I felt sure Thorvald was telling the truth. I was bitterly disappointed. If it wasn't Thorvald, then who could it be? 'Very well,' I said slowly. 'I believe you. But I need to see Leif.'

'That's out of the question,' said Thorvald at once. 'No visitors. The king's orders. Sorry.'

'I helped you when you needed it,' I said quietly.

'And you were paid well for your trouble.'

'I was, but that's not why I came. I would have done the same for you if you'd been too poor to pay at all. Please,' I said earnestly. 'I beg you. I just need to see him.'

We stared at one another, eyes locked, a silent struggle taking place. I knew Thorvald had felt some remorse or discomfort for my sake yesterday when he took Leif from us. I'd seen it in his hesitation and his apology to me, and the amulet had helped me sense it. He owed me a debt and he knew it.

'You're a cursed troublesome healer-wench,' exclaimed Thorvald at last. 'If you get me into trouble with my father, I'll kill you myself. Wait here.'

Thorvald slammed out of the room. I clasped my hands together to stop them shaking. After only a few moments, Thorvald came back, a bunch of keys at his waist. 'I'll take you to see him once only,' he said. 'But on two conditions. You tell no one of the visit and you never speak to my father of my connection with that Saxon girl.'

'If you were telling the truth, I'll never need to,' I said.

'I suppose that'll do. Let's go,' he said and strode out of the room. I followed him closely, out of the back of the house, down the length of a narrow street and around the corner. There was the lock-up, guarded by two men standing just inside the door; swords hung at their waists.

'The king's business,' said Thorvald curtly, and led me into the prison.

The place was dirty, cold, and vermin-infested. I was appalled at the thought of Leif here. Thorvald unlocked a heavy wooden door and nodded for me to step inside. I stepped into a tiny, dark room, with only a small hole high up in the wall to let a little light in.

'Sigrun!' cried Leif as soon as he saw me. He came towards me, arms held out, and swept me into a hug.

'Touching,' remarked Thorvald sardonically. 'You have a short time to talk, and I shall have to lock you in here.'

I agreed and he went out, securing the heavy door behind him.

'I'm so glad to see you, I can't tell you,' said Leif. 'Is everything sorted out? Have they found Leola?' He released me and looked at me eagerly. I shook my head.

'I'm sorry, Leif. They haven't. I persuaded Thorvald to let me see you so I could discover what you know.'

'I? I know nothing. I already told the king. I saw Leola that afternoon, was thrown out of the house and didn't go back. I can't imagine where she could be. I'm so worried about her.'

I took Leif's hands and drew him to the bed which was the only place to sit down in the room. 'That's the honest truth? It's very, very important you tell me everything you know,' I said earnestly. 'It's the only way I can help you.'

'I wouldn't lie to you,' Leif promised me earnestly. 'I meant what I said yesterday. I love you like a sister.'

'I'm so relieved,' I said. 'I was so afraid that perhaps in a desperate moment you may have persuaded Leola to run away with you. It didn't seem likely, but I couldn't be certain.'

'Does the king believe me though?' asked Leif eagerly. 'Will he let me go?'

I shook my head sadly. 'I'm very sorry,' I said. 'The king has gone away. You're locked in here until he gets back. I mean to search for Leola, but I need you to tell me all the people she knows, because I don't know where to start.'

Leif was bitterly disappointed. He got up and paced the cell restlessly. 'I'm to be shut away until some time in the future when the king gets back?' he demanded angrily. 'Where's he gone? It's the middle of the winter! It's not the time for travelling or war.'

'I don't know; no one's told me,' I said. 'I'm so sorry. I keep saying that, but I am. I feel so helpless.'

Leif resumed his pacing, clenching and unclenching his fists. 'We're very short of time,' I told him apologetically. 'Thorvald will be back any minute.'

'Leola knows everyone!' exclaimed Leif impatiently. 'Every young man of good family in Jorvik is in love with her, and more besides.'

'Is there anyone specific?' I asked.

Leif frowned. 'Thorvald himself is one of her favourites,' he said. 'Perhaps it's him, and that's why he's been so keen to lock me up.'

'I thought so too,' I said. 'But I don't think he knows where she is.'

Leif threw up his arms in despair. 'I just don't know,' he said. 'I have no idea. I thought Leola favoured me.'

'I'm afraid that looks unlikely,' I said as gently as I could.

The key rattled in the lock behind us, the door opened and Thorvald stood there.

'That's all the time I can allow you,' he said firmly. 'You must leave now.'

I hugged Leif tightly in farewell. 'I'll do everything I can,' I promised him. I felt dreadful leaving him in this desolate place. But Thorvald was already ushering me out, hurrying me from the building.

'He knows nothing,' I told Thorvald. 'Is it really necessary to keep him imprisoned here?'

'Until we know where Leola is, he stays here,' replied Thorvald. 'Anyway, if I let him out, Eadred would kill him.'

That was a frightening thought. And quite possibly true. Poor Leif. He'd drawn such consequences on himself and all he'd done was fall in love unwisely.

'You're keeping him in such squalor,' I complained as we reached the outer door. 'It's freezing cold, he has no covers and the place is filthy. Does he even get fed here? He could die waiting for justice.'

'I've done enough for you, healer,' said Thorvald abruptly. 'If you want to send him food or furs you'll have to bribe the guards like everyone else.' So saying, he left me outside the door of the prison-house and strode away.

CHAPTER TWENTY-FOUR

'Where in Thor's name have you been, Sigrun?' my father cried when I got home. 'We've been looking for you! Thrang and Erik are still out trying to get word of you. I was worried sick.'

Maria stood beside him looking reproachfully at me.

'I'm so sorry,' I said. 'It took much longer than I expected.'

'You've been gone for hours, and without Maria! Promise you won't go out alone again. Or at least without leaving word where you've gone.'

'I promise, father. But it was important.'

'It's not safe for you to wander the city alone, going into people's houses as you do. It's bad enough worrying you're going to catch some infectious disease from all those poor people you tend. There are all sorts of dangers in a city like this, Sigrun, that you have no idea about. It's not like at home where the greatest danger is the weather.'

'I said I'm sorry, father,' I said, trying to stem his flood of angry words. 'I do understand the dangers. I was quite safe today.'

'How can anyone be safe when a girl has disappeared from her own home? I can't stop thinking about it.

You're all I have left here, Sigrun.'

My father pulled me into a hug, holding me close. Then he held me at arm's length to look at me. 'How you've grown up,' he said. 'When did that happen?'

I smiled slightly, and felt myself blush. I touched my father's cheek lightly with one finger. 'I'm the same person I've always been,' I said. 'Just, as you said, a little older.'

At that moment Thrang returned. After his exclamations of relief were over, we all sat down by the fire. I gathered my courage to tell them where I'd really been.

'I have news of Leif,' I said. They all looked up at once.

'What news?' asked Thrang urgently.

'You've seen him?' asked my father astonished. 'How?'

'Thorvald let me in to see him. He's cold and hungry, but unhurt. We need to get him some warmer clothes and some food. But most importantly, he swears to me he knows absolutely nothing of Leola.'

There were questions, exclamations, more reproaches for putting myself in danger. Thrang wanted to go immediately to see his son too, but I had to tell him that any further visits had been absolutely forbidden.

'I knew he was innocent,' said Thrang. 'I knew the stories of him and that girl were invented.'

'Eadred isn't lying about what he saw,' I said. 'Leif admits that, and it's what makes him look guilty. But he didn't see her again, and had nothing to do with her disappearance.'

'Who took her then if it wasn't my son?' asked Thrang.

* * *

The talk went on most of the day on and off. Who could be behind Leola's strange disappearance? We discussed every possibility, including that Leola could have run away alone. When father and Thrang had gone out on business, I turned to Maria.

'You probably know as many of Leola's secrets as anyone. Can you think where she could be?'

Maria looked at me helplessly. 'I think and think,' she said. 'But I don't know.'

'Who are her particular friends? Does she have any favourite admirers?'

Maria threw up her hands. 'Friends? Not really. Admirers? Half the city. The men half.'

I bit my lip. 'Yes, that's what Leif said. But it makes it very hard to trace her. Was there no one she favoured above the others?'

'All of them,' said Maria. 'She make all men think they are favourite.'

I thought back to the feast at Eadred's house and I knew what Maria meant. This was going to be even more difficult than I'd imagined.

The winter became colder, but there was no change in Leif's situation. I asked in every household I visited if anyone had any clue to Leola's whereabouts, but no one did. It was as though she'd vanished from the city altogether.

Snow fell and turned black and slushy in the busy streets. I walked with Maria through the wet and the dirt each day, to take food to Leif. We had no word from him, but the guards assured me he was well. I didn't trust them and wondered how much of the good food they ate themselves.

'If only the king would return,' I said to Maria on the way home one overcast, windy afternoon. 'He might decide Leif is innocent.'

'Or maybe punish him,' said Maria, and I shivered inside my heavy cloak. She was right, but it was a possibility none of us wanted to face.

'How is it possible for her to be so well hidden?' I said. 'It's been weeks now.'

'Perhaps Leola murdered,' said Maria. 'By jealous woman. And buried somewhere.'

We'd talked about this many times. We knew Leola's disappearance might never be solved, and Leif might perish unjustly. 'If anyone killed her though, it was her uncle, in a fit of rage,' I said. 'And he's just pretending to be distressed.'

'Possible,' agreed Maria.

'No, I don't think so,' I sighed. 'There's no guilt in him. Only anguish. I don't think he's pretending.'

'How you know that?' asked Maria.

'I feel people's moods,' I admitted. I thought of the amulet still hidden inside my kirtle. I'd never told Maria what it meant to me or how powerful I believed it to be. It was my secret.

'All healers do that?' she asked curiously.

'I don't know,' I said truthfully. 'My mother reads auras.'

Maria looked puzzled so I explained: 'Everyone has a cloud of colours around them, especially around the head. They change all the time with moods and thoughts and health. My mother can see them and read them. She tried to teach me, but I'm no good at it.'

The thought of my mother made me feel homesick. I wondered how she was. If I'd made a good job of setting her leg, she'd be walking normally again by now. How I wished I could see her just once, to be assured she was well.

We reached home, and pulled the front door open, trying not to look at Unn who was using the latrine at the front of the house. I still hadn't accustomed myself to the outdoor latrines in Jorvik, where the user was clearly visible to all passers by above a waist-high woven fence. I tried to visit it myself mainly in the hours of darkness.

We poured ourselves a drink of whey and warmed a little porridge and sat down.

'It comes down again to who was missing from the Yule feast that night,' I said as we ate.

'No one missing except Leif,' said Maria. 'We ask Bjorn and Thrang many times.'

'I know,' I sighed. 'We keep going over the same ground. But the alternative is to give up, and I won't do that.'

Father and Erik came down the stairs and joined us. 'This is taking its toll on Thrang,' said father, hearing what we were talking about. 'He's looking years older.'

'And no one but us is trying to solve the mystery of what happened to her,' I said, bitterly.

'That, Sigrun, as we've said before, is because everyone is sure it's already solved,' said my father. 'As far as the king and Eadred are concerned, Leif has spirited

Leola away, and the only thing keeping him alive is their hope he may say where she is.'

There was a knock on the door, and Unn struggled down the stairs to say I was needed to deliver a baby on the other side of the city. I hurriedly gathered the medicines I might need, while Maria fetched the cloaks we had only just taken off.

'I'll be out when you get back,' said my father. 'I'm invited to tell stories at a feast again tonight, and Erik's coming with me. I'll listen out for any gossip about Leola as always.'

'Yes, of course,' I said. 'We're both city people now, working for our living, aren't we?' I felt a mixture of pride and sadness at the thought. We were both successful at what we did but this wasn't the life I'd choose to lead.

'Indeed,' said my father. 'I'd never have expected to see you so sought after. You always seemed so timid and reluctant about your trade at home. Your mother told me she feared you lacked confidence and perhaps even talent.'

His words would have hurt me and made me feel ashamed just half a year before. But I had fewer doubts of my abilities now, and was growing in experience daily. I wasn't surprised to hear my mother had doubted me. After all, I'd been certain myself that I lacked healer qualities.

'And you were so unwilling to part with your stories,' I teased him in return. 'I see all we had to do was to pay you, and you would have told them to us.'

CHAPTER TWENTY-FIVE

'There's a ship just arrived from Iceland at the quay,' said Thrang one spring evening at nightmeal. 'It's early in the year, isn't it? It's not four months since Yule.'

A tiny, irrational flame of hope leapt into being within me. It couldn't possibly be Ingvar, could it? Had he persuaded his father to follow us? I suppressed the idea at once, knowing how impossible that was. Just because the ship was from Iceland, didn't mean it had Ingvar aboard.

My father had another, equally unlikely thought: 'It would be too much to hope that it's my son with our ship?' he asked.

'I'm sorry,' said Thrang. 'They are strangers, so I hear. But I'm sure you'll hear from Asgrim before long, now that spring's here.'

A shadow passed over my father's face. 'I wish I could believe that,' he said sadly. 'So, a ship has sailed here from Iceland? How I wish I were sailing in the other direction. It's hard to have to stay put here, knowing that the days are lengthening and growing milder and the seed will soon need planting in the fields at home.'

'Of course,' said Thrang with gruff sympathy. 'And I can hardly believe I need to begin sailing again myself tomorrow.' He sighed. 'I was so determined not to leave

Jorvik with my son's case still unsettled.'

We all thought of the second half of the winter which Leif had spent nearby and yet completely cut off from us. It was utterly unjust. But after all this time, I still had no clue as to what had happened to Leola on Yule night.

'Are you sure you don't want me to accompany you on this trip?' my father asked Thrang.

'No,' said Thrang at once. 'You're sending your men with me; that's help enough. I'll be more comfortable knowing you're here while I'm away. In case . . . anything can be done for Leif.'

We all knew how unlikely that was. The king had returned weeks ago and Thrang had called on him. Leif would be released, he was told, when he was prepared to reveal Leola's whereabouts. Or else eventually put to death. He'd tried to go back again, to plead Leif's case, but had been turned away at the door.

'Very well,' said Bjorn. 'If I'm to stay here, I'll go and look for that Icelandic ship in the river tomorrow, and find out what news there is from Iceland. Though it's hardly likely I'll know the people. Will you come with me, Sigrun?'

'Certainly,' I agreed at once, glad of the prospect of an outing with my father. I mustn't let myself dream of seeing Ingvar. I must simply remember that I liked to walk down to the Ouse, where the wind often blew in from the sea and was free of the stink of the city.

We saw Thrang off at dawn the next morning, and left the house ourselves shortly after.

'Wouldn't it be wonderful if the Icelanders had brought news of mother?' I said. 'I'd give anything to hear she's well.' I was too shy to mention Ingvar to my father.

'Me too,' said father. 'But it's impossible. None of our neighbours sail to Jorvik.'

We'd only just turned the first corner when a slave came running up to us.

'Are you the healer?' he asked me. My heart sank. I could never plan even an hour without it being interrupted by a summons to some distant part of the city. But then I put aside such selfish feeling. There were sick people needing my help, and they paid me for my trouble and my skills, often very generously.

'I am,' I said.

'Knut Siefredsson wants to see you,' said the woman. 'In Petergate . . . '

'I know Knut,' I said, remembering the king's younger son. 'Is he ill?'

'He's very sick with a high fever,' he said. 'If you're willing, I could take you there now.'

I turned to my father. 'I'm so sorry to miss our walk, and the chance of perhaps meeting people from home,' I said to him.

'Don't worry,' said my father with a smile. 'If they're worth meeting, I'll offer them hospitality this evening.'

On impulse, I reached up and hugged him. Seeing him out in the spring sunshine this morning, I suddenly noticed he was ageing. There was grey in his dark hair and deep lines around his eyes. We'd grown closer than ever before over the winter, and I felt a rush of affection for him. Perhaps my mother had done the right thing, sending me to take care of him, however hard I'd found it to leave home.

Father headed towards the river and I fetched Maria and my medicines. 'I haven't seen Knut for ages,' I said to Maria as we walked. 'Not since . . . well, not since before Yule in fact.'

It struck me that it might be useful for me to ask Knut a few questions. I hadn't thought of him until now, but he'd certainly been one of Leola's admirers. But I'd had my hopes of solving this mystery dashed so many times that I wasn't optimistic.

Maria and I found Knut lying in a makeshift bed in the upstairs room. He was wrapped in furs, shivering, flushed and clearly very ill. He tried to lift his head as we came in, but let it drop back down with a groan. 'I can hardly move,' he said in a faint voice. 'I've never felt so ill. Is it brain fever? Or some deadly plague?'

I laid a hand on his brow and noted the high fever, the dry burning skin. Then I checked his arms and torso for rashes.

'Has your stomach been upset?' I asked him.

'Yes.'

'Have you passed blood?'

'Yes . . . no . . . I don't know. What's wrong with me? Am I dying?'

'You're not dying,' I told him. 'I suspect you have the influenza. As long as you follow my instructions and take the medicines I give you, there should be no complications.'

Knut sighed with relief and then shivered violently.

'You should be down by the fire,' I said to him. 'Not up here in the cold.'

'I thought it might be contagious,' he said weakly.

'It is, of course,' I agreed. 'But that can't be helped. Do you have men in the house who can carry you, or support you? We must get you back downstairs, and then I'll need to brew some medicinal tea for you.' I got up to go to the stairs, but Knut called me back, his voice suddenly stronger and urgent.

'Wait! Can't my slaves brew the medicine?'

'I suppose so,' I said doubtfully, turning back to look at him. 'But I'd rather do it myself, or Maria can . . . '

My voice tailed off. I'd heard something. A short dry cough from below stairs. I recognized it immediately. It sounded just like Leola's cough. I snatched up the powdered willow bark and headed for the stairs. I had to know at once if I was right. The cough sounded again. Dry and distinct from the cellar room.

I paused and looked back at Knut. He opened his bloodshot eyes, suddenly wide awake, and they met mine. I could see that he knew I knew.

'She's *here*,' I said accusingly. 'How could you?'

I ran down the stairs just in time to see the skirts of a kirtle whisk behind a door, and to hear the thud of wood on wood as it closed. I ran towards it.

'You can't go in there,' said a slave woman rising to her feet, agitated.

I ignored her and pulled the door open. There, hiding in the food store, paler than I remembered her, stood Leola. She crossed her arms over her chest and stared at me defiantly.

'Hello, healer,' she said. 'I can't remember your name. So what are you going to do? Tell my uncle where I am? Well, I don't care. I'm sick of hiding here. I want to be married.'

'Do you even care that someone who loves you has been imprisoned while you've been hiding here?' I asked her angrily. I wanted to slap her face.

Leola snorted impatiently and looked away.

'Maria!' I called.

'Yes?' Maria was near the top of the stairs waiting, and came down at my words.

'Go and tell the king we've found Leola, please,' I said in a shaking voice.

Maria gasped. 'You . . . ' she said. 'You *here*?'

It seemed a very long time until the king's men arrived. Leola sat down by the fire and stared into the flickering flames in sullen silence, and I could hear Knut's fevered breathing upstairs. He must know he would be in deep trouble with his father, but perhaps he was too ill to care. At last there was a commotion upstairs and a band of armed warriors arrived with Maria.

When we reached the king's house, the king was waiting in the same carved chair I'd last seen his eldest son in. He looked old and careworn in the light of day. Thorvald stood by his side with a face like thunder. He glared at Leola as she stood before his father.

'So, Leola, Eadred's niece,' said the king sternly. 'You've caused us a great deal of trouble. Would you like to explain yourself?'

'I'm engaged to your son, Knut,' she said. 'I wear his token.'

So saying, she held up a ring on her little finger. The king held out his hand, and rather than remove the ring,

Leola put her hand into the king's. It lay there, small and delicate in his huge fist. The king was stunned into silence for a second, gaping at her, then he brusquely turned her hand over to examine the ring before pushing her away.

'It bears the royal seal,' he said. 'But do you tell me it was my son who stole you from your uncle's house?'

'Oh, he didn't steal me,' she said blithely. 'I ran away while my uncle was out at the Yule feast and waited at his house. My uncle had been most cruel to me, and I needed protection.'

I stood silently by, piecing this together. Knut had been at the Yule feast. So I'd ruled him out. I didn't think he could have been involved. But Leola must have been waiting on his doorstep when he got home. At this moment I really hated her for all the suffering she'd caused.

The king looked furious. He'd made such a fuss about pursuing and punishing the guilty person, and all this time his own son had been hiding the runaway.

'Where's Knut?' he snapped.

'He's ill, my lord,' I said, stepping forward. 'He has a high fever.'

'Tell him to wait on me the moment he's able to get up. I want the truth of this,' snarled the king to Thorvald, who bowed politely. 'Meanwhile take the girl back to her uncle and tell him to keep a closer eye on her in future. You can go, all of you. I'm sick of this whole business.'

I spoke before anyone could move. 'Please, my lord,' I said. 'An innocent man has spent three months in prison because of this. Can he be freed?'

'We don't know that he's innocent,' said the king, raising his voice angrily. I could feel he didn't want to accept that his son was to blame. 'How do we know that he wasn't involved in spiriting her away from her uncle's house?'

'I think, my lord,' said Thorvald, taking a step forward, 'that you'll find all this is a plot to unseat you from your rightful place as king. As you know, this girl is daughter to the former Saxon king of Northumbria. And you know that my brother has been planning to visit Northumbria as soon as the weather improves. I think he feels that as your son and married to the princess, he may get support to raise troops against you.'

Thorvald looked pleased with himself as he delivered this speech. I remembered Knut's callous hope that Thorvald would die of his wound last autumn, and realized the animosity between the brothers ran deep. I could feel the suppressed hatred in Thorvald, until it was blotted out by a surge of pure rage from the king, who had now absorbed his words and their implications.

'Are you saying my own son is plotting with the enemy against me?' he shouted.

'No!' cried Leola. 'He's marrying me because he loves me!'

No one took any notice of her.

'He's ambitious, father, and it's never suited him to be the younger son,' said Thorvald. 'He knows I'm loyal to you, and will always serve you faithfully.' There was a calculating look in his eye as he spoke, and I suddenly remembered the bracelet Leola still wore. He was as big a traitor as his brother.

'Are you sure that wasn't your own plan?' I asked. 'When you were meeting her in secret last year?'

'What nonsense is this?' said Thorvald quickly.

I grasped Leola by the arm and pulled up her sleeve, praying that the bracelet would still be there. To my relief, it was. Concealed on her arm was the Midgaard Serpent, glowing gold for all to see.

'She had this from Thorvald as a gift,' I said.

'He promised me!' cried Leola, starting to weep. 'He *promised* he'd marry me if I did what he said and I'd be queen. And then even though he got me with child, he broke his word!'

I'd unleashed a torrent of secrets. It was out of my hands now, and I wasn't sorry. These people had let Leif suffer for their underhand schemes. The king gaped at Leola speechlessly for a moment and then bent a furious stare on his eldest son. 'Thorvald?' he asked.

'It's a lie, father,' Thorvald said smoothly. 'I never promised marriage.'

His father gave him a look of withering scorn. 'So you went running to his brother?' said the king, turning back to the weeping girl in front of him. 'Hoping to become queen that way instead? There is no word bad enough for you, you scheming vixen!'

He turned to his men.

'Seize Thorvald!' he cried.

There was a moment's appalled silence as his warriors hesitated, thinking they couldn't have heard aright. 'Do it!' shouted Siefred. 'Throw him into the prison!'

Thorvald was dragged from the room, shouting that it was all a lie. The king turned to the remainder of his men.

'Fetch Knut and lock him up too,' he ordered. 'I don't care how ill he is. Oh, and wait! Arrest Eadred too! The rest of you get out! Get out!'

It was clear the king was humiliated at having so many witnesses to his family quarrel. He was purple with rage, his fists clenched.

'Please, my lord king,' I begged, throwing myself onto my knees at his feet. 'Please let Leif Thrangsson go. He had nothing to do with any of this. He was falsely accused to hide the truth.'

The king dashed a hand in front of his eyes and took a shuddering breath before he could focus either his gaze or his mind on me.

'And you're to be his wife, aren't you?' he said. 'I remember your father telling me.'

Feeling guilty at the lie, I nodded. 'Yes, my lord. So you see, he had nothing to do with Leola.'

'Is this true, girl?' barked the king at Leola.

'What would I want with him?' she said scornfully through her tears. 'He's nothing.'

'Release Leif!' ordered the king, pointing to one of his guards. 'At once! We shall give him recompense in due course. Eadred's possessions perhaps.'

I caught the king's hand, kissed it. 'Thank you and may the goddess bless you with good health,' I said, and turned to walk to the door. I passed Leola, who was weeping stormily at the news her uncle was to be punished.

'And what shall I do?' she screamed in her distress at losing all her prospects at once. The king grasped her by the wrist and pulled her towards him.

'I'll tell you what you'll do, Saxon princess,' he said

deliberately. 'You will become queen after all.'

Leola gulped and paused in her weeping. 'What?' she asked, confused. 'How?'

I paused at the door, curious to hear the outcome.

'I have two choices, you see,' said Siefred. 'You're clearly a danger to me. So I can either have you executed, or I can marry you myself. I think there should be a wedding this evening, don't you?'

I couldn't help but smile at Leola's shocked face as I left the room. Her dreams were to come true at last. As long as she didn't mind a husband older than her uncle.

'Leif is to be set free!' I whispered excitedly to Maria who'd stayed outside the door. After all this time, it seemed too good to be true. 'Hurry!' I grabbed her hand and pulled her after me, almost running after the guard who was striding away towards the prison.

We waited outside the building, straining to hear what was going on inside, longing for a first glimpse of our friend. I could feel my heart pounding in my chest with excitement and nervousness. How would he look? How would he react to the news that he was free at long last?

Leif appeared, blinking in the daylight, thin, pale, and dirty. He saw us waiting for him and tears of gratitude and joy rose to his eyes.

'Oh, Sigrun!' he said shakily. 'Maria! How happy I am to see you both.'

We both hugged him, despite his dirt, ecstatic to see him free.

'Forgive me my weakness,' he said, hastily wiping away the unmanly tears he was shedding. 'I've been ill, I've been afraid, and thought I'd never be allowed home.'

We each took one of his hands in ours and led him back to his house. Leif walked slowly, leaning on us, weak after his long incarceration.

'Your father's away for a few days,' I said. 'He'll be overjoyed when he gets back. But my father is here, and will celebrate with us.'

'So to what do I . . . owe my release?' asked Leif, short of breath and struggling to talk as well as walk.

I recounted the events of the morning as briefly as I could, and he shook his head, trying to stop the tears that forced their way into his eyes.

'Oh, Leola,' he cried. 'How could she do that to me? I loved her. I thought she cared for me! I prayed that she was safe. But she left me in prison for months when she could so easily have cleared my name . . . '

Leif stopped, overcome. He turned away from us, wiping his face with his dirty sleeves.

I gave him a few moments and then put a hand on his shoulder.

'You're ill,' I said. 'Come home now, and we can talk more.'

CHAPTER TWENTY-SIX

Despite Leif's distress over Leola's betrayal, I felt elated as we approached home. A long spell of threat and fear had ended, and we were bringing Leif back safely. I couldn't wait to tell my father. I hoped he hadn't invited the visiting Icelanders home to nightmeal after all. It would be much more fun to have Leif to ourselves tonight. There was so much to tell, and to hear too.

As I thought of my father, I felt suddenly uneasy. At first, I didn't know why. But the feeling grew stronger with each step I took closer to the house.

'Father!' I whispered to myself. I could feel him nearby, and he was mortally afraid. 'I shouldn't have left him!' I cried.

'What's wrong?' asked Leif. 'Sigrun, what's the matter? You've gone as white as a new-shorn lamb.'

But I was already running ahead, pushing open the door of the house. It wasn't locked, because we'd left Unn and Erik there. So my father couldn't be in danger, could he? I must be imagining it.

As I ran through the door, a stranger lunged at me out of the gloom and my worst fears were realized. I dodged him, and ran for the stairs, flinging my bag to the floor as I went. I heard Maria scream as she was caught, but I couldn't stop. I had to get down the stairs to the source of the fear and despair I could feel there.

As I ran downstairs the most appalling scene unfolded before my eyes. My father was fighting for his life, his sword Foe Biter in his hands. A much taller man was attacking him, raining blow after vicious blow down on him. The noise of iron on steel in the confined space was ear-splitting. It was a man with hair as red as fire and a black tunic, and I was almost sure I recognized him.

I grasped all this in an instant and screamed in terror. A blow fell that I thought must split my father's skull in two. He heard me and spun round. I cried out again and he twisted, dodging the blade by a hair's breadth. At the same moment, a man leapt at me and caught me hard against him, clamping his hand down over my mouth.

'Be silent,' he growled in my ear.

I had no intention of distracting my father again, but I was desperate to be free. I fought my captor with all my strength, writhing and twisting in his arms, biting down on the foul-smelling hand that was half suffocating me. The man cursed but didn't loose his hold.

Father was fighting hard now, beating his opponent back towards the fire, making him give ground. Both men were running with sweat, their blows fierce, their concentration intense. I could see veins standing out in my father's forehead, and the muscles rigid in his neck as he gave every last vestige of power in his body to this battle. Father swung round, forcing the other man to turn too, and I saw his face at last. It was Halfgrim, of course. Who else could it be?

He'd broken his agreement with us and had pursued us to get his revenge. So these were the Icelanders my father had gone to greet with an offer of hospitality. The terrible irony made me feel sick. What had happened? Had he recognized them and fled back here? If so, they'd tracked him down quickly. I fought wildly to escape the iron grip that held me.

Father slipped suddenly on the earth floor and fell to one knee. My scream of terror was muffled by the hand still holding my mouth tight shut. With a massive effort, my father turned the fall to his advantage, turning aside the blow that Halfgrim struck with his blade and then thrusting upwards towards his opponent's unprotected belly.

With a shout, Halfgrim fell back. Instead of bringing him down, the sword sliced only through the sleeve of his tunic, drawing blood. He stumbled further back, right into the fire, nursing his right arm. With a cry of pain and shock, he leapt out of the embers again, throwing himself at father, wielding his sword with renewed fury, ignoring the blood that flowed down his arm and the smell of singed leather and wool that filled the room.

A movement to my left caught my eye. I'd been so intent on the two men fighting that I hadn't noticed there were other people in the room. They stood still and quiet, intent upon the fight. One, two, three, four, five men, drawn swords in their hands. If Halfgrim fell, or even looked likely to fall, they were ready to strike my father down. This wasn't a fair fight. It was a murder. He had no chance.

It came to me all at once that my father knew this. He

fought on, bravely. Honourably, even without hope. Just as I kept fighting my captor, knowing that even if I could escape, there was absolutely nothing I could do to help. I couldn't give up a last, desperate hope that somehow I could save father.

Halfgrim had borne my father back until he could go no further. Pressed up against the house wall, he fought on, bracing his body against the timbers, using their unyielding force to give power to his blows which were weakening now as his strength began to fail. Halfgrim was tiring too, both men breathing in noisy gasps, grunting with every blow, every parry. My father had the support of the wall, but he was also trapped, unable to fall back to dodge blows. He made one last, powerful lunge forward, aiming for Halfgrim's heart. Halfgrim turned the thrust aside and drove his sword straight into my father. There was a sickening sound; the severing of fabric, flesh, and organs, and my father groaned aloud in pain and despair. Halfgrim stepped back, his reddened sword still held defensively, and watched as my father slid slowly down the wall onto the ground, blood soaking his tunic.

'No!' I screamed, tearing free at last, now that it was too late. I flung myself across the room, dodging Halfgrim, and fell on my knees beside my father. It was silent around me. Everything but the two of us and my utter despair ceased to exist. I grasped my father's hands, slippery with blood and sweat.

'Sigrun,' he whispered faintly. 'I'm so sorry.'

I tore off my cloak and used it to staunch the blood that was flowing from the wound. I didn't need to examine it to know it was fatal. Halfgrim had pierced the stomach, and that could not be healed with any skill or plant I knew of. I could feel tears flowing hot from my eyes as I pressed my cloak down.

'I'll help you, father,' I lied, my voice a broken whisper. I could feel his agony as though it was my own.

There was a thundering on the stairs behind me, voices raised, shouts and the clash of metal on metal once more. Glancing round, I saw Leif and some other men attacking the intruders. I put my arms around my father, cradling him protectively, terrified of losing him. I smoothed his long, dark hair and saw his eyes cloud with pain. If only the men would stop fighting and go away. I longed to be left in peace.

'Sigrun,' I saw rather than heard my father whisper. He drew me closer, and I bent over him, straining to hear him over the commotion behind me.

'Don't grieve for me,' he whispered, as I bent low over him to catch his faint words. 'I regret nothing. I've had . . . ' he paused, as a spasm of pain passed though him.

'Don't try to speak, please, father,' I begged him, tears running down my face and dripping onto him. But he was determined. The hand on my wrist tightened once more.

'Twenty . . . happy years. Who could ask for more of life? Sigrun, promise me . . . don't . . . let them avenge me. I want . . . peace.'

'I promise,' I whispered earnestly. 'I swear it to you.'

My father fell back exhausted. He moved once more, to push Foe Biter feebly into my hand. I took it from him, and then he lay still. I could feel his strength draining from him, his spirit failing. As I held him, his eyes dimmed, the life leaving them.

Two powerful arms grasped me from behind, tearing me away from my father. I dropped father's sword and screamed out in distress, trying to claw my way back to him. There were confused shouts all around me. 'Out! Get out!' someone cried. I reached out desperately for my father as I was dragged away from him.

'Father!' I yelled to him. He didn't respond. Then Halfgrim stood between us, looking down at him, a long knife in his left hand.

'Die, you murdering slave,' he shouted. I looked away as he stabbed viciously downwards with the knife.

I was lifted bodily from the ground and carried up the stairs at a run. My father's pain was gone from me, and I knew he no longer felt it either.

He was dead.

CHAPTER TWENTY-SEVEN

I woke with a splitting headache. The sun was bright in my face and the ground sickeningly unsteady. I couldn't imagine where I was. I tried to move and noticed that I couldn't. My wrists hurt. My head hurt. In fact, I hurt everywhere.

'Sigrun?' asked a soft voice. 'Are you awake?' A gentle hand was laid on my brow. It was unbelievably painful to open my eyes, but I did. I thought I could make out Maria next to me, but it was too bright, so I shut my eyes again. There was a pain in my feet too, and when I tried to move them I couldn't.

'Where am I?' I asked, surprised at how faint my voice was.

'We prisoners on bad man's ship.'

Maria's words made no sense to me. Who was a bad man and why would I be on his ship? I should be . . . where? In Jorvik. With my father.

With a sickening plunge of despair deep inside me, I remembered. Father was dead. Halfgrim had killed him. Maria was right to call him a bad man.

The grief rushed into me like the tide rushing onto the beach. Hot tears stung my sore eyes.

'Father . . . '

'I'm so sorry, Sigrun,' said Maria, softly, stroking my face.

I wept unrestrainedly, racked by the pain of loss, the sobs hard in my chest. When I wanted to wipe my eyes, I realized I couldn't. My hands were bound.

'Why?' I asked, tugging uselessly at the cruel ropes.

'You not stop scream and fight them,' Maria told me. 'We left Thrang's house, you scream and scream. Everyone stare. So bad man hit you on head. Now we tied up.'

I struggled to remember. It was all a confused blur; being pulled away from father, being slung painfully over somebody's shoulder, and jarred as he ran with me.

'He hit you very hard,' said Maria.

'Why have they taken us? Where are we going?' I asked. I struggled to sit up and see what was going on, but I was tied too tightly.

'I not know,' said Maria. 'I think they take us to get out of house; so Leif not dare kill them. I afraid they throw us in sea.'

I went cold at Maria's words. But there were other things worrying me too. 'Was Leif hurt?' I asked. 'And what about Erik and my father's other men? What about Thrang?'

'Thrang and other men still away. I not see what happen Leif and Erik,' said Maria sadly. She was tied only at the ankles, and unlike me, her hands were free. She stroked my hair soothingly.

I lay still on the heaving deck, wrestling with my sorrow and my fears. I was grateful for Maria's affection, though for her sake I wished she wasn't in this dangerous predicament with me. I imagined Leif, still weak from his time in prison, fearing for us and unable to do anything to help. I thought of my mother and her great sorrow when at the end of three years neither her husband nor her daughter returned. And who knew where Asgrim was and what he intended? Perhaps she would never know what became of any of us.

I remembered how Halfgrim had killed my father and the sorrow was so acute I was nearly sick. Despair was overwhelming me but I had to fight it somehow. Maria and I couldn't simply succumb to our fate.

A shadow loomed over me. I opened my sore eyes and squinted up against the strong sunshine.

'Ha, you're awake at last, slave's daughter,' said Halfgrim. 'I thought perhaps I'd done for you, and that would have been a waste. You'll fetch a pretty penny at Hedeby market. You both look just like the slaves you are, so we won't have any trouble.' He bent over me, taking my chin in his cruel fingers and twisted my face towards him. 'You're a pretty thing, as far as slaves go. You'll appeal, and so will the other one.'

He released me and I glared at him, loathing him. My hatred burned in my veins like poison.

'My father kept the agreement you made. You broke it coming after us. You had no right to kill him. Breaking your word brings shame and dishonour,' I cried furiously.

Halfgrim raised a hand threatening to strike me, and I couldn't help flinching away from him.

'You can talk about dishonour!' Halfgrim shouted. 'I found out the *godi* who negotiated that deal between us was your father's blood brother! He wasn't neutral. That made the agreement void.'

'Helgi would always have been fair,' I said. 'And no one forced you to agree.'

Then I noticed Foe Biter hanging in a scabbard at his side and rage took hold of me. My father had given his sword to me. It was the last thing he'd done. I strained to get my hands free so that I could hit Halfgrim. I wanted to scratch him, bite him and hurt him in any way I could, but the ropes at my wrists might as well have been iron bands.

'Such a shame your murdering dog of a slave-father won't know his precious daughter was sold into slavery,' Halfgrim said, watching my struggles with a detached satisfaction. 'Perhaps death was too good for him after all.' He walked away, chuckling at his own wit.

I opened my mouth to hurl abuse at him, but Maria laid a finger softly on my lips. 'Don't,' she whispered. 'He *want* to make you angry.'

I knew she was right and stayed silent, but inside my head I used every foul word I'd ever learned from my brother.

Much later that day as the sun was dropping towards the horizon, a man paused by us and offered a water-skin. Maria thanked him, accepted it, and helped me drink a little. The man squatted down.

'I'd know how to treat a couple of pretty girls better than Halfgrim,' he said with a smile. His words were kind enough, but I disliked the smile that accompanied them. As I finished drinking, I realized his hand was on my leg.

'Get off me!' I cried, trying to pull away, but unable to because the ropes were too tight.

'Stop!' said Maria, slapping the man's hand. He ignored

her, leering at me. And then abruptly he was plucked violently away from us and thrown to the deck. Halfgrim stood over him, one foot on his chest, drew his sword and held it to his throat.

'If I catch anyone going near these two, for any reason,' he said deliberately, 'that person dies at my hand.' He lifted his head and repeated his words for the whole ship to hear. 'Do you understand me?' he shouted.

There was a muttering of assent and the man who'd given us water crawled away looking furious. 'No food and drink but from my hand, no speech and absolutely no touching,' Halfgrim ordered.

He turned to us. 'And don't think I'm doing this from the kindness of my heart,' he said. 'I'll make sure I find the filthiest, foulest, most vicious old man in the whole of Hedeby market to sell you to. But I will have a good price.'

Maria and I huddled together, too frightened and miserable to speak. We took comfort in each other's presence, but it was the only solace we had. The horrifying prospect of slavery loomed before us.

We sailed for several days and nights on the open sea. I lay bound most of the time, ropes chaffing my wrists and ankles, feeling nothing but misery and discomfort, only a bleak and uncertain future ahead of us. I lay on the hard deck in the cold and thought of Ingvar and the hopes I'd had that we would one day be together. They were gone now. I thought of poor Maria and hoped that her fate now would not be worse than the one I had snatched her from.

'There's a ship behind us,' I said to Maria as I sat up,

still bound by the ankles, one afternoon.

'Yes, I see him yesterday also,' said Maria, using her hand to shade her eyes from the bright light as she looked behind us.

'This is probably a busy route,' I sighed. 'Jorvik to Hedeby: lots of ships must sail this way.' For my own sake I tried to stifle the hope that Thrang might have arrived back in Jorvik in time to pursue us. It was impossible. He could have no idea where we were heading or what Halfgrim's ship looked like.

Once or twice Halfgrim brought us food and drink. Mostly he didn't bother. On the third day, both of us weak with hunger and lack of water, we beached on a broad sandy shore. Halfgrim ordered his men to carry us off the ship. They dropped us on the sand, laid a fire and went to barter for fresh food and drink.

'Welcome to the Mark, slave girl,' Halfgrim said, giving me a kick in the side. 'We've made land just south of Hedeby, and we'll move on at first light.'

'Why are you bothering to tell me?' I asked him, my hatred burning fiercely.

Halfgrim leered down at me. 'I want you to be able to look forward to the morrow with a proper degree of dread.' He looked me up and down. 'I considered killing you,' he said. 'But I think this is more fitting.'

'I've never harmed you,' I said to him.

He grasped me by the hair, twisting it. 'Oh, but you have,' he said softly, his face very close to mine. 'Your family stole my inheritance.'

'That was before I was born. And from what I heard, your father had stolen most of it from others in the first place.'

His cold, dead-fish eyes looked into mine for a long moment.

'Liar,' he said at last.

I lay sleepless that night, as Halfgrim had intended, dreading the morning. The men had all drunk deeply, celebrating the success of their mission, my father's death and being safely on land once more. My loathing of Halfgrim knew no bounds as he toasted 'the stinking slave's death'. Eventually they all grew so drunk they keeled over where they sat by the fire, forgetting even to post a guard, and snored heavily. Halfgrim lay next to me reeking sourly of mead, his breath like a latrine. I turned and wriggled a little to get away from him, but Maria lay on my other side, huddled close for warmth and shivering in the bitter chill of the spring night.

It was the darkest part of the night, and the fire had burned down to a faint glow, when I felt the shadow of a new presence among us. A creeping form, more impenetrable than the darkness, moved nearby. I tensed, unsure whether I should cry out and raise the alarm, or hope that whoever this was, they couldn't be worse than Halfgrim.

I stayed silent, and nudged Maria softly. She nudged me back, her breathing soft, and I realized she was awake too. I hoped none of the men were. Halfgrim farted loudly beside me, disturbed himself by choking on a snore and rolled over, flinging one arm across me. I wrinkled my nose in disgust as the stench engulfed me and turned my head away.

The dark shape had frozen as Halfgrim had stirred, and I could no longer see it. I could still sense it though. I realized it wasn't alone: men filled with tension, fear, and excitement were all around us. I prayed they were about to fall upon our enemy, and only hoped they would not kill us too. The shadow moved again, slowly. I strained my eyes in the darkness and thought it looked like a man carrying some bulky object.

Halfgrim was grunting piggy snores into my ear. I tried to ease myself away from him, but it was hard to move, bound at the wrists and ankles. My whole body was tensed with anticipation. A light touch on my arm almost made me scream. I swallowed the sound, and stared into the darkness trying to make something out. I could smell death and decay, which frightened me. For a moment I thought of trolls or ogres and had to repress the instinct to cry out.

A pale face loomed close and I recoiled, startled. The figure laid a finger gently on my lips and I understood I was to be silent. I felt the cold touch of steel at my wrist and tried to keep absolutely still as the rope was cut. Any movement of mine could alert Halfgrim.

Who was helping me? Was it a member of the crew? I didn't think so. My hope was that somehow, incredibly, Leif and Thrang had come after us, but it seemed too good to be true.

The knife moved to my ankles and sliced through the rope there too. The stranger knew I was bound and where the ropes were. My limbs were free, but Halfgrim

238

still snored beside me and I didn't know how to get out from under his arm. When I tried to move, his hold tightened. I stared into the darkness, hoping the mysterious stranger would help me. The soft hiss of more rope being cut close by told me he was freeing Maria too.

The stranger bent over me and mouthed in my ear: 'When I lift his arm, roll free.' I did so, rolling into Maria, who clutched at me in the darkness, shivering with cold and fear.

Though there was no moon, the clouds had cleared a little from the stars and I could just make out the stranger as he held Halfgrim's arm and then, with an effort, rolled a large, heavy object under his arm in my place. Whatever it was, it stank.

The stranger then rose and began to creep away, beckoning us to follow. I took one shaky step, but then turned back to Halfgrim. He had no right to Foe Biter. That had come to us through my mother's family. Very carefully, very slowly, I knelt down and tried to draw my father's sword from the scabbard, terrified that Halfgrim would wake at any second. He didn't, but the movement disturbed him and he rolled over with a grunt. He was now lying on the sword.

Reluctantly, I gave up and tried to push myself upright, but my legs were numb and unresponsive from being tied so long. I realized with a shock that I couldn't walk. Maria took my arm and tried to support me but she was unsteady herself. I stumbled again, and this time fell, narrowly missing a sleeping crew member.

The stranger appeared at my side again, scooped me up and carried me. I could hear Maria staggering next to us as she tried to pick her way through the sleeping figures. Another dark shape emerged from the shadows and picked her up too. It was almost dream-like, this fleeing in the darkness with strangers who could be friends or enemies: both exhilarating and terrifying. My overriding feeling was relief at escaping my bitterest enemy. As for the future: could it be worse than what we were fleeing from?

We were borne swiftly away from the camp, striding out into the darkness of the night, along the beach. I kept waiting to hear the sounds of men waking, of pursuit, but they didn't come. I was both relieved and afraid. Who had taken us and why? Had we just allowed ourselves to be taken into another danger? To judge by the stench that still lingered on the man who carried me, these men certainly had no sense of hygiene. I'd hoped with all my heart it might be Leif, but I was no longer sure.

'Who are you?' I asked my companion at last.

'Hush,' he whispered. 'I'm a friend, but we're not safe yet.'

So saying, he threw me onto his shoulder and broke into a run. I clung to him and for the second time in a few days I was bumped and jarred over a man's shoulder, the breath knocked from my body. I could hear other men running beside us in the darkness, and hoped Maria was all right.

And then we were slowing, stopping. I was lifted clear of this man's shoulders by someone else, lifted onto a ship, put down on the deck, and Maria was beside me. I clung to her, glad to be together.

'Who are they?' she whispered to me. 'Is Leif or Thrang?'

'I've no idea,' I replied.

The ship surged forward on the sand, and we had to grasp the sides to keep our balance. Then we were afloat and moving out to sea with swift, ordered strokes of the many oars. I could see the starlight shining on the water around us. We'd escaped. Had we done right?

There was the click of flint and the flare of a light being struck nearby and a lantern flickered into life. A man stepped forward holding it aloft so that the light fell on our faces. Judging by the smell, it was the man who'd carried me here.

'You're not hurt?' he asked anxiously. I could suddenly sense other feelings besides anxiety in him. I could sense . . . love. Then the light of the lantern fell onto his face, lighting up his long, fair hair, his blue eyes, the familiar and beloved face and I cried out in joy and astonishment. 'Ingvar! How . . . what are you doing here?'

CHAPTER TWENTY-EIGHT

Ingvar passed the lantern to another figure in the darkness and before I knew it, I was in his arms, hugging him, pressing my face into his scratchy, smelly woollen tunic, laughing, crying and asking questions all at once.

'Is it really you? How can it be you?' I asked over and over again, hardly able to believe it.

'Of course it's me, Sigrun,' he said, holding me very tight.

'Maria!' I cried. 'It's Ingvar! All the way from Iceland! We're safe . . . we're really safe!' I let go of Ingvar and hugged her, pulling her over to meet him. They shook hands, Maria laughing with relief.

'And here's Erik,' said Ingvar. Erik's familiar figure emerged out of the darkness to embrace me.

'I thought I'd lost you,' he said. 'I didn't know how I'd ever be able to go back to Iceland with such dreadful news for your poor mother.'

'It's bad enough, even now, isn't it?' I said, my delight tempered at once. 'Father . . . '

'Yes,' he agreed soberly. 'It's very bad.' Erik turned to hug Maria, and I looked back at Ingvar, hardly able to believe he was really here with us.

'How do you come to be here?' I asked wonderingly.

'I came looking for you,' he explained.

'Then you know . . . ?'

'About your father? Yes, and I am deeply, deeply sorry. He was a fine man.'

Ingvar fell silent a moment and then spoke again: 'I set out to warn him that Halfgrim had broken the agreement,' he said. 'We heard from neighbours that he'd had word your father was in Jorvik and had set out intending to kill him. So I borrowed my father's ship and set sail in pursuit. I wanted to warn Bjorn, and fight by his side if necessary. Our ship is faster than Halfgrim's tub and I hoped to overtake him. But we suffered a broken rudder off the Shetlands and reached Jorvik a day after him. Forgive me.'

'It's not your fault,' I whispered. 'It's mine. My mother trusted me to protect him. But I failed.'

'It's *not* your fault,' Ingvar said fiercely. 'How could it be your fault?' He drew me aside to a seat at the side of the ship, where we could sit down close together. 'Don't ever blame yourself,' he said. He put his arm around me and I leaned against him, rubbing my cheek against his tunic.

'Ingvar,' I said, 'I don't mean to complain, but you smell repulsive.'

To my surprise, Ingvar chuckled. 'That's a story to chase away these tears,' he said, gently wiping the wetness from my cheek. 'The men whose ship was berthed next to Halfgrim's in Jorvik described his ship to me and told me he was bound for Hedeby. We caught up with you halfway here: you might have seen our ship if you'd looked aft.'

'Oh, we did!' I said, remembering. 'But too far away to recognize the sail. I never dreamed it was you.'

Ingvar's arms tightened around me, holding me close. 'We arrived on the beach just after Halfgrim last night,' he continued. 'We watched you from the dunes. I saw how jealously he guarded you, how he even dared to sleep with his arm around you, the murdering cur. He didn't . . . hurt you, did he?'

'He didn't,' I assured him. 'But he was going to sell us. *Sell* us, Ingvar!'

'We feared as much,' said Ingvar. 'I stayed in Jorvik only long enough to learn what I needed and arrange everything. Leif helped us discover where Halfgrim had gone and Erik packed up all your things. Three other men of your party were still away with Thrang. I couldn't wait for them when you were in such danger. I've left money for them to pay passage back when they can get one.

'When we reached this place, I could see how difficult it was going to be to get you away. We were outnumbered, and my men are slaves and farmers not warriors. We couldn't take you and your friend by force. So we needed a strategy. When I stumbled over a dead sheep in the dunes behind the beach, it gave me the idea.'

'Dead sheep?' I asked, bewildered.

'I decided the best plan would be to sneak you out from under their very noses in the night,' grinned Ingvar, his teeth gleaming white in the darkness. 'And to give Halfgrim a more fitting bedfellow in your place.'

'You didn't!' I asked, awed. 'That wasn't a dead sheep you put into his arms?'

'It was. I only wish I could be there to see his fury when he wakes,' said Ingvar. He threw back his head and laughed; his familiar, merry laugh that always made me smile and I smiled now too, filled with warmth and comfort at the sound of it, and at Ingvar's nearness.

'So that's the terrible smell?'

'It is. The creature was more rotted than I realized and carrying it was a messy task.'

'Disgusting!' I smiled at the image of Halfgrim waking up with a hangover and a rotting sheep in his arms.

'Where do we go now?' I asked. 'Back to Jorvik?'

'No. Leif promised to bury your father with every honour,' said Ingvar. 'It will be done by now.' He tightened his hold, knowing how distressed I must be. 'I'm taking you home,' he whispered. 'If that's what you want. Unless there are new ties that bind you more strongly elsewhere?'

I shed tears of relief, tears of longing, because I was so relieved to be safe with him and couldn't wait to see my mother and my home again.

'There are *new* ties of friendship,' I said when I could speak. 'I'll be truly sorry not to see Leif and Thrang again. They were very good to us. And poor Leif was only just out of prison. But . . . *stronger* ties? No.'

I knew what he was asking me, or I hoped I did. I was afraid of saying too much or too little, wondering where we stood with one another after such a long separation.

The ordeal of the past days had left both Maria and me exhausted. Very soon we couldn't keep our eyes open. Ingvar piled furs onto a sheltered spot of the deck for us and left us to rest while he went to the tiller, choosing to risk sailing on into the darkness to put distance between us and Halfgrim.

The two of us lay down side by side, enjoying the luxury of warm covers in the cold night air.

'Maria,' I said, taking her hand in the darkness. 'I meant to offer you a choice when I finally quitted Jorvik. To accompany me home to Iceland or to stay as a free woman. But I'm afraid there's no choice now. We're going home.'

Maria uttered something between a sob and a laugh.

'I thought we being drowned by Halfgrim, or slaves,' said Maria. 'Now we free. I very happy to go to Iceland with you.'

The following days sped by in talk and exchange of news, just as the waves sped past under our keel. The sail was constantly full and there was no need for oars except the one night we stopped at Jarlshof for supplies and shore leave.

I told Ingvar of Asgrim's treachery, of our winter in Jorvik and the story of Leola's disappearance. In return he gave me news of my mother and of his own family. 'She's as well as can be expected,' he said. 'She's missing you all badly of course.'

After only eight nights we sighted Iceland on the horizon. I stood in the prow gazing on the distant mountains, a mixture of joy and sadness filling me at the sight of my home country. I'd longed all winter to be home again, but had never imagined returning without my father.

We sailed around the easternmost reach of our island, sighting glaciers, countless fjords, and dizzyingly tall, rugged cliffs filled with thousands upon thousands of sea birds, so that it made my mouth water just to look at them.

'It must be time for guillemot eggs,' I said to Ingvar, 'if the birds are here.' I thought of the delicious blue eggs, collected at great risk from the cliffs in early summer; the first fresh food of the year.

'Soon,' said Ingvar with a warm smile. 'When we get back, I'll collect some especially for you.'

I felt a jolt of pleasure at his words. 'Thank you,' I said. Then I sighed, thinking of my father again. 'How shall I break the news to mother?'

Ingvar looked at me. 'Don't you think Thora already knows?' he asked quietly.

I realized he was right. The goddess wouldn't have left her ignorant of such a tragedy. My task would not be to break the news, but to comfort her.

Ingvar was right. When we sailed into the bay some days later, it was a sad group collected at the shore to greet us. My mother stood bowed, red-eyed, her face shadowed with grief. She sought my eye as soon as we were close enough, looking for confirmation of what she'd already seen. As I nodded sadly, she turned and fled, her grief trailing behind her like a dense fog. But even at that moment I noticed that she didn't limp. Her leg had healed.

I knew it wasn't lack of love for me that had sent her running away instead of staying to greet me. It was simple, overwhelming grief for my father, who had been everything to her. She kept to her room, and I felt her distress and despair. She wouldn't come to the door no matter how much I knocked and called to her, and she wouldn't take any food or drink.

Helgi and Bera came to visit, and hugged me tightly, offering words of comfort. They welcomed Maria to Iceland, treating her with great kindness. And they made no secret of their relief at having Ingvar restored safely to them.

'How long has mother been like this?' I asked Bera. 'She looks very thin.'

Bera hesitated. 'For many days,' she said. 'Since she saw the vision of your father's death. She took some courage from the fact that she foresaw Bjorn's death once before, and he didn't die. But now there's no hope.'

'I'm frightened for her,' I said. 'She loved my father so much.'

'I know,' said Bera. 'But she'll be glad to have you back, Sigrun. She loves you too.'

On the second evening after my return, I told the sad tale of my father's death to the whole household and to many of Helgi's. I wanted to tell it well; to honour his bravery and fearlessness. I kept my voice steady throughout, though I shed tears as I described his final moments. I wasn't the only one to weep. As I finished speaking, I saw my mother had come out of her room and was standing quietly by the door, listening to me with tears running down her face.

I got up shakily and went to her, and she folded me in her arms. We stood together for a long, long time and I knew at last that I had truly come home, and that I was loved.

'Take comfort, Thora. And Sigrun,' said Helgi to us at

last, coming over, and laying a hand on each of us. 'Bjorn died honourably and is now drinking mead and feasting in Odin's hall with the other warriors.'

I caught my mother's eye and knew we were both thinking the same thing. Would he be comfortable in Valhalla? Father had never seen himself as a warrior, though he had been forced to make his end as one.

CHAPTER TWENTY-NINE

There was a commotion before rising time the next morning. I heard the hammering on the door and loud voices and was wide awake instantly, my mouth dry and my heart pounding with fear. Had Halfgrim pursued us to Iceland already? Were we under attack again?

I'd scrambled into my clothes and was halfway down the ladder before the other women in the sleeping loft had even finished rubbing their eyes and yawning. Bera and my mother stood by the remains of last night's fire. Mother was tousled with sleep, dark shadows under her eyes.

'Of course I'll come,' she was saying in a tired voice to a desperate-looking stranger. 'I just need a few moments to prepare for the journey.'

'What is it?' I asked Bera.

'This is Arnor, the *godi* from across the mountains. His wife's in labour,' said Bera. She looked deeply concerned and turned to my mother: 'Thora, please. You're not well enough to go such a distance in this cold.'

'I must,' said my mother, turning away to pick up her cloak. Astrid was hurrying to pack some food for the journey and Asgerd went to unlock my mother's medicine chest. All was suddenly bustle and noise.

Mother never spared herself when other people needed her, but I'd never heard her sound so weary. I, on the other hand, was rested and full of energy. And so relieved to hear that there were no assassins at our door that I thought a woman in labour sounded a simple matter. I spoke without thinking:

'Mother, you need to rest. I'll go.'

There was a sudden silence as everyone stopped what they were doing and looked around at me.

'Really,' I said, flustered by so much attention. 'I'd enjoy the ride and I'm quite recovered from the journey home.'

Slowly my mother turned to stare at me. 'It's likely to be a difficult birth,' she said.

I nodded. I was only half aware of my hand going to my amulet beneath the neck of my kirtle. 'I delivered a breech baby in Jorvik,' I said.

My mother blinked in surprise and the silence in the room deepened. I looked around uncomfortably, wondering what all the fuss was about. It took me a few moments to remember how frightened I used to be of working alone. That time seemed so far away now.

'Very well,' said my mother at last. 'Thank you, Sigrun. Make sure you dress warmly. It's a long way. I'll send someone tomorrow to fetch you home.'

'Thank you,' I said, hurrying to fetch my warmest clothes, my medicines, and my pouch of runes. 'Remind me, when I get home, mother, to show you all the medicines I was able to buy in Jorvik. I think you'll find it exciting.'

Surprise held my mother silent.

'Would you like to come with me?' I asked Maria. 'We can saddle another horse.'

'I not ride horse,' said Maria sadly. She looked forlorn at the prospect of being left, and I hugged her before I went. 'I'm sorry to leave you,' I told her. 'Our family will look after you. When I get back, I'll teach you to "ride horse",' I added teasingly, drawing a small smile from her.

'We won't let you feel lonely while Sigrun's away,' said my mother kindly to Maria. 'We can spend some time getting to know each other.'

It was a hard ride across the mountain pass at the back of the bay. Arnor was unwilling to waste a moment, even on sparing the horses, so we cantered and galloped much of the way in an exhilarating race against time. Once we arrived, there was a long, traumatic labour. I supported the poor woman as best I could, brewed medicines for the pain, and finally, towards morning the next day, she was delivered of a healthy daughter.

'Thank you, Sigrun,' said Arnor, shaking my hand energetically, his voice quivering with emotion. 'We're deep in your debt. You're a worthy daughter and apprentice of Thora the Healer.'

For the first time, I truly felt that perhaps he might be right.

I slept deeply for a few hours, and woke to the sound of Ingvar's voice. I sat up, surprised and pleased, and peeped down from the strange sleeping loft, to see him drinking a glass of breakfast ale with our host.

'Good morning, Sigrun,' he said, catching the movement from the corner of his eye and looking up.

'Good morning,' I said withdrawing hurriedly, aware of my uncombed hair and half-dressed state.

Washed, dressed, and groomed, I joined him and Arnor for breakfast. Arnor's wife Thurid was sitting by the fire nursing her newborn, looking content.

'I wasn't expecting you,' I said to Ingvar.

'How could I let anyone else have the pleasure of accompanying you?' he asked. 'Besides, this is a small journey compared to last time I fetched you home!'

I laughed a little, and acknowledged the truth of it.

The return journey was very different to the outward one. It was much milder, the sunshine warming us. We lingered over the ride, talking, remembering our childhood, stopping to look at the views I'd missed while I was away.

'I didn't know how I was going to make it through three summers in exile,' I told Ingvar. 'Not that I wasn't pleased to be with father, of course. But we were so far from home! I thought my heart would break.'

'I was afraid you wouldn't want to return,' confessed Ingvar. 'Once you'd experienced city life.'

'I hated it, honestly,' I assured him. 'I missed the open spaces, the views, the fresh air and the horses. And you must know from Dublin how badly a city stinks.'

'Yes, I do,' Ingvar agreed. 'You've thrived on it though. You're a different person.'

I raised my brows and he hurried to reassure me: 'I mean that well,' he said. 'You're more self-assured, and it suits you. But while you were away . . . I was afraid you might forget me.'

'I had your amulet,' I told him, flushing with pleasure.

'It gave me such abilities and courage too. You told me it was powerful and you were right. And it reminded me of you every day. Not that I needed reminding.'

Ingvar brought his horse close beside mine, reached out and caught my fingers in his, pressing them gently.

'I missed you,' he said.

My heart beat quickly as I heard the words I'd been longing to hear all the long months of my exile and the days since my return. I smiled shyly up at him.

'And I you,' I said.

Ingvar halted his horse, and mine stopped too. Ingvar slid down out of his saddle and lifted me down from mine. Before I properly understood his intention, he was drawing me into his arms. I forgot all about my horse, abandoning the reins, resting my hands instead on the woollen sleeves of Ingvar's tunic. He was looking down into my eyes, and his were such an intense blue, the expression in them so fierce and at the same time so tender that it took my breath away. The wind whipped some strands of my hair across my face, and Ingvar stroked them softly away again. He ran his thumb over my lips, then bent his fair head and kissed me.

I'd dreamed of kissing him so often that it felt both familiar and terrifyingly strange. As he tightened his arms around me, I yielded completely, wishing I could melt into his embrace and stay there for ever. I felt as though nothing could hurt me, and even the loss of my father faded to a dull ache.

We kissed for a long, long time, until I was dizzy with love. When Ingvar finally released me, I was vaguely surprised to see the world unchanged around me, and the horses quietly grazing nearby. I rested my cheek against him, feeling the warmth of his chest through the fabric of his tunic.

'There's something I must say to you,' said Ingvar seriously.

I looked up questioningly.

'I love you. Shall we get married?'

I blushed, half laughing, half crying with surprise and pleasure. 'Yes,' I said, hugging him. 'I love you too. Let's get married.'

It was late in the afternoon before we climbed the final slope, and saw both our farms on the coast before us.

'Home,' I sighed happily.

Then I rubbed my hand across my eyes and looked again, not at the farms but out into the bay. I could hardly take in what I was seeing, wondering if it was a trick of the light.

'Bjorn's ship?' said Ingvar slowly, as though he too had trouble believing his eyes.

'Yes,' I said. For a wild moment, I thought there had been a mistake, and my father wasn't dead after all, but come home safe and well to us. Then with a sickening lurch, I realized who it must be. 'Asgrim,' I said heavily. 'Asgrim's returned. Much too late.'

I was right. My brother had come home. When we walked into the house, he was bowed before my mother, down on one knee, his face dark red with shame, while she berated him for his betrayal. He was silent, neither arguing nor defending himself. We stood quietly until she ran out of breath. Erik stood nearby, fists clenched, looking as though he'd dearly like to punch my brother.

At last Asgrim spoke, his voice low with emotion and shame. 'I've been ignorant and headstrong, mother,' he said. 'I did wrong and I'm more sorry than I can say. I spent some days in Jorvik with Thrang. He explained a lot of things to me about your past and father's too. He made me ashamed of what I'd done. If only you or father had told me!'

'Don't blame us!' said mother angrily. 'You owed your father your duty and your loyalty. Instead you betrayed him and behaved without honour.'

Asgrim flinched. 'Mother, this winter, I've experienced things that have changed me. I'm older and wiser now, I swear to you.' He passed his hand over his face. I saw a scar running from his ear to his chin, and guessed that his adventures hadn't gone as smoothly as he'd hoped. Good, I thought. He deserved to be as miserable as he'd made us.

'I've come home a wealthy man,' Asgrim told mother. He turned and pointed at three locked chests that had been placed beside the wall. 'I know it's no compensation. But I'm ready now to take on my responsibilities and look after you all.'

My mother sniffed scornfully. 'Are you trying to buy my forgiveness, Asgrim? I have no use for wealth.'

Asgrim blushed scarlet. 'No, of course not,' he mumbled.

'You have a great deal to make up for,' mother said. 'If you hadn't abandoned your father, he might be alive today. Neither words nor wealth can suffice to earn for-giveness for that.'

'I intend to prove myself,' Asgrim said. 'I intend to—'

'That's enough,' snapped Thora. She turned away from him. She would forgive him I knew. With the help of the amulet, I could already feel her softening. Beneath her anger, she was relieved her son was alive and back home. But she wasn't going to tell him so yet. Instead she looked straight at me.

'Welcome home, Sigrun,' she said. 'The goddess showed me that you have news for us.' A smile lit her sad countenance briefly. 'A rare vision; I usually only see danger approaching.'

Everyone who'd been pretending not to listen to the exchange between Thora and my brother now turned to me. I blushed deeply wondering what my mother had seen.

'I . . . I've delivered a healthy baby girl . . . ' I said.

'That's very good news,' said my mother. 'But it's not that.'

Ingvar stepped forward and took my hand in his.

'Sigrun and I have agreed to marry,' he said.

There was an outcry. My mother embraced me first. 'I'm happy for you both,' she said, turning to Ingvar, and taking both his hands. 'You'll suit each other so well. I wish you every happiness.' Then she turned away, tears filling her eyes as our love brought back her own heart-breaking loss. I wanted to go to her, to comfort her, but my brother was standing before me.

'Will you still take my hand and my good wishes for your future?' he muttered, staring at the ground.

He glanced up briefly but couldn't hold my gaze. I felt the regret, the remorse, the guilt that was in him, but I couldn't forgive so quickly.

'Perhaps I could if father hadn't died,' I said in a hard voice, not taking his hand. 'But as it is, you'll have to give me time.'

Asgrim let his hand drop and looked miserable.

'But there's someone I must introduce to you,' I said a little more kindly, not for his sake, but for Maria's. 'Someone I hope you will treat with more honour and respect than you showed us last winter. She came to us the same day you robbed and deserted us and has been a *true* friend.'

I found Maria standing nearby, took her hand and drew her forward.

'You have a new foster sister,' I told Asgrim. 'This is Maria. Maria, this is my wayward brother Asgrim.'

My brother stared at Maria, stunned. 'Foster sister?' he said, as though he'd never heard the words before.

'Yes. She's been a good friend to me. Father chose to foster her before he . . . died.'

Maria stood blushing and fearful. Perhaps she was worried that Asgrim would disapprove of her inclusion in the family. But he bowed and took Maria's small hand in his large one.

'In that case, welcome to the family, Maria,' he said, not taking his eyes from her face. Her blush deepened.

Everyone was waiting impatiently to congratulate me on my betrothal. I was hugged and kissed by most of the household. I laughed and felt my happiness growing once more.

'I very happy for you, Sigrun,' said Maria, smiling when she could get near me once more.

'I hope you'll be as happy one day,' I whispered. She shook her head and smiled. Bera was beside me now, drawing my attention from Maria.

'Sigrun, my dearest girl, we look forward to welcoming you to the family,' she said. Her lips smiled but her eyes were bleak. I could feel heaviness in her heart. I stood frozen with shock, unable to respond properly to her embrace. I could sense dread, despair, even anger in her. What had I done to deserve this? I'd always thought she loved me.

'You're not pleased?' I asked, unable to stop myself.

'Nonsense, child,' said Bera, tears in her eyes. 'It's what . . . what I've always hoped for. Thora and I talked about it when you were just babies.'

I knew she was lying, but I had no idea why. I couldn't understand it. For some reason this betrothal had distressed her. I let it pass. At this moment, I wished I didn't have the powers the amulet gave me. They'd spoiled a moment of happiness by allowing me to see feelings that should be private.

Nightmeal was going to be a feast in celebration of my betrothal to Ingvar. Mother told Asgrim very pointedly that it wasn't to welcome *him* home and he should behave modestly and stay sober.

Before the feast began, I climbed into the sleeping loft. I sat still on my bed for a few moments, waiting for a calmness to settle over me. When it did, I took a deep breath and untied the horse amulet from around my neck. Except for the time I'd offered it to Eadred in exchange for Maria, it was the first time I'd taken it off since Ingvar had given it to me.

I didn't want to spy on anyone else's feelings tonight. I didn't want to know that Bera was unhappy about her son's betrothal to me, or that some of the other young women were fiercely jealous. I wanted to enjoy the evening without other people's feelings intruding into my hard-won happiness. I tucked the amulet inside my sleeping furs where it would be safe. It was valuable to me both because of its powers and because Ingvar had given it to me. But I wanted to be without it tonight.

I climbed down the ladder and joined the supper party. I'd expected to feel more different. To my astonishment, I could still feel my mother's mixture of happiness and deep grief, and Bera's sadness. It's because you already know that's how they're feeling, I told myself. So you imagine you can still feel it. Or perhaps the amulet can still work its magic just by being nearby. But I was puzzled.

Helgi arrived. He was weighed down by grief inside, even though he hugged me and said how happy he was. How did I know? How could I feel this, when I'd taken the amulet off? It shouldn't be possible. I felt tears start to my eyes at the thought that Ingvar's parents didn't want us to be together. I was hurt and confused. Didn't they like me? Had I been blind to that all my life?

Ingvar came to find me, taking my hand in his. I could feel his love, his warmth, his happiness as he smiled down at me, and it lifted my spirits to look up into his glowing face. I loved him more than anything in the world. My heart turned over with love. I decided to be happy tonight, no matter what. I smiled up at Ingvar and pressed his hand. He bent down and kissed me gently, not caring who was watching.

The meal was a strange mixture of merriment and sadness. We were toasted, but we also drank to my father's memory, falling silent and sad. I wished with all my heart he could be here now, to celebrate with us. I kept thinking he would walk in at any moment and take his place beside my mother; the seat she kept empty in his memory. It was impossible to believe that he would never do so again.

CHAPTER THIRTY

The following morning, I walked out with my mother, at her request, to collect plants. She looked pale and drawn, as though she hadn't slept much. It was too early in the year for anything much to be growing, but I thought perhaps the fresh air would do her good, so I agreed to go.

'You've changed a great deal while you've been away, Sigrun,' she said as soon as we'd left the house behind us.

'For the better, I hope,' I said anxiously.

Thora smiled.

'Of course. It makes me very happy to see how you've grown and flourished while you've been away. Tell me, what happened to change you so much?'

'Noth—nothing happened,' I faltered. 'What do you mean? I've already told you what we did and where we went.'

'But what finally gave you confidence in yourself?' asked my mother. 'Before you went, you'd almost rather have jumped off a cliff than gone to a birth by yourself. I did everything I could to encourage you, but nothing worked. It seems it was my absence you needed, not my help. Have I overshadowed you, do you think, Sigrun?'

'Oh, no,' I cried, distressed that she should think that.

'Not at all! You taught me everything I know. Well, nearly everything. I love you dearly!'

My mother smiled sadly. 'I know that,' she said. 'And I love you too, my daughter. But I've wondered, since I saw the change in you, whether it was hard for you to develop with me standing over you with all my knowledge and experience.'

'No,' I said eager to reassure her. 'It wasn't that, truly it wasn't. It's a secret, but . . . it was the amulet Ingvar gave me.'

My mother stopped and stared at me. 'Amulet?' she asked disbelievingly.

I was already pulling the horse out from under my tunic, untying it so that I could hand it to her.

'It gave me such powers,' I told her in a rush. 'Suddenly I could sense people's moods and intentions. And the runes spoke to me. They'd never done so before.'

My mother took the amulet in the palm of her hand and looked at it closely, examining the beautiful craftsmanship. Then she looked up at me, a searching stare. I looked back at her, disconcerted to see a trace of amusement creeping into her eyes.

'What is it?' I asked.

'Sigrun, I thought I'd taught you better than that,' said my mother gently.

'What do you mean? Don't you believe me? It really does have powers. It helps me read people. Not see their auras. You know I've never been good at that. But *sense* what they are feeling.' I was desperate to convince her. Perhaps because the amulet had worked such changes in my life, I wanted my mother to understand.

'It's a beautiful piece of jewellery,' said my mother giving it back. 'Made by a very skilled silversmith. But the goddess doesn't need trinkets to speak through. A piece of silver can't give you powers, Sigrun. You know that.'

'But it *did*!' I insisted. 'How else would you explain it?'

'Tell me about what happened when Ingvar gave it to you,' my mother asked. I did so. I told her how he had spoken to me before I went away, given the amulet to me as a parting gift with the hope that we'd meet again. I omitted to tell her of the kiss, of my own feelings for Ingvar at the time. Although everyone knew now, how we felt about each other, I still felt shy about discussing it with my mother. But I didn't need to. She saw the connection at once. When I finished speaking, she turned and hugged me.

'My foolish child,' she said fondly. 'Don't you see? It was falling in love that brought your powers alive. They were there, but latent. You needed to grow into womanhood for them to develop fully. It's often the way with seers and healers. The gift of the amulet just happened to coincide with the discovery of your love.'

I blushed and stared at the ground as we started walking again.

'Really? Was it . . . was it that way for you too?' I asked.

Thora shook her head.

'No, Sigrun, it wasn't. I had my visions and my ability to see auras from childhood. But everyone is different. I can see now that it was all lying within you, ready to blossom.'

'So the amulet made no difference at all?' I asked in a

small voice. I felt I was betraying it to admit such a thing; betraying Ingvar's valuable gift to me.

'Of course it did. Because you believed in it,' said Thora simply. 'It's the same reason charms and spells often work as cures. You'd already learned all the skills a healer needs. But you needed to believe in yourself.'

I held the amulet tightly. I didn't know whether I was relieved or disappointed. But in my heart I knew my mother was right.

'Yesterday,' I said, 'I sensed . . . '

I paused, unsure how to continue. Then I reasoned my mother had similar skills to me. With her ability to read auras she might already know what I was about to say, so I continued.

'I saw that Bera was grieved that I was marrying Ingvar. It upset me. So before nightmeal, I took it off. I left it in the sleeping loft.'

'And it made no difference,' said my mother. 'You could feel it anyway.'

I nodded. 'Yes. And Helgi too. And some of the girls are . . . '

'Jealous,' finished my mother. 'Yes, that was to be expected. We're short of young men of marriageable age, and Ingvar is . . . well, the biggest catch.'

'But Helgi and Bera,' I asked. 'Why?' I could feel myself close to tears.

'I think . . . ' said Thora. She stopped walking, her eyes glazed and she stood quite still. I waited quietly, knowing she was seeing the future. After a few moments she came back to herself. She looked tired and years older.

'What did you see?' I asked tentatively.

'You'll know soon enough,' she replied sadly. 'You mustn't think they don't love you. They do.'

We turned for home in silence. I wanted to ask my mother to explain what she'd seen. I didn't want more secrets. But her sadness was so strong, that despite my dread, I couldn't bear to force her to speak.

When we returned, Ingvar and Asgrim had just come back from collecting eggs from the cliffs. They were elated and full of their success.

'I promised you guillemot eggs, Sigrun,' said Ingvar with his beautiful smile. 'And here they are!' He put a blue egg into my hand and I felt the weight of it, anticipating the taste. It was so good to be home. Ingvar was here, he was full of love and life and fun. What could be so terrible about our marrying?

At nightmeal, my brother called for a barrel of mead to be opened. There was a wind blowing up outside, making the fire smoke, but it was cosy to be indoors. Maria walked around the tables, pouring each man a drink as I helped serving and passing out the food. I happened to see her pause beside my brother and fill his horn, and I noticed Asgrim raise his eyes to smile warmly up at her. She smiled back. Then Asgrim raised his horn to Ingvar.

'A toast!' he called out over the chatter and the noise of eating. 'To our success, my new brother!'

There was a light in his eyes that made me uneasy. It had nothing to do with the mead; it was an elation that I could feel from across the room.

'Success in what?' I asked.

My brother rose to his feet and a hush fell over the hall as everyone turned to look.

'I've had word that Halfgrim has slunk back to Iceland, the dog,' he said. 'This is my oath before Odin the Allfather and the mighty Thor: by midsummer, I shall avenge my father, and restore our family's honour!'

Ingvar lifted his horn in support of the pledge. There were no cheers, only a few mutterings. Most people were silent. Bera burst into tears and moaned quietly with distress. I looked at my mother. She'd covered her face with her hands and was rocking slightly in her seat. I realized this was what she had foreseen.

'Are you mad?' I asked my brother, aghast. 'Father wouldn't want this; he specifically said he didn't want to be avenged!'

Asgrim frowned angrily at me. 'His soul won't rest until he's avenged. Honour is men's business,' he said sharply. 'You deliver the babies and leave this to us.'

I stared at him in disbelief and anger for a moment and then stalked out of the house, banging the heavy door closed behind me.

Fury consumed me. Asgrim had abandoned father when he'd needed his son. He'd left us stranded in Jorvik, penniless and exposed to attack. And now, when it was all too late, his idea of shouldering responsibility was to ride off to commit more killings; to deepen the feud between the families. Such idiocy. Such stupidity. I could feel my jaw and my fists clenching as the anger tore through me.

I walked swiftly uphill away from the house, out towards the cliff where the horse had nearly galloped to his death on that day Asgrim and father had returned. It seemed so long ago now. I'd changed. I was no longer naïve and trusting, and no longer expected the world to be a safe, happy place. But to seek out violence and danger? It was madness.

The wind tore at my kirtle as I walked. My dark hair was whipped into a tangle. I pulled it angrily out of my eyes. The sea was a dull grey, heaving and churning in the bay. It looked as angry as I felt.

I sensed Ingvar's presence long before he reached me. 'You'll freeze up here,' he said, offering my cloak. I allowed him to fasten it at my neck, and wrap it around me. His own cloak streamed down from his shoulders and flapped in the strong wind. He put his arms around me and I leaned gratefully against him.

'Please don't support Asgrim in this,' I begged him. 'It's suicide. You could be killed.'

'I won't be,' Ingvar said. 'You needn't be afraid, Sigrun. We can muster a strong force. We can take on Halfgrim.'

I couldn't believe what I was hearing. I pulled away from Ingvar and stood at the cliff edge, the wind clawing at me.

'Are you insane too?' I asked him. 'Even if Asgrim isn't killed in this attack, sooner or later Halfgrim's kin will make sure he dies in revenge and so it goes on. One attack after another until our whole family is wiped out. Asgrim, his children, our children, Halfgrim's children. For what?'

'Asgrim needs to keep his honour. It would be cowardly to let be,' Ingvar said. He reached out his arms for me, but I pushed him angrily away. 'Your father won't be able to rest in his grave until he's avenged,' Ingvar added. The wind took his fair hair and blew it into his face, but he dragged it out of the way. 'He'll have no peace. Is that what you want for him?'

'He made me promise *not* to avenge him!' I cried. 'It was one of the last things he said. He didn't want it.'

'Sigrun, I'm sorry, but Asgrim will never believe that,' said Ingvar earnestly. 'Bjorn agreed to go into exile, but Halfgrim came after him anyway. He broke his word and murdered him. That was against any law and all honour. Asgrim knows he'll be despised as a coward throughout Iceland if he lets Halfgrim get away with that. Don't you understand?'

'No I don't! And even if it's true, why do you have to support him?' I shouted against the wind. 'Why must you encourage him?'

'Because we're family now,' said Ingvar. 'Or we soon will be.' There was a sudden lull in the wind and he dropped his voice. 'As your future husband, I'm obliged to support him. Otherwise his shame will be my shame.'

'Because of *me*?' I asked, my voice loud in the relative stillness. I could hear the swell heaving and breaking against the cliffs below me.

'Yes, when we marry.' Ingvar's face was open and determined. He believed what he was saying. Perhaps my brother was right and these ideas of honour were something only men understood, because I certainly didn't. Ingvar was going to risk getting himself killed because of me, even though I was begging him not to.

'That's why your parents don't want you to marry me,' I said, realization dawning. 'I couldn't understand it. I thought they didn't like me, or thought I wasn't good enough for you. But it's because they don't want you drawn into our family's feud. Well, I don't blame them. I don't want it either.'

Ingvar's face was so sad as he stood there listening to me, that it made me ache. I loved him; I loved him with my whole heart and soul, but there was only one way to keep him safe. We couldn't be together.

'I won't marry you,' I told him fiercely.

He looked as though I'd slapped him. He stood quite still, staring at me. 'But you . . . we . . . Sigrun, please! Be reasonable. How can I go in to Asgrim now and tell him I've changed my mind? He'll think I'm afraid.'

The wind roared in from the sea again, almost taking my breath away and buffeting us both. 'I don't care what you tell him, and I don't care what he thinks. I have the lowest possible opinion of Asgrim right now. He causes nothing but trouble. Ingvar, *please* say you won't support him.'

Ingvar stood looking wretched. His face wore a look of agonized indecision and I could sense the battle raging within him. I held my breath, praying I had persuaded him to see sense. Ingvar turned and looked out to sea for a moment. Then, taking a deep breath, he turned back.

'Sigrun, believe me, I love you more than you can possibly imagine. You're everything to me. But I cannot in all honour break my word to your brother after I've given it.'

'I don't want anyone to support my brother in this bloodlust. It's madness, and will only make things worse. If you won't listen, then it's over. You're nothing more to me than a neighbour.'

I turned away from him, unable to bear the pain I could feel in him. I'd offered him an impossible choice, but all I could think of was that he hadn't chosen me. I ran along the cliff. The wind battered me, stealing my breath, numbing my terrible pain. I wasn't saying no to Ingvar just for a short time. If this feud went on, I'd never be able to marry him. It would be exposing him and any sons we ever had to mortal danger.

When I was sure Ingvar wasn't trying to follow me, I cut up the hill to the horses. The wind was in my back now, and blew me along, the great gusts making me stumble, whipping my hair into my eyes so it was hard to see where I was going. I had to say those things to Ingvar. I had to hurt him. I wanted to run back and tell him I didn't mean them. But I didn't let myself, because this was the only way I could think of to keep him safe.

There were four riding horses picketed on the hillside, beyond the burnt-out shell of what had once been their stable. I hugged them and breathed their familiar scent, comforted by their calm presence. It was balm to the appalling emptiness inside me. The happiness and the hope I'd carried with me for so long was gone: I could no longer believe that Ingvar and I had a future together.

I stayed with the horses a long time, until the evening light dimmed in the sky and it grew too cold to remain outdoors. I hoped Ingvar would have left by now, but when I walked into the house, he was sitting by the door waiting for me. It was almost dark inside the longhouse. Everyone else was asleep, but Ingvar caught my wrist as I tried to push past him.

'I know why you said what you did,' he said in a hurt

voice. 'You're trying to stop me going with Asgrim. But I think he's right. He can't have everyone saying he has only the courage of a slave. He has to prove himself and end this. And Sigrun: I'll go with him anyway. As his friend.'

I tore away from Ingvar. I was so angry, so distressed, I wouldn't look at him or speak to him. He waited a few moments and then flung his cloak around himself and left.

I leaned against the wall, prey to the darkest despair. I'd quarrelled with Ingvar and for what? He was risking his life anyway.

'Sigrun!' a voice whispered in the gloom.

I looked up and saw my mother beckoning me from the door of her room. I went softly over to her and she drew me inside. We sat down on the bed, looking at each other by the flickering light of a fish-oil lamp. I could feel her grief, and I knew she saw mine radiating in my aura.

'You can't stop them,' she whispered. 'For men, concepts of honour are absolute.'

'But it's senseless,' I said. 'It's a pointless waste of life. And it won't end anything, can't they see that? It'll carry on and on.'

'You and I see that. We bring life into the world and nurture it. They see it quite differently.'

'Have you seen the outcome of this?' I asked, dreading the answer.

But Thora shook her head. 'I saw only the intention to seek revenge,' she said. 'Not what will happen. Sigrun, you can't change their idea of what's right.'

CHAPTER THIRTY-ONE

I didn't go to bed. Instead, I sat by the embers of the fire, and held my amulet in my hand. It was growing light before I knew what to do. The idea came to me in a rush. It was so brilliant that it could only have come from the goddess.

I climbed softly into the sleeping loft and woke Maria. She sat up at once, alert and ready. I whispered a few words in her ear and then she dressed quickly for a journey. When she came down, I was waiting by one of the chests Asgrim had brought home with him. I bent to lift it, indicating to Maria that she should take the other end. Her eyes widened as she realized what I intended, but she did as I asked. The chest was heavy and we staggered as we crept silently out of the house, carrying it as far as we could.

'One more,' I said, still panting with effort. Maria looked awed.

'He be so angry!' she said breathlessly.

'I couldn't care less.' I was completely focused, and nothing as trivial as my brother's anger would turn me from it. 'He stole from us. I'm stealing back, and for a much better purpose.'

'What purpose?' Maria asked.

'I'm going to settle the dispute. With your help, if you will, and without violence,' I said. 'There are ways it can be done, but it will involve large gifts.'

'I help you,' said Maria at once.

The second chest was even heavier than the first, but we managed to drag it out too. I fetched all four horses from the pickets, buckling on the largest saddlebags I could find. I took my father's axe down from the wall, and took it with me.

With the blunt back of the axe, I smashed the locks from the chests. Inside were bags and bags of coins, gold and silver jewellery, goblets, pearls and rolls of silk. We both gasped when we saw the contents.

'Help me stuff it all in the saddlebags,' I told Maria. 'As quickly as we can. We mustn't be caught.'

We both worked to transfer as much as we could, and then we abandoned the bulkier items and the chests.

'I wish I'd had time to teach you to ride,' I said apologetically. 'You'll just have to hang on and do your best.'

I helped Maria climb onto her horse and put her feet into the stirrups.

'Oh,' she gasped, clutching at its mane. 'It's so high up . . . and oooh!' She squealed as the horse took a step forward. 'It *wobbles*!'

'Hush,' I begged her. 'Just hang on tight. Hold the mane or the saddle. You'll be all right. She'll follow the other horses.'

I swung myself onto my own horse. Turning towards the mountains, I pushed my mount swiftly forward, leading the two spare, heavily-laden horses. Maria's horse followed more slowly, knowing it had a novice on its back, stopping to snatch mouthfuls of grass from time to time. I could hear Maria's half-suppressed squeaks and gasps of fear. It was very unfortunate she'd never learned to ride, but there was no one else I could trust. Even my mother wouldn't do what I was doing now.

By the time the sun rose, we were out of sight of the house and over the pass. I'd been forced to lead Maria's horse as well as the spare ones, because it was more interested in grazing than in keeping up, but we'd covered more ground than I'd hoped for. Maria was hanging on tightly to the front of the saddle, looking slightly green, her face screwed up.

'What's wrong?' I asked her. 'Are you in pain?'

'Yes. My back end on fire, my legs all stretched and my tummy go up and down like on ship,' said Maria, summing up her sufferings.

I couldn't help grinning. 'That bad? I'm very sorry. Do you wish you hadn't come?'

'Oh, no. I very glad I not home. Your brother be soooo angry,' said Maria, and then she winced again as her horse broke into a trot. 'I just big hope he not catch us.'

'He won't. The other horses are all up in the hills, grazing on the spring grass,' I said. I smiled to myself as I thought of my brother's rage. 'He'll have to find them or walk to Helgi's to borrow a horse. By then we should be at Arnor's, and Asgrim can be as angry as he likes.'

'Your brother young and very brave,' said Maria. 'He settle down when he older. Who Arnor and why we go to him?'

'Arnor is the man whose baby daughter I delivered two days ago. He's a *godi*, which means that he can intercede with the gods, leading sacrifices and so on, and also deal with matters of law. I plan to ask him to negotiate with Halfgrim for us,' I explained. 'The treasure is our bargaining tool. Halfgrim thinks my father robbed his father.' I paused, remembering what my father had told me. 'Well, in fact, I believe he did. So we owe him. And the only way to end a dispute without bloodshed, is by settlement. Payment. I remembered in the night. I thought through all the tales of feuds I'd ever listened to and that was how they were eventually settled.'

'But how paying Halfgrim make your brother honour again?' asked Maria puzzled, and struggling to find the words in my language for these difficult concepts. 'Surely it make him feel worse? Sigrun, Halfgrim *kill* your father.'

'I haven't forgotten,' I said bitterly. 'And I'm still working on how it will solve things exactly. I hope Arnor will advise us. It won't just be a payment, it'll be a sort of exchange or bargain for peace.'

Arnor was surprised when we arrived at his farm, our horses sweating with the heavy load and the fast ride. He came out to greet us, brows raised.

'What can I do for you, Sigrun?' he asked.

'I need your help urgently,' I told him. 'In a matter of a delicate negotiation. I'm right, aren't I? As *godi*, you are the person to come to?'

His brow creased slightly.

'Of course. Forgive me if I'm taken by surprise. I would have thought your brother would take on such a task, not you.'

News travelled fast despite the distances between

farms, and I wasn't surprised to hear that Arnor already knew of my brother's return. 'I've taken it upon myself to act in this matter,' I said. 'It's not impossible for a woman to do so, I believe.'

'Not impossible, merely rare,' said Arnor. 'I'll be happy to help you if I can. But why didn't you go to Helgi? He has the same powers as me.'

'Because he was my father's blood-brother,' I said. 'He isn't neutral in our family affairs.'

'Very well,' nodded Arnor and I breathed a sigh of relief. 'Won't you come in, you and your friend, and tell me the problem over refreshments?' He took my horse's bridle to make it easier for me to dismount. I hesitated. I was going to have to tell Arnor the truth about Asgrim after all.

'I am concerned my brother could be on our heels,' I admitted. 'He prefers the course of violence to settlement.'

'I see. I'll order fresh horses to be made ready for us all while you take a drink,' Arnor promised.

I dismounted then, sliding to the ground and giving my weary horse a pat, while Arnor lifted Maria down from the saddle. She groaned and hobbled as she tried to walk, and I took her arm to support her.

I poured out our whole family history over refreshments, or at least what I knew of it. It was a strange experience to speak openly about what had been such a closely-guarded secret for so many years. Arnor's wife, Thurid, listened, horror-struck, clutching her baby to her. Arnor on the other hand heard me calmly and nodded. 'I've heard of this Halfgrim. He's only recently settled near here. It'll be tricky if he's broken one agreement already. But I think we might arrange a settlement both families can live with. Especially as you're disposed to be generous.'

He got up and began to give orders. I quickly understood he was bringing quite a number of men. I was glad of that, not wanting to be at Halfgrim's mercy again. All over the house, men of Arnor's household were rolling bedding furs and packing food into saddlebags. I felt guilty for the disruption. But I was trying to save lives; to avoid bloodshed, misery, and grief for my family.

'Why don't you leave Maria with me?' Thurid asked me. 'She's much too tired to ride on. It's at least two days' ride to Halfgrim's farm.'

I glanced at Maria, who was leaning wearily against the table looking pale and shaken from the long ride.

'I *want* to go,' Maria said sorrowfully. 'But . . . '

I hugged my foster sister close. 'You helped me when I needed you most,' I told her. 'Thank you. Stay here and recover. I'll be fine now.'

CHAPTER THIRTY-TWO

My hands were chilled on the reins, and the dark clouds above us promised rain at any moment. Two days' hard riding had brought us to Halfgrim's farmstead, a shabby, cobbled-together place on poor land. It had taken half of another morning for Arnor to persuade him to meet me. Now I sat waiting on horseback on this cold, exposed hillside for Halfgrim to appear. The wind blew steadily, stealing all the warmth from me, and making me shiver. Perhaps I shivered, too, because I dreaded seeing my father's killer again. I loathed the idea of having to speak to him.

We'd agreed to come unarmed, but I was almost certain, as Halfgrim and his men finally rode towards us, that they had weapons concealed beneath their bulky cloaks. My horse sidestepped restlessly and I knew she was picking up on my fear.

Arnor rode forward a few steps and greeted Halfgrim, who grunted something unintelligible in reply.

'We are here to try to reach a settlement over the feud that has arisen between your families,' Arnor began formally.

'Yes, yes, we know all that,' snapped Halfgrim. He leaned forward over his saddle, breathing heavily.

'Very well,' said Arnor, clearly thrown off his stride by Halfgrim's rudeness. 'Do you both accept that I'm a neutral negotiator? That's important before we move on. I barely know Bjorn's family, and I know you only by reputation. Will you state your satisfaction with that before we go any further?'

'Pah!' said Halfgrim scornfully and spat on the ground. His face was flushed and his eyes bloodshot. I wondered whether he'd been drinking, but it seemed early in the day for that. I noticed him tug awkwardly on the reins with his left hand. Some memory stirred in me, but I couldn't quite think what.

'I see no need for any settlement,' Halfgrim said. 'No need for any negotiation at all by you or anyone else. I avenged my father, there's an end to it.'

'It's not an end,' said Arnor. 'Bjorn went into exile according to the agreement you made. His life was no longer forfeit. But you pursued him and killed him any-way. And Bjorn has a son who now intends to avenge *his* father. You can prepare to protect yourself and your family, or you can agree to a settlement that will be to your advantage. My task is to bring an end to the dispute so that both families keep their honour and there is no more killing.'

I heard a crunching sound and realized Halfgrim was grinding his teeth in rage.

'The only settlement I'll consider,' he said angrily, 'is the usurper's farm, house, and all its contents, includ-ing the slaves. They all belonged to my father.' A gust of wind bringing the first drops of rain blew over us all, and Halfgrim shivered. I looked at him closely, noticing how he held his right hand awkwardly cradled over the pommel of his saddle. I had a sudden, painful memory of Halfgrim fighting my father. He was right-handed. Something was wrong with his right arm.

'Your father stole many of those possessions from others including *my* grandparents,' I said, half my mind still on the argument, but the other half distracted as I diagnosed my enemy's health. 'And there are no slaves at Thorastead.'

'There soon will be,' said Halfgrim with an unpleasant smile. 'And anyway, I won't do business with a wench. That would shame me. Send your brother, or is he afraid?'

'He's so unafraid that he's sworn you'll be dead by midsummer,' I told him.

Halfgrim laughed scornfully. 'Let him try,' he said. 'As if I'd be afraid of an untried stripling like him!' As he spoke he jerked suddenly on the reins, pulling his horse around to ride away. My stomach lurched, knowing this was my last chance to stop him, to persuade him to settle with me.

'Wait, please!' I cried.

But Halfgrim's horse had thrown up his head as he turned and the movement had buffeted Halfgrim's right arm, making him groan and bend forward in pain. His high colour faded to a sickly grey as he swayed in the saddle. Beneath his anger, I could suddenly sense overwhelming pain and sickness.

I watched as he slid helplessly off his horse and fell to the ground. His attendants jumped off their horses to help him. One grabbed his arm and Halfgrim screamed in pain, startling us all.

I knew I should help. I suspected the wound my father had given him had festered. If I left him, he would probably die and a part of me wanted to let him do just that. He'd murdered my father in cold blood. His death now would keep Ingvar and Asgrim safe.

Halfgrim muttered something, his words slurred and indistinct. Then he fainted.

'What's wrong?' asked Arnor. 'Is he sick?'

'Wounded,' said one of his men, looking helplessly at us. 'I think he's had it. I don't know what to do.'

Arnor looked sideways at me, but I pretended not to see. I knew what he was going to ask of me, and I didn't know how to respond.

'He needs a healer,' said Arnor. He was still looking at me.

'There aren't any round here,' said the man. 'Only the old woman at the farm a days' ride away who delivers babies, but she won't come here. She's no good anyway.' He looked back at his injured friend.

Arnor turned to me. 'Sigrun,' he said quietly, so the others wouldn't hear, 'I know he's your bitter enemy. We both know what he did. You have a choice now: you can watch him die and see it as the gods' justice, or you can try and help him.'

I bit my lip, my training and my conscience at war with my instinct. My hatred for Halfgrim still burned so fiercely within me. I could never, ever forgive him for what he'd done to my family.

'What do *you* think I should do?' I asked, torn and unhappy.

Arnor shrugged. 'It's not for me to say. It may be too late to save him anyway.'

I sat frozen with indecision. My horse dropped her head, sensing I was distracted, and snatched a mouthful of grass. I pulled her up absent-mindedly. Arnor would always know, I thought, that I could have helped Halfgrim and didn't. Worst of all, *I* would always know it. Right now, I didn't care. But would it weigh on me for the rest of my life afterwards?

I tried to imagine what my mother would want me to do; what she would do herself. And then I knew, as clearly as if she had spoken to me, that I must try and help this man. No matter how much I loathed him and no matter how much I thought he deserved an excruciating death in the grip of fever.

I slid down from my horse and gave her a pat before handing the reins to Arnor,

'Very well,' I said. 'I'll look at his arm.'

I knelt beside the unconscious man, the wetness from the grass soaking my tunic, and forced myself to take hold of his wrist. His skin burned with fever. The infection must be very bad. I pushed his sleeve carefully back and revealed what I had guessed I'd see; the sword slash given to him by my father in their last fight, now swollen and dark, angry red. Foe Biter had been true to its name.

'I can't treat this out here,' I said to Arnor. 'I'd need hot water, clean cloths, and I'd have to brew some medicines.'

'Are you a healer?' asked Halfgrim's companion in surprise.

'I am,' I said. 'But I don't have many of my remedies with me.'

'Please try,' he said. 'Otherwise he'll die, won't he?'

'It's likely,' I agreed. I swung myself back onto my horse and we followed the group slowly down to the house. Halfgrim had been slung across his horse, head and legs lolling to either side as the horse walked. It was raining in earnest now, drenching all of us. The skies were dark and clouds were rolling down from the mountains, engulfing the landscape in thick fog.

Halfgrim's longhouse was smaller than my home; the building materials a shabby mixture of rocks, imported timber, and driftwood. There were hardly any women, and the house, though new, was dirty, smelly, and neglected. Everyone stared at me suspiciously as we entered. At first the women were reluctant to help me, but once I'd laid out my medicines and explained my intentions, they began to co-operate.

I lanced the wound to drain the pus. That brought Halfgrim round, but after a few delirious cries of pain, he fainted again. Once the injury was clean, I bound it in a cooling, disinfecting poultice. I also brewed a tea that would help his body work against the infection. As I worked, I tried to close my mind to the thought that this man had killed my father. I tried to think of him as just another patient, but it was difficult. My skin crawled every time I had to touch him.

'He's been ill since he came home,' one of the women said, as she watched me. 'Getting steadily worse. But when you came here demanding to talk, he got so angry he got up and rode out anyway. Will you be able to cure him?'

'I don't know,' I said. 'It'll be down to how strong he is and how well he responds to the medicines.'

As I was speaking to her, I noticed a grubby boy clinging to her skirts and peeping out at me. His face was smeared with dirt and his hair was long and tangled, hanging down over his eyes. I smiled at him, and he ducked back behind the woman's kirtle, putting his thumb in his mouth.

'Is he yours?' I asked the woman pointing at the boy.

'No,' she said quickly, twitching her kirtle away from his grasp. 'He's master's son.'

'Oh, I see. I didn't know he had a son,' I said, surprised. 'I didn't even know he was married.' There'd been no sign of a wife, or any kind of mistress of the house. How little I actually knew of this man who'd almost destroyed my life.

'Dead,' said the woman with a sniff. 'Two winters ago.'

I crouched down, my sympathy for the boy stirred, but also alert to the danger he represented. If Halfgrim died, it still might not be an end to the violence. In a few years, this son might want to avenge him.

'What's your name?' I asked the boy. He stared at me, poised for flight, uncertain if I was a threat or not.

'Bjorn,' he said at last.

'Named for his grandfather,' said the woman. There was no softness in her voice nor any apparent affection for the little boy.

Named for his grandfather using the name my father had taken as his new identity. All this had been going on while I lived quietly on our farm unaware of my family's dark past. It was a strange thought.

I left Halfgrim's servants with instructions and quitted the house accompanied by Arnor. We rejoined his men in the rough camp they'd made nearby. The rain had stopped and everyone had gathered around the fire.

'Will he live?' Arnor asked me as we warmed our hands.

'I think so,' I said. 'But cases like this are difficult to predict.'

Arnor nodded. 'It'll take him time to recover,' he said.

'I'm afraid it will,' I said, feeling guilty at keeping him and all his men kicking their heels here. 'And I'd expected my brother would have tracked me down by now. We've wasted so much time. If Asgrim gets here before we've agreed anything, all this will have been for nothing.'

'Don't worry,' Arnor said. 'If he tracks you to my house I've told my people to send him in the wrong direction. Meanwhile, I've had an idea that will take a day at least to put into action. Halfgrim won't be up and about by tomorrow, will he?'

'I doubt it,' I said. 'Even when the fever breaks, he'll be as weak as a kitten.'

'All the better,' said Arnor. 'Perhaps he'll be more malleable.'

CHAPTER THIRTY-THREE

When I tried to visit Halfgrim the following day, he was awake enough to recognize me and order me out of the house. I went swiftly, glad not to be forced to tend him again. I spent an interminable day waiting, while Arnor planned and talked and sent his men off in different directions on horseback.

'Halfgrim doesn't trust me,' he explained. 'He thinks I'm on your side. So I've sent my men out to gather all the neighbours within a day's ride of here. Especially the men who come to the Northern Quarter Assembly in the spring.'

'Assembly?' I asked. I had a vague memory of Helgi talking about this, but no clear idea what it was.

'We decide on laws, deal with disputes and so on. Halfgrim won't be in a hurry to alienate all his closest neighbours. He has to live among them. I think that will give him better manners and make him think twice about breaking an agreement a second time.'

I was impressed by Arnor's wisdom and foresight. 'I'm very grateful for all your trouble,' I told him. 'I can never repay you.'

'You delivered my daughter,' he reminded me. 'There's nothing to repay. In any case, we don't have a settlement yet.'

The neighbours started to arrive at our camp the following day, appearing like shadows out of the early morning mist. The sun hadn't yet risen above the mountains when I struggled out of my furs, sleep still fogging my brain. I tied my shoes, dragged a comb through my hair and began preparing a hot breakfast of barley porridge for everyone.

I could feel an atmosphere of expectation, almost of excitement around me. People had few opportunities to gather together, spread out as they were on distant farms and were eagerly exchanging news and stories. Arnor moved among the new arrivals, the mist hanging in beads in his beard, greeting them and informing them about the conflict they'd come to help settle.

Once the sun was up and the mist had dispersed, there was a fair crowd of people standing around the fire. The noise of cheerful voices grew as more people arrived. It was almost like a party, I thought. For me, of course, there was nothing festive about it. I had the deadly-earnest task of preventing my brother and Ingvar from risking their lives. I was also uncomfortably aware I would have to speak before all these people. Not only was that the thing I hated most, but it was unusual for a woman to take on such a task. Disputes were normally settled by men.

I reminded myself how much more confident I'd become during the months in Jorvik, and touched my amulet for luck. I would find the courage I needed and I'd succeed. I was determined.

When the sun reached its highest point in the sky, Arnor led the way down to the meadow where we'd met Halfgrim before. I stopped in surprise. It had been transformed. Posts had been driven into the ground and rope tied between them, marking out a large circle.

'What . . . ?' I began.

'It's like a *Thing*; an assembly,' Arnor told me enthusiastically. 'This is how we hold the spring assemblies. We've even found a rock for the speakers to stand on. We thought it would be more impressive, more binding a settlement, if we make it look as formal as possible.'

I looked around me in amazement. Everyone was laying aside their weapons as they entered the circle, leaving them with friends or slaves who formed an outer circle at a distance. The clouds parted for a moment allowing the sun to gleam on the mountain tops, its bright light spilling over them, reaching out towards us, turning the sky blue and filling the landscape with richer, deeper colours. I felt a moment of awe. It was as though the whole of the world, gods and all, were smiling on what Arnor had organized.

The men around me fell quiet, but not because they were silenced by the natural beauty around us: Halfgrim was riding up the hill. He got down from his horse at the edge of the circle, glaring around suspiciously. He looked pale and unsteady, but his colour was better than the last time I'd seen him.

'What's this?' he demanded, his voice weak but angry. 'Am I on trial for some crime?'

Arnor stepped forward. 'No one is on trial,' he said. 'This is an assembly formed to settle a dispute. You have the right to choose representatives, as does Sigrun. If you agree, they will hear what you have to say and take a decision which you will both abide by.'

Halfgrim let go of his horse and took an angry step forward towards the edge of the circle. Two men stopped him.

'Your weapons, please, before you enter,' they said.

'Curse you!' shouted Halfgrim. 'I'm not giving you my sword!'

'My sword,' I muttered angrily under my breath, seeing it was Foe Biter he wore at his waist.

Halfgrim fell back and bent double, panting after his outburst. Several men stepped up to him, speaking quietly so that I couldn't hear what was said. It took time, but to my relief, they convinced him to hand over the sword and enter the circle.

The sunshine was warm now, making the ground steam, and many of us cast off our cloaks. I sat down on mine, and others did the same. I had real hope, looking around me, that we could achieve something.

I chose Arnor and one other neighbour called Thorbjorn as my representatives. Halfgrim also picked two. I wasn't sure if these were neighbours he knew or not; he didn't seem to be acquainted with many of the men present. Arnor and Thorbjorn took me aside to discuss the terms I was proposing.

'I've brought payment that I'm willing to make in recompense for the goods my parents stole,' I said.

'And what will you ask in return?' asked Arnor. 'The killing of your father was unlawful, whatever Halfgrim says. He'd agreed to accept exile.'

'Apart from wanting my father's sword back, I'm not sure,' I said. 'That's my unresolved point. It needs to be something Asgrim will consider satisfies his honour.'

'You could do with some kind of surety,' Thorbjorn suggested. 'Something that will prevent Halfgrim from attacking you again.'

'That's exactly what I think,' said Arnor enthusiastically. 'And I think I've come up with just the thing. We should suggest that your family foster Halfgrim's son. That way he won't be brought up to hate you.'

'His little boy?' I asked, rather shocked at the thought of tearing him away from his home and his father at such a tender age. However loathsome I found Halfgrim, I was sure little Bjorn loved him. 'But he can't be more than five winters.'

'It's a very usual arrangement,' said Thorbjorn at once. 'Even without a dispute to settle, boys are often fostered. Your family give him his education and in return, once he's older, he works for you. Halfgrim is spared the expense of raising him.'

I looked from one to the other of them, remembering Ulf, our neighbour's child whom my own parents had fostered when his father couldn't raise him alone. But his father had lived just across the bay and had visited frequently.

'The child looked rather neglected from what I saw,' added Arnor. 'It would be a highly suitable arrangement.'

'Is it likely to satisfy my brother?' I asked dubiously.

'I'll do my best to get him to see the sense of it,' Arnor assured me. 'The child will be a type of hostage after all. A guarantee of Halfgrim's intention to honour the settlement. He can hardly burn your house down with the lad inside, can he?'

'Very well,' I said slowly. 'I certainly see the benefits. I just hope he won't be too unhappy.'

'He'll soon adjust,' Thorbjorn assured me.

Arnor opened the meeting and spoke first. Standing on the low rock, he talked of our new country finding its feet, becoming a land of fairness and justice, without kings or taxes, a country where the people chose the laws and decided how to live together in peace. It was stirring, and made me feel proud to be part of the young nation emerging on this wild, beautiful island. Then he turned to me.

'Sigrun Bjornsdottir has come to me because she wants to find a way to live in peace with her countryman Halfgrim Bjornsson, despite a troubled past. As she's bringing this action, I'm inviting her to speak first. Sigrun Bjornsdottir, do you swear by Odin the all-seeing to speak only the truth?'

I felt my mouth go dry and my hands go cold, as my fear of speaking before people returned. I got up, aware I was shaking. I stumbled as I tried to step up onto the rock. Could I speak coherently to all these people?

Waves of nauseous panic rose in me. I put my hand to the amulet and thought of Ingvar and of my mother. I was doing this for them. So that there would be a future for Ingvar and me. So that our children need not grow up fearing vengeance.

Feeling calmer, I looked out at all the upturned faces and began to speak.

'I swear,' I said. Then I took a deep breath. 'Between my family and Halfgrim's,' I said, my voice shaking a little, 'there's been a history of wrongs stretching back twenty years and more. His father persecuted and stole from my mother's family, and took my mother forcibly from them when she was just my age. Halfgrim's father, Bjorn Svanson, killed my aunt, and in retribution, my father killed Svanson and stole his ships and possessions.'

I hoped I'd pieced the history together correctly from the snippets my father had told me. But of the next part of the story, I had no doubts: 'Halfgrim attempted to burn our house down last summer. This spring, he killed my father even though he'd agreed to go into exile.' I looked at Halfgrim as I spoke. I was trying to be fair. But I couldn't help the sadness that welled up in me as I remembered, nor the anger that burned in my veins.

I paused, and looked around at my audience, my courage growing. 'But the time has come to put this behind us,' I said. 'I want to make a settlement we can both live with. One that doesn't disadvantage either family or harm their sense of honour.'

I stumbled over the last word, knowing it meant something different to all the men present than it did to me.

'In recompense for my father's theft, I offer two chests of valuable treasure. They would make Halfgrim a man of wealth and standing. In compensation for my father's death,' I said, 'I demand the return of the four horses Halfgrim stole from our farm last summer, and of my father's sword which came to him from my mother's father, and which he gave to me. Furthermore, I ask . . . '

My voice failed as I tried to mention Halfgrim's son. I

didn't know how to put a demand that was likely to make him furious. I looked pleadingly to Arnor, my tongue suddenly glued to the roof of my mouth, my whole body trembling with the strain of saying so much. Arnor must have recognized the desperation in my face, because he got up and came to stand beside me.

'As Sigrun's representative, I propose a further measure to recompense her family for the loss of her father and to ensure lasting peace between the families,' he said clearly. I envied him his confident manner and his strong, carrying voice. 'I suggest that Halfgrim gives his son to be fostered by Sigrun's family.'

A buzz of talk rose around me and then faded again as everyone waited for Arnor to go on. 'Little Bjorn would grow up with his new family, forming a bond of love and duty that would ensure this feud doesn't continue into the next generation,' Arnor said.

Halfgrim jumped to his feet. 'He's my only son, you she-dog,' he shouted at me. 'This is your idea!' I could feel his rage as well as hear it.

'You'll have a chance to speak in a moment,' said Arnor sternly, frowning at Halfgrim.

'Bjorn was my only father,' I said quietly, mastering my impulse to shout back, to vent some of my rage and grief. 'You took his life brutally and against the agreement you'd made. I, on the other hand, intend to care for your son.'

Arnor helped me step down from the rock. I was trembling but relieved. I'd done what I could; it was out of my hands now.

Halfgrim got onto the rock. I could feel his anger had

faded and a look of cunning had come into his face.

'My father never stole from her family,' he said. 'He was a wealthy man and her mother was merely a slave. But she and the impostor murdered him and stole everything my father owned, leaving me practically penniless. The penalty for a slave that kills his master is death. The only recompense she can offer is the farm, and everything in it, slaves included. That's my birthright.

'I refuse to hand over my son. She'd teach him to hate me. But I accept in principle that we should tie the families to avoid future bloodshed. It seems fitting that Sigrun and I should wed. Then she doesn't lose her home when I claim it.'

I caught my breath with shock and horror. This appalling proposal took me utterly by surprise.

'I also want to know what guarantees you can give me that your brother will abide by any settlement we make here,' Halfgrim concluded. He stood down looking pale and exhausted but pleased with himself. He got off the rock and sat down heavily between his representatives, passing a shaking hand over his face. He was struggling to keep going with his wound barely healed and the poison of it still running in his blood.

I felt sick and my stomach was tying itself in knots. Marriage to Halfgrim? It was enough to make me abandon this whole plan. If that was the way the decision went, I would be begging my brother and Ingvar to kill him.

At this point, our representatives and another group of men chosen to adjudicate the settlement stayed in the circle whilst the rest of us withdrew. I paced restlessly, some distance from the fire in our camp, wringing my hands in distress. This turn of events had shaken me badly and I was now in mortal fear of the outcome. I'd come here with the hope of settling the dispute, of securing Ingvar's safety, not of sacrificing myself to the brute who'd killed my father. The mere thought of marriage to him was repulsive and abhorrent. But Halfgrim was cleverer than I'd expected. They were unlikely to award him the farm, but they might well think his suggestion of marriage was a good way to unite the families. And I'd agreed to abide by their decision.

It was late afternoon when one of Arnor's men came with a summons to the assembly. I walked down with him, trembling and afraid. Halfgrim arrived from the other direction, and joined us. I averted my eyes from the face I hated.

'We have a few questions to ask you both on points we think need clarifying,' said one of the men, a tall, fair-haired neighbour, who seemed to have taken charge for the time being. 'I've been appointed the speaker. Sigrun, is it true, to your knowledge, that your mother was Svanson's slave?'

I shook my head. 'Absolutely not. My mother has often spoken of her childhood. Her father was a wealthy and respected man, but was later persecuted by the local chieftain: Halfgrim's father. Father told me she was taken forcibly from her family because he needed a healer in his settlement. He was ill-treating her and that's what provoked my father to kill him. That and the fact that he'd murdered his sister earlier that day, even though she was with child.'

There was a gasp of outrage from several of the men, and even Halfgrim looked taken aback. 'I don't believe you,' he said at once, but was hushed by the speaker.

'Are you currently betrothed or promised to anyone?' he asked me.

I hesitated. What could I say? I'd sworn by Odin to tell the truth, and I could not honestly say that I was.

'I was, but broke it off when I found my . . . he'd committed himself to avenge my father,' I said, blushing deeply. 'If only this dispute can be resolved, we would . . . ' I broke off in embarrassment, hoping they understood my tangled speech.

'Do we take it then, that you don't favour the suggestion of marrying Halfgrim?' asked the speaker.

I hesitated, wanting to find the right balance between making the strength of my feelings clear without antagonizing anyone.

'I don't want to marry the man who murdered my father,' I said. 'I couldn't be a proper wife to him.'

'Do you hate him?'

I glanced across to Halfgrim who was clearly enjoying watching me squirm.

'When I think of my father, I do,' I said, a note of bitterness creeping into my voice.

'In that case, how can we be sure you can be trusted with his son?' asked the speaker.

'I can answer that,' said Arnor from his place in the circle. 'If I may?'

The speaker nodded and Arnor stood up.

'I'm witness to the fact that when we arrived here, Halfgrim was very sick of a festering wound. Despite her dislike of him, Sigrun nursed him. If she hadn't done so, he might be dying by now.'

There was a murmur of approval, and Halfgrim scowled fiercely. Arnor's words had made me look noble and forgiving, and I was only glad they couldn't see into my heart to the angry, resentful feelings I had.

The speaker turned to Halfgrim. 'You say that Sigrun's father deprived you of your father's wealth?'

'Of course,' growled Halfgrim.

'But you weren't aboard the ship bound for Iceland with him?'

'Obviously not,' said Halfgrim angrily. 'I've only just come here to settle. I grew up in Norway. In poverty, thanks to *her* father's actions.' As he spoke, Halfgrim stabbed an angry finger in my direction.

'This is something we don't understand,' said the speaker. 'Your father wasn't taking you with him to his new life. You appear to have had no expectation or right to share or inherit any of his possessions.'

Halfgrim leapt to his feet, his face darkening in rage. I saw his hand go automatically to his side, reaching for a sword, but it wasn't there. It lay safely outside the circle. 'He thought it would be too dangerous for me. I was only five! He promised he'd come back for me and my mother,' Halfgrim shouted. 'And he would have done if *her* slave-father hadn't unlawfully killed him!' He pointed at me, his face contorted with fury and hate.

The speaker turned to me. 'Were there other women and children aboard that settlement ship?' he asked. I thought of Asgerd and her daughter Astrid who was just ten winters old when she sailed to Iceland.

'Yes, there were,' I said. 'Several women and one child I know of.'

'Thank you, both of you. You've been very helpful,' said the speaker. 'We'll call you back when we've reached a decision.'

He nodded dismissal to us, and I left as quickly as I could to avoid any confrontation with Halfgrim.

The afternoon dragged into evening. The sun was low over the mountains in the north-west and the air had turned cold before we were called back to the men with whom we had entrusted our fate.

They were standing as we approached, solemnly awaiting us. I could feel how seriously they were taking this meeting and the decision they'd made. I felt comforted even though I shook with dread. This was it. I was going to hear their ruling, and we had both sworn to abide by it.

Halfgrim stepped into the circle and the speaker stood up on the rock to announce the verdict.

'We've heard the facts, insofar as they can be known, given that the original men in this dispute are dead,' he said. 'We've discussed the matter carefully and taken our decision: we see no reason to doubt that the real chieftain Bjorn Svanson was the father of Halfgrim. But we doubt Svanson's intention to share his life or goods with his son. It strikes us all as very unusual to leave a son behind when emigrating. We therefore judge that Halfgrim has no claim on his father's possessions. However, he is entitled to vengeance for his father's killing.'

The speaker paused and I clenched my hands into fists, trying to stay level-headed enough to take in what he was saying. Was it good or bad for me and my family? Breathe, I told myself. Stay calm.

'Halfgrim, you agreed to be satisfied if the imposter Bjorn would go into exile from Iceland for three years. But you didn't keep your word. We therefore rule that you should have no further claim on his family or goods, and no right to any further settlement.'

Halfgrim had been looking steadily more thunderous, and at this he let out an angry bellow, but the speaker went on.

'Sigrun, you demand the return of the horses that were stolen and your father's sword. This is agreed.

'The last point is your intention to make peace between the two families. We find this a good and just aim, and feel it would be better served by the fostering of Halfgrim's son than by your marriage. We trust you to bring him up as a valued member of your family and always to speak respectfully of his real father in his hearing. Do you agree?'

I tried to speak and failed. I nodded, then had to sit down and duck my head between my knees, weak and sick with relief. All I could think about was that I didn't have to marry Halfgrim.

'Halfgrim will bring his son and the goods here to hand over,' said the speaker, 'and then I declare this meeting at an end.'

'You are unjust!' shouted Halfgrim. 'You give her

everything and me nothing! How is that fair?'

'You agreed to abide by our ruling,' the speaker reminded him. 'You won't find yourself welcome here if you go back on your word at any time.'

I got shakily to my feet. I didn't want Halfgrim left humiliated and angry. That would be storing up trouble for the future.

'I offered you compensation for the theft of your father's goods,' I said, my voice faint. 'I will voluntarily give you a payment still.'

My voice was faint, but the speaker repeated my offer for everyone to hear. I could both sense and see Halfgrim's pride battling with his greed. He wanted to make a grand gesture and fling it all in my face, but he also wanted the riches.

'It's my right to be paid,' he muttered at last.

I nodded and left the circle, climbing the hill on shaking legs to decide how much of the treasure to give to my enemy. Although, of course, I shouldn't any longer think of him as such.

CHAPTER THIRTY-FOUR

In the end I selected most of the wealth I'd brought with me, knowing a generous gift would reflect well on my family. Several of Arnor's men carried the valuables down to the assembly circle. I could see Halfgrim waiting for me there, his son beside him. Before I reached them, the ground began to shake. The tremors resolved into the thundering of hooves as a group of horsemen rode at breakneck speed towards us.

'Stop!' shouted a voice. I recognized my brother's voice at once, and my heart sank. Just as everything was about to be concluded. I noticed with a jolt of surprise that he was leading a spare horse with Maria mounted on it. She looked pale and weary and sent me an apologetic look.

Asgrim flung himself from his horse, grabbed me by the shoulders and shook me; his rage was clear for everyone to see.

'How *dare* you, sister, steal *my* possessions and . . . and betray your own family like this?' he demanded, almost incoherent with fury.

'I'm trying to *save* our family,' I answered. Asgrim shook me again so that my sight blurred and my teeth rattled together.

'Let her be!' said another familiar voice, and I looked

up to see Ingvar dismounting and hurrying towards us. My heart lurched with relief and happiness at the sight of him.

'You're supposed to be on *my* side!' Asgrim shouted at Ingvar.

'Don't fight with your friends,' said Maria's soft voice, and she stepped forward to tug at Asgrim's arm. He paused a moment, the furious fire in his eyes fading a little.

'I'm on your family's side and what's best for all of them,' said Ingvar firmly. 'I see there's been a hearing here. Shouldn't we know what decision has been reached before we object?'

I looked gratefully up at him. To my relief, Asgrim released me. Ingvar stepped forward and took my hand, looking questioningly at me. I could see Maria was still gently restraining Asgrim.

'Come and join us, Asgrim Bjornsson,' Arnor said. 'And hear what your sister, Sigrun Peacemaker, has brought about.'

It took several hours to convince Asgrim that he should abide by the agreement that had been reached. At first he shouted and argued, and refused to accept it.

'Halfgrim should be outlawed!' he demanded. 'Not given my wealth!'

Between them, Ingvar, Arnor, and the speaker persuaded him to back down. They convinced him the settlement was honourable and fair. He wasn't happy, but eventually he was resigned. Maria came into the circle once everything was over and spoke to him. To my surprise, I saw him listening and nodding. She seemed to know how to soothe him.

'He make me come with him,' she whispered to me as she hugged me. 'And I hope stop him fighting if I come.'

'You seem to have a way with him,' I said. 'Thank you.'

Maria smiled to herself, and I could feel how she cared for Asgrim. It seemed to me that there was a softness in his eyes too, when they rested on her, that I hadn't seen in him for a long time. I couldn't sense how he felt about her, but perhaps he didn't know himself yet. I thought how good Maria would be for him, how much such a marriage would benefit her too.

The goods were exchanged and the meeting ended. Asgrim and I both stepped forward to take the sword, Foe Biter, but I got there first.

'Sigrun, that sword belongs to me now,' said Asgrim, holding out his hand.

I buckled Foe Biter to my belt, dwelling for a moment on the memory of my father that it evoked. 'No, it doesn't,' I said. 'Father gave it to me when he died. You weren't there, remember?'

Asgrim stepped back looking confused and ashamed and didn't argue.

Halfgrim left with his saddle-bags brimming with valuables, and the other men dispersed slowly in twos and threes to return to their farms. Arnor, my brother, and Maria waited for us a short way off. I looked down at little Bjorn standing forlornly in the middle of the circle.

'Hello, Bjorn,' I said gently, holding out my hand.

'You're going to come and live with us.'

'I don't want to,' said Bjorn. His lower lip puckered and he looked as though he might cry at any moment. Fostering of children was commonplace, but looking at the young boy, I thought how hard it must be for the child at first. I could sense his confusion and unhappiness.

Ingvar spoke from my side. 'We have the best horses in Iceland in our bay,' he said. 'Just wait till you see our herd. If you like, you can choose a horse of your own.'

I felt a rush of love and gratitude to him for his kindness to the child.

'Really?' asked little Bjorn, in a wobbly voice, mastering his impulse to cry with an effort. I watched as he took Ingvar's hand instead of mine, and followed him bravely back up to our horses.

Ingvar swung the lad onto his own horse. 'For today, you can ride with me,' he said. 'But first I just have to speak to this lady.'

Ingvar walked over to me, took my hand and spoke quietly so that only I could hear his words. 'I'm in awe of you now, Sigrun Peacemaker,' he said with a slight smile. 'And with that sword at your side too!'

'Don't be foolish,' I said, laughing a little to cover my embarrassment. Was all well between us now, or had my words to him all those days ago spoiled everything?

'Shall we agree to forget what was said?' he asked, almost as if he could read my thoughts. 'We know the reasons for our misunderstanding, don't we?'

There were tears of relief pricking at my eyes. I brushed a hand quickly over them, tried to speak, and failed, and ended up nodding wordlessly, unable to meet his eyes.

'Sigrun?' he asked softly. When I still didn't look up, he put his fingers under my chin and gently lifted it until our eyes met. 'My love for you is stronger than ever,' he said. 'Do you still care for me?'

'Of course I do,' I whispered. 'I only thought of protecting you.'

'I'm really very capable of looking after myself, you know,' said Ingvar, a hint of sternness in his voice.

I looked at him reproachfully. 'You wanted to make war on Halfgrim and get people killed,' I said.

'I was supporting your brother and what he wanted. But I'm sorry I took his side against you. I'll never do so again. Do you forgive me?'

I nodded, fighting the tears that wanted to come. The relief was almost overwhelming. I'd been so afraid I'd lost Ingvar for ever. But now he was drawing me into his arms, caressing my face, and looking down at me so lovingly that it took my breath away and brought the colour rushing to my face.

'I'm in admiration of the way you outsmarted Asgrim,' Ingvar said.

'Was he furious?' I asked.

'You can't imagine how furious,' Ingvar said. 'He was intolerable. I couldn't stand to hear the things he said about you.' Ingvar drew me close, bent his head and kissed me. I'd almost forgotten how soft his lips were against mine, how good his kisses made me feel. I closed my eyes and threaded my fingers into his long hair, forgetting all about the people and horses all around me. Only Ingvar existed for me.

When we remembered that we had companions and

horses waiting for us, we broke apart. I drew a deep breath and tried to gather my thoughts and my dignity, and mount my horse.

'I thought you said you were going to *talk* to the lady,' I heard little Bjorn saying in a disgusted voice as Ingvar took his horse's reins in his hand.

'That's the very best way to speak to ladies,' said Ingvar with a grin. 'When you're about to marry them.'

Little Bjorn made sick noises. 'Just so long as you don't ever expect *me* to talk to one like that,' he said.

Ingvar looked across at me and we exchanged a smile. The kind of smile that you can only share with someone you love and understand. Then Ingvar ruffled the boy's hair. 'Wait until you're older, lad,' he said.

Marie-Louise Jensen (née Chalcraft) was born in Henley-on-Thames of an English father and a Danish mother. Her early years were plagued by teachers telling her to stop reading and stop writing stories and do long division instead. Marie-Louise studied Scandinavian and German with literature at the UEA and has lived in both Denmark and Germany. After teaching English at a German university for four years, Marie-Louise returned to England to care for her children full time. She completed an MA in Writing for Young People at the Bath Spa University in 2005.

Her first novel, *Between Two Seas*, was shortlisted for the Waterstone's Children's Book Prize (2008), the Glen Dimplex New Writers Awards (2008), the Hampshire Book Award (2009), and the Branford Boase Award (2009). Her second novel, *The Lady in the Tower*, was shortlisted for the Waterstone's Children's Book Prize (2009), and the Wirral Paperback of the Year (2010).

Marie-Louise lives in Bath with her two sons.

Also by Marie-Louise Jensen

'Travel to Skagen and find him. Give him my letter. Seek a better life, Marianne! Promise!'

Bound by a vow made to her dying mother,
Marianne sells her few belongings and
leaves Grimsby. Her destination? Denmark, where she will
search for her father, Lars Christensen—the golden-haired
fisherman her mother fell in love with many years before.

The journey will be long—and dangerous for a young girl
travelling alone. As Marianne boards the fishing boat that will
carry her across the North Sea, she wonders: will Denmark
be the fairy-tale land she has dreamt of?
Will she find happiness there? Will the father she has never
met welcome the arrival of his illegitimate child?

And why didn't he return for her mother,
as he promised he would?

'a riveting read.'
Guardian

Spring 1540

I am afraid. You are in grave danger.
Mother, will you run away with me if I can free you?

The servants call it The Lady Tower: the isolated part of the
castle where Eleanor's mother is imprisoned following a
terrible accusation. For four years Eleanor's only comfort has
been their secret notes to one another.

A chance discovery reveals a plot to murder her mother. Now
Eleanor must free her before it's too late. But with danger and
betrayal at every turn, she can trust no one. Not even her father.

Eleanor must use all her cunning to survive.
For it is not just her mother she needs to save . . . but also herself.

'a perfectly sweet, dreamy romantic fantasy'
Amanda Craig, *The Times*